CALA

Laura Legge is a former winner of the
PEN International New Voices Award.
This is her first novel.

CALA

LAURA LEGGE

HEAD
of ZEUS

ISBN (PB): 9781788547475
ISBN (E): 9781788547482

Typeset by e-type

Printed and bound in Great Britain by
CPI Group (UK) Ltd, Croydon CR0 4YY

Head of Zeus Ltd
First Floor East
5–8 Hardwick Street
London EC1R 4RG

WWW.HEADOFZEUS.COM

We are working all the season, boat near to boat in the
    nights,
And danger may come on us quick, no time to stand
    upon rights,
When our hands are net-cut, and our eyes as sore from
    the spray,
How can we think of our neighbours except in a
    neighbourly way?

'The Alban Goes Out', Naomi Mitchison

One fisherman alongside the other
one seagull alongside the other
seagulls over the fishermen.

'Congregations', Omar Pérez

PART 1

I

IN PULLHAIR, A small village in the Outer Hebrides, there was a church, a school, and a fire station. The school and the fire station were seldom used.

In Pullhair, also, was a stone farmhouse, known by the four women who lived there as Cala, haven, and by the villagers as Gainntir, place of confinement. It faced the sealoch and on the rare clear day, one could look toward the mainland and imagine herself connected to a larger body. If she were so inclined.

The four women of Cala sat in its dining room on the autumn equinox, wearing garlands of ash and hazel, visible to one another only by candlelight. It was a few years into the twenty-first century, but their leader, Muireall, had banned all *modern implements* from the house, including electricity. On the walls hung cords of redcurrants, and on each plate sat a small finger puppet, knitted by Lili, holding a nametag. She, like Euna, had been exiled to Cala when she was eight, and it was as if the stone walls had preserved her exactly as she had been then, a child-fossil. After a decade together they did not need the nametags, but they indulged their sweet girl, or ossified her.

Most days they wore grim and identical outfits – linen shirts, tweed trousers, an optional sweater for heat – but on each equinox, they were allowed to embellish. Today Muireall was in a leather jumpsuit, one that bound her skin tightly, and a gold chain at once necklace and body harness. Pass the food clockwise, she said.

Euna, who had chosen to wear the linen and tweed, now submitted to Muireall. She passed bowls of foraged hedgehog fungus, sea lettuce boiled into stew, blaeberries blended into curd cheese. Everything they ate came from the Cala grounds, barren though they had been lately. Euna was used to these lean meals, but she still cleaved to her image of an equinox feast. She asked Grace, Is there a roast coming?

Grace tinkered with her necklace, moving its moonstone pendant left to right, jerking the chain until it seemed to choke her. Euna knew the answer. Their most recent butchery had been of a cow, in early summer, which they had skinned and hung in the icebox. But like all of their meat stores, those bones had gone bare. Muireall, who assured them she was the only one with powers, oil-chumhachd, had been angry for months – ever since Euna had started to ask questions about the world outside of Cala, and worse, outside of Pullhair. The women now stopped passing bowls and held hands around the table, a custom when they sensed one of their coven was feeling ashamed, or lonely, or low. Through those points of touch, Euna felt a kind of unalloyed love move, and when they let go, she saw that Grace's face had changed from dull to polished.

I checked the icebox and the outbuildings, Grace said.

Muireall said, Don't worry, lamb. We always find a way.

A few weeks before, Euna had noticed a new fish farm a kilometre down the coast. Just past the patch of wych elms she had seen lights, then heard men's shouts and motor mowers across the water. And a strange thing had happened – one man had seen her staring, all those metres away, and he had waved. He had not turned away, or spat, or called *bitch* across the water. He had waved. Euna had not been allowed, nor had she wanted, to leave Cala in the last decade. But now the seed was in her, she was tending to it.

Open Forum, she said. They conducted Open Fora when they wanted to do anything that required others' consent, no matter where they all were, in the latrine or around the dining table. They would run to the sound of any woman's whistle.

I noticed a new fish farm down the seaboard, she went on. I could go there and see if they would give us any shellfish.

Grace said, ruffling Euna's long red hair, That sounds a bit frightening, doesn't it, bana-churaidh? This had always been Euna's favourite term of endearment – heroine, female champion – and Grace knew that.

It does, Euna said. But we're starving here.

Muireall pronged potatoes into her mouth and chewed on them. She dug the tines of her fork into her forearm, just below the stiff leather cuff, though her face remained calm. What have I always told you? she asked. We're not welcome there.

Yes, Euna said, you have always told me that.

Muireall had inherited this farm from her ancestor, Cairstìne Bruce, who had been drowned by neighbours for practising witchery in public. She had been skyclad, culling the sea for kelp for a ceremony. Some of those neighbours were still living, filling the eaglais pews each Sunday, or so Muireall had told her.

After everything I've done for you, Muireall said, you call me a liar.

I'm sorry, Euna said. I didn't mean to insult you.

Though Euna was being vinegary, unlovable, Grace was still stroking her hair. Euna teemed with shame. She had lost her appetite entirely. It's okay, Grace said. But no more of that talk.

Under the table, Euna could feel Muireall's foot hook around her calf. Above it, her expression shifted from friendly to unfeeling. Go ahead, she said.

But you've never let anyone leave, Lili said. Not even to go swimming. Not even that time you gave us henbane and Euna saw a kelpie down the loch.

Muireall took a handful of fungus from Lili's salver and put it into the girl's mouth, pretending tenderness.

Euna, you were always trouble, Muireall said. You have never deserved all I do for you. If you want to risk the good life you've been given, go ahead.

The shame came chopping up Euna's stomach now, waves in a wind storm. She did not say sorry for fear she would eject her meal, and that would seem ungrateful, after Muireall had spent so much time at the farm edge, foraging.

When they were all finished eating, Euna made a slow show of licking the plates clean.

*

That night, she had the nightmare that had been recurring to her since she was a child, since the day it really happened. She and Lili were seven years old, living in Bucksburn in bordering houses. Their fathers, who were brothers, were rigid and religious. Hard work, self-control, economy. At night, their mothers would get rat-faced and rubbered, for reasons then unclear to the girls. Never enough money for milk or meat, always enough for white cider.

To go to the church that night? It had been Lili's idea.

They rode their bikes past the old stone houses, the dispensary. Lili had pink streamers on her handlebars and a clear pack full of pastel crayons. Under the world's grey roof, she was the only bright furniture.

They were going to eat the treats reserved for the after-service fellowship, some shortbread and cranachan. That was all. To warm them? It had been Lili's idea. In the dream, lighting the gas flame, Lili's face was sweet and juvenile, brave. But after they ran outside, and were watching the old church burn to the earth, her face looked as it did now, ten years older, still watching.

Alarms, demonic. In the dream it was a farmer who came first, a warm man from down the road who said, It's not your fault, you're only children. In truth it had been the police who came first, then Euna's and Lili's bewildered families, and over time the neighbours, the other folks of Bucksburn, who egged their houses, broke the windows, set fire to effigies of the girls.

Her father's shame in the dream was so heavy that Euna now felt flattened, as if a body were sleeping directly on hers. And the body, passive and impossible to lift, was steadily stifling her breath.

Euna woke to find herself gnawing deeply on her down pillow, her mouth overfed with feathers. In the same bed, too

7

close beside her, Lili was sleeping untouched. For the rest of the night Euna lay awake, sifting through memories of the past. Muireall and her then girlfriend, Grace, had read the news story and come to rescue the two girls; Euna's and Lili's fathers had been willing, if not thrilled, to let this happen. Muireall had called it her mission. Mission. Mission. Euna said the word in her head so many times now that it completely lost meaning, the way a problem held too close or too long can be leached of perspective.

Cala was the down pillow, deep in her mouth, and she needed air. By the time the sun made pink streamers of the clouds, she had decided to go out, just for a few hours.

She slipped from the house while the others were sleeping, as she often did when she felt the urge to do something illicit, like carve distress signals into her skin, or kneel to pray. She followed the lochside, a straight route to the fish farm, clear of Pullhair. Each time she started to shake or turn back, she thought of the man waving. He had not said anything so lavish as *Welcome* or *You are forgiven*. But he had shown she was not grisly or worse, invisible. He had proved to her she still existed.

*

Inside the Scottish Salmon Company hut she found a man, maybe forty, in a torn and tawny sweater. A prawn caught in his belt buckle, a langoustine clinging to his longest finger. She held herself at the threshold.

What a day for Euna to look ugly. Roseate from the wind across the heath, still dressed in tweed, hair a nest not fit for sparrows. Though the farmer was covered in dirt, she was mortified to be so grimy in front of him. She licked her palm and smoothed the nest as best she could, then pinched her lips to bring the blood nearer to the surface. At Cala, only Grace was allowed makeup, so Euna had learned the body's own beauty tricks.

May I help you? Beautiful ban-Leòdhasach, are you lost? He flung the sea creatures away from his fingers as she took a step inside the hut.

I'm sorry, she said. She was aware of how strangely she spoke, as did the other women in the coven. Over time they had settled into a common accent, fish hooks at random places in their sentences, highs where they did not belong. She thought she heard a brogue when he spoke, too, but she was not confident enough in her standard to mention it. I was hoping to buy some salmon, she said.

He laughed and clapped his hand between her shoulder-blades as if they were old friends. We don't sell fish here, he said. They do sell it at the guest house in town. Your best bet is to ask one of the kind women there.

She was stunned. Surely everyone in Pullhair knew her, she-spirit, young hag, a badhbh who needed to be sealed in her stone house so everyone could sleep at night. But here he was, chapped and compassionate, telling her to ask the women in town. She wondered if maybe he was new to the Hebrides, shipped in for a few months to fish. She was roused by a sudden energy she had not expected to feel – he did not know her from Eve, so in front of him she had the remarkable power to rewrite herself.

Thank you so much, she said. I'll try that.

If you're stuck, he said, come back. This land is fertile. No pretty girl should go without. He winked.

Strange. Cala's acreage had been bleak for so long that the women were starving. And he was saying the land here was lush?

She left the hut with a wave of her empty hands. On the long walk back to Cala, she gathered what she could, hawthorn for their hearts and juniper for their gin cylinder. She was exact with the trees. With her penknife she severed the branches, separated the berries from the wood. She would be saddled with two kinds of guilt if she came back with nothing, for failing at her task and for trying to earn a stranger's attention. One of which was shameful, the other of which was forbidden.

Euna noticed she had nicked her finger while pruning, leaving a crescent of blood above her nail. She had thought herself precise, adept, in perfect control. Yet somehow the knife had slipped.

*

Inside the farmhouse, Euna struggled to read *The Witches Speak* by candlelight. This was one of the many peculiar books Cairstìne had collected in her lifetime, which, together, formed Euna's exposure to the broader world. She squinted. She thought her eyes had grown used to the house's mood after all these years. But now she could not discern *goddess* from *goodness*, *ritual* from *rightful*. And the harder she worked to focus, the wetter the word-edges got. In much the same way, she strained to forget the fish farmer, and in so straining, the farther he bled into her.

Lili lowered her hand by the candlelight, casting a cat shadow onto the stone wall. She ran the animal across that grey span, then forced it to heel and beg for scraps. Euna did not laugh. This was a very old game. All of their games were. This one, sgàilich, was especially stale. Only Lili liked it, and so she was forever acting out shadowplays, recreating the one or two harmless experiences she remembered from her life before the coven. Euna felt an urge to burn her friend's hand on the open flame, not to punish her, but to give her a new story to tell.

You don't want to play? Lili asked. She was dressed in her pink playclothes, which she kept in a chest by the firebox.

Most days Euna would have joined in on this round of sgàilich. She hated to hurt Lili by saying no. Now she said, Leave me alone.

She saw herself in the door of the hut, hair loose.

Want had washed her feral.

Piss off, Lili said. The cat shadow curled into a circle, and then disappeared from the stone. Euna could not look at her friend directly.

The farmhouse had a kitchen, dining room, library, and pantry on the main floor, and two bedrooms upstairs, a canopy bed and a fanlight in each. So they would not grow overly attached to any particular friend, the four women had agreed to rotate beds on a monthly basis. For the month of October, Euna and Lili were to lie, tightly, in a single. And though Euna was desperate now to go upstairs and think about the fish farmer, she knew that bed could hold no secrets. Instead she took her turtleneck from the wool basket and went outside, so distracted she forgot to wear boots. Her feet unfelt the heath.

The women held ten acres. Euna walked across their plot, past a gorse copse and a range of rusting farm tools. She was headed for one of several outbuildings – the others being the latrine, sheds for their cows and goats, and a silo, all rundown past the point of even rustic beauty. She was going instead to the greenhouse, an architectural anomaly in this town of stone and timber, an all-glass address. There life bloomed well beyond its backcloth. Colour endured. Seasons burnished and then bleached; with that building, she had a living relationship.

It had been foolish of her to step outside barefoot. Her toes, death-cold, no longer seemed attached to her feet, and her soles stung. Then she came to the greenhouse and forgot quickly about her body. The flowers and ferns were her only focus. She pushed open the steam-sealed door.

Who goes? a voice asked.

Oich. Damataidh. Even in the dark, Euna could see Muireall's shape, tall, all torso.

Euna said her name out loud. It sounded odd, as if she were trying to get her own attention. But then, perhaps she had been. Muireall came ruffling through the toad rush. She was wearing her slippers and her half-slip.

In the *Life Grammar*, a book Cairstìne had conceived and then bound in a flesh of leather, were two hundred rules for a coven she had always wanted to run, but had never been able to, in want of converts.

Euna had learned to read in Sunday School until she was seven, and then she had studied the books at Cala on her own. For some of the more difficult language in the *Life Grammar*, she relied on Muireall's explanations. For instance, *CXX. No resident of Cala is to be out gallivanting after nightfall. This is to protect all women from feelings of jealousy and abandonment. And moreover to protect them from the prying eyes of the villagers.*

Euna, it's dark, Muireall said. You should be back at home reading.

I got sick of that, Euna said.

So you came here to pick some peonies? Muireall asked. Or nibble on a head of cabbage?

Suddenly Euna felt very naked, though Muireall was the one in the half-slip. She hid her bare feet under a mandevilla bush.

Go back to the house, Muireall said. Lili will be so lonely.

If only Euna could steep the starwash above the glass roof. She needed to see her friend's face more clearly, to know how stern this demand was meant to be. Sometimes Muireall had a bit of play in her. But sometimes, sombre and firm, she meant to punish. With strops and school rulers, if needed, she meant to punish. I just wanted a minute on my own, Euna said, trying to sound dutiful.

Muireall broke several flowers from a nearby stem, wee and white in the low light. Euna could not be sure, but she worried by their shape and shade they might be foxglove. Take this back to the house, Muireall said. Tell Grace to make you a tincture.

Euna knew she would have no privacy tonight. What she wanted now was much simpler: to avoid punishment. To keep her body free of this tincture. She took the plant from Muireall and in so doing grazed her hand. Her interaction with the fish farmer had stirred up so many feelings, desire

13

and fear and frustration, that she needed a place to rest them. And why not in Muireall's hand, caked with loam and clay? It tingled, that fleeting touch.

Thank you, Euna said. Muireall struck her on her flank, surely, as if Euna were one of their two stabled horses.

Euna left the greenhouse and headed back across the heath. Somehow the ground had grown colder. She walked as quickly as she could, to keep her feet in perfect tact. The fish farmer had been kind – why had Muireall told her for years that everyone was a possible enemy? Now her trust had a hairline crack in it; a trace of red marrow was showing. She glanced down at the possibly poisonous flowers in her arms.

When she got to the door, she was grateful not to hear any sound in the house. Then, entering, she ruptured the thing she had so loved. She wanted to be air, as here and gone as air, but she was far from pure. She was inexact, embodied, the long nails that turned into trimmings, the long hair that clogged the bath drain. The feet that forked the perfect dark.

She stubbed her toe on the grandmother clock by the library door. The hulking thing clanked and shook. Then Euna heard footsteps coming from upstairs – by the pointed sound, she knew they belonged to Grace. She always wore Florentine heels, even when inside, which made a fine art of her legs. Her beauty had in many ways made her life more difficult; these hang-ups, the heels, a habit of smearing her cheeks with rouge even before sleep, were more obligation than choice. They had only worsened after Muireall broke off her relationship with Grace, choosing instead to follow a life of celibacy.

At the top of the stairs, a torch illuminated Grace. She gestured with her free hand for Euna to come up the stairs.

Euna obeyed. She was still carrying the plant, and when she reached Grace she handed the blossoms to her without saying a word.

Through the thin door, Euna could hear Lili singing her nightly devotions. She would be in her sleep tunic, on her knees beside the bed. *A chrostag! Today I smelled like an old reindeer. A chrostag! Today I wore dirty nylons.* The chorus, *A chrostag!* – naughty girl! – never changed, though each day she added the particulars. Euna wondered what would happen if she were to kneel now and sing her own version.

Grace smelled the flowers, then let Euna do the same. It was not foxglove at all. It was full, holy hyacinth. Had Muireall really been trying to comfort her – had she sensed a pit and aimed to fill it with flowers? Fear had such a loud way of speaking. Maybe all of these acts had been tender, plucking the plant, striking the flank, and the violence had not been in Muireall's hands but in Euna's mind.

A chrostag! Today I was a very bad girl but oh, I will be better tomorrow. This was always the final line of the song. Soon Euna would hear the sounds of Lili snoring, as she had every night that month. In the lull between sing and snore, Euna said, Muireall wanted you to make a tincture of that.

Grace's grin had a cutting edge. She wants to make you smell beautiful, she said.

The women had many ways of furnishing their time: weaving on their grand loom, divining using frogs and figs, playing their synthesizer, making perfumes for one another. This last pastime often ended in an odd stridency of smells, especially when all four of them wore different scents on the same calendar day. Euna's tended to be bloomy, big, and exceedingly sweet, though she had never chosen that character and in fact got the occasional rash because of it.

Grace patted Euna on the top of her head, as if a mother sending her girl to bed. She and Muireall were twenty-eight, Euna and Lili eighteen, and in moments like this the smallish gap felt mammoth. Euna took her nightgown from their communal dresser, which was nestled into a nook close to where Grace had been standing at the top of the stairs. They were not allowed to keep clothing anywhere else in the house. All of it had to be folded in the same way, sweaters with the arms pulled forcefully behind the back, underwear rolled into pipes. As Grace descended the stairs, presumably to trim and vase the hyacinth, Euna moved behind the paper screen and changed into the nightgown. She neatly gathered her linen shirt and trousers, then placed them in the bottom of their shared laundry hamper. The next day, she would beat them with salt and flat-edged stones, along with the rest of the garments of the coven.

She felt her way into the bedroom, as Lili had already blown out the eventide candle. She laid on her side of the bed, closest to the porthole. From that window, there was a ladder one could climb if she needed to use the latrine. Euna rarely woke in the night, but if she were to sleep on the far side of the bed, she would almost certainly feel trapped. She would toss for hours, wondering what would happen if she needed to pee and did not want to wake Lili and her thousand attendant remarks.

The bed would have been perfectly comfortable, had it been larger. The mattress was filled well with foam, and the pillows were cased in antique silk. But in order to lie down, Euna had to turn onto her side and align her hips to Lili's, rest one hand on her own leg and tuck the other near Lili's backside. This was the part that made her feel rangy and inelegant. Each night the same question: what to do with her hands?

She lifted the coverlet to her jaw and then creased it between their two bodies as a kind of border. Lili was snoring, but gently. Through the porthole, the moon floodlit one feature of the room – a painting of Cairstìne Bruce.

Over the curve of Lili's ear, Euna watched the image. Watched and watched and in the moonlight watched. After a long while her eyes were scraped dry. And then she had no choice but to close them, and hope she would not dream.

*

Two weeks later, the women had started to feel downcast by the short, sunless days. Every year was the same, a slow decline in their energy, starting in October. That was the heaviest month, the evening light first excised. Lili had suggested they distract themselves by celebrating Samhain a few weeks early, and at breakfast, no less – to everyone's surprise, Muireall had agreed.

The four of them were sitting around the table in their usual seats, Euna on a campstool, Muireall on a bishop's throne they had found abandoned by the edge of their property. Muireall had made a tart of common nettles and some unnameable kind of mince. It was a chore to choke each bite down. If bland were a colour; if beige were a taste. But it was an offence to use sauce or seasoning on others' cooking, so Euna worked her fork in and out of the tart without a word.

Where did this meat come from? Grace asked Muireall. I didn't think we had anything left.

Muireall drank from her tankard of tea. She was in the business of withholding – rationing their bath salts one day, their rhubarb preserves the next. She seemed to be relishing this moment she was presiding over.

I need to know what I'm eating, Grace said. I don't want to get fat again, like I did when you hid whey in our food.

Muireall drank her tea with a little satisfied smile.

Grace said, Just answer. Christ.

The word clanged. Against their copper mugs, their cuts of maybe-mutton, the strange thing rang. *Life Grammar, CIX. No discussions of religion or overtly religious language will be tolerated inside Cala. In the fern garden, residents are allowed to whistle hymns, provided they omit all lyrics.* Muireall straightened the neck of her black tunic, which she sometimes wore over her uniform linen shirt for warmth. She was looking straight at Grace. Pardon, she said. It's just crushed mushrooms and a slice of pig fat.

Euna blamed herself for the tension. Since meeting the fish farmer she had become increasingly sullen, sometimes rude, and she could only imagine the effects of her behaviour on the other women in such a sealed environment. And so she tried to calm everyone by pouring a round of water, rearranging the posies at the centre of their table. She was desperate for conversation. But she could only think of the fish farm. Do you know, she asked, that salmon eat their own kind? At the farm they're fed fishmeal and oil.

Lili touched the pompoms in her pigtails, mismatched, one large and one tiny. They don't really have a choice, she said.

Her fingers were swift, lifting the curled ends of her hair. She asked, Would they be better off dying?

The wind tossed a pale detail at the bay window, antler, branch, or bone. The sound was sharp, and they started. Nature, here, tended to encroach. Euna said, I don't know what it's like to be a fish. I wish I did.

Muireall's laugh was bright and genuine. You can be so strange, she said, pinching a sprig of parsley from Euna's lips. As it had in the greenhouse, their touch felt charged. And perhaps even more so, this being an act of care.

Euna is a damp lump lately, Lili said. She's making the walls mouldy. She won't even play sgàilich.

You naughty goat, Grace said, winking at Euna.

All the women kept speaking, one over the other, but Euna was no longer among them. The touch from Muireall had reminded her of a more vital touch, in the fish farmer's hut – so brief and unobtrusive, that clap on her upper back. Between the two of them had moved a dark, flickering current, a sort of pop and snap. Mearanach, she heard someone say now, another word for delirious. The -nach sparkling and black, like a horsewhip through air, morning light catching leather.

An idea penetrated Euna. She felt the tip of that dark current again. When I went to get the fish, the – she improvised a title – foreman said I could come back if we were really stuck, she said.

Muireall took a slow drag of her tea. From the mug came the smell of peat, a sea-mossy sweetness. Is my food not good enough for you? she asked.

Truth was Euna was sick of the tart and the earth tea and the burned ends of tree resins that always fucked with the vibe

19

of the table. She was sick of tucking her ankles underneath it while her thighs pulsed, pretending the tick of the grandmother clock was discreet, even pleasant. It was killing her to be sinless. Through the window she looked at the mattock. They used it mostly when gardening, tilling ground that could house bushes. For a pulse she saw blood on its metal head.

I've been so hungry lately, Euna said, coolly as she could. It's nearly winter, you know. I need to feed myself.

XXX. No woman living at Cala shall develop feelings for anyone outside of the coven. XXXI. A woman in the coven may unintentionally contravene XXX; should this happen, she will under no condition explore the feelings in a physical manner. This is for the safety and well-being of all parties involved.

On the table they kept an unopened bottle of wine, a token of some untouched, luscious future. They all wanted to drink it; Euna, deeply. But they restrained themselves each meal. They knew an occasion would come. Some special day would swoop down on Cala and the women would need a red. Until then they would find other ways to hold off their thirst.

Why don't you go hunting if you need meat so badly? Muireall asked Euna. I saw a few hares last time I was out on the heath.

Rabbit was Euna's favourite food, braised, slow-roasted. Most days the animal would get her mouth wet. Now the idea of eating it disgusted her. The bodies that lived on land – badgers, deer, rodents she could not name – seemed tainted. Even vegetables, the leeks and the white-skinned turnips, were thick with earth funk. Not the sea creatures. All salted, clean as a loch.

Lili, Euna said, turning to her friend. Do you remember how good that salmon we had on the equinox was, covered in ginger?

The girl perked up. She seemed thrilled by this memory. Of course, she said. I think about it all the time.

Grace said, I could use some of that oil. This weather is ravaging my face.

Absently, Muireall had started to play with the wine bottle. Euna waited for her to speak. Her grip tightened when she reached its neck; rare for the other women to express an opinion contrary to hers. I don't care what you do, she said. But if you see another soul, you will come back here right away. I won't let you parade around, getting the attention of everyone in town. It's not all about you, Euna.

Euna nodded. She finished her tart and waited for the others to do the same before carrying their plates outside and scraping them into the compost drum. She brought the plates inside and, with a pail of water from their storage cask, rinsed them one by one, chary of chipping the porcelain. The other people in town, according to Grace, had taps. But Muireall insisted they honour the legacy of Cairstìne Bruce, who had been unable to afford plumbing. They showered in the latrine, even in winter, water going rigid on their clavicles. Ice hitched to their small notches.

As she cleaned the dishes, Euna heard the squeak of the cork in the dining room. She was shocked. She took her time, poured washing soda, scoured the last traces of fat from the plates. Then she came back into the dining room to see Muireall's mouth stained red, as if blood-fed. Grace lipping the top of the bottle, Lili sitting spellbound. Euna had to leave. She felt, at any moment, her friends could equally get naked, wield the mattock, throw fake meat at the wall, dance in open ecstasy. Wild women, caged in peeling wallpaper.

She took her turtleneck from the wool basket. The frost would have dissipated a bit by now, it being mid-morning. Still the world was bound to be cold, especially by the loch. I'll come back soon, she said.

We haven't even celebrated Samhain yet, Muireall said.

Euna said, I know. But I'm doing this for Cala. She thought she heard a small growl from Muireall, a cornered creature. Euna knew it would be wiser to wait until Muireall was calmer before leaving the grounds. But wisdom, in her life, had been a weak master. She crossed the threshold, into the frost.

*

The hut was empty when she arrived an hour later, having walked her feet into strident pain. At least this time she had remembered to wear boots. Having taken the path along the sealoch, she had managed to avoid all of the townsfolk. But any pride she felt in her stealth now disappeared. He was not here. She had deluded herself. She did not even know how fish farmers worked, if they were given temporary contracts, if they sailed from port to port. No wonder he had not known who she was.

She was too drained to return to the farmhouse right away. So she closed the door of the hut and lay down on its hard cot. A hundred hard thoughts lay down beside her. Her life was going to continue exactly as it had been. And so she would have ice on her collarbones all winter. And so she would eat nettles at the same time every day, and fall asleep each night to the sound of Lili snoring. And so she would never bear children. And so she would lose her looks and be a wretched, run-of-the-mill witch. And so, after all the hard work of enduring, she would just die bored.

She had started to sweat. She ran her hands along the rough blanket the fish farmer, or whoever now inhabited this hut, slept under. It was terribly thin, as if military issue, and it was peppered with small holes. There was no pillow. The only way she could make herself comfortable was to rest on her back with one leg straight and the other folded in a triangle, her head turned to the right.

Her fear had a form, of a wave moving over her, polished and black. There were no windows in the hut. Pale light filtered only through tiny pits in its door. Before long, the wave was indiscernible against her skin.

*

Euna opened her eyes in a state of confusion. She had woken in one of two bedrooms for the last decade, and this was neither. This place was cooler, less adorned. And then she made out the fish farmer's face, cragged and attentive, a foot above hers.

I hope it's okay that I touched you, he said. You weren't answering.

She had been so timid the last time that she had hardly allowed herself to look at him. She saw now that he had thick, black eyebrows connected above the bridge of his nose, and a full head of silver-flecked hair. Around his neck, where she expected to see iconography – Jesus on the cross, a pentagram

– was a plain pendant made of driftwood, a thick block with no other markings.

Euna sat up and felt the cot shift beneath her. I shouldn't be here, she said.

The farmer was looking at her with something close to concern, or pity, and she did not like to be looked at in that way. She wanted to be desirable. Magnificent. A horse loose on the heath, not a bird in need of feeding.

I came to get some food, she said, nuzzling a little into her turtleneck. Her face was icy and she worried it was lined from sleep. So she thought it best to hide everything but her eyes, which were green and lovely in most water surfaces. Muireall had banned mirrors in the house.

The farmer said, smiling, I already told you we don't sell fish here.

Euna could not move farther into her turtleneck without disappearing entirely, so she sat there wondering about the parting in her hair. Was it dry, dandruffed? He would never love such a saltine. She felt much worse than she had walking into the empty hut. At least then her future plans had been deferred, not rejected.

I'll catch my own, she said. I should never have bothered you here. Standing, she realized her foot had fallen asleep.

One chapped hand, on her breastplate, held her in place. With the other hand he tugged down her turtleneck, baring her lips. The damage of autumn on her mouth – he dampened it. He dulled its brand. Her skin lit up like an electric cage. He asked her to lift her arms and then removed her turtleneck and linen shirt, leaving her uncovered. He did the same with her trousers. No ritual. The hut was so cold that once she was

24

nude, she was in pain. Her scalloped underclothing, at least, was washed.

Some animal scraped the door, trying to enter the hut. Its claw fitted into one of the small holes in the wood. Mink, maybe, or marten. The farmer's instinct was to wrap his arm tightly around her neck, an act both protective and threatening – a defensive hold or a headlock, she could not tell. The animal clawed and clawed, desperately trying to enter, and then it conceded. Euna heard its footsteps on the frozen ground as it withdrew. The farmer did not ease his hold, even when the animal was gone.

His teeth were on her trap muscle. She liked the way it felt, until the bright stir gave way to a sting, a pang. She touched her fingertips to the place he had been feeding and found blood. Was this what people did to one another? She had learned of intimacy from her poetry books. Maybe that cut of love, tender, well considered, did not exist in the real world. For a few minutes, they did the forbidden act. It hurt, in part. Still, she had come through many seasons of non-feeling, and even a sting, a pang, did not bother her as much as that numbness had.

When they were finished, he whispered in her ear, You're a very special girl. Then he drew back completely so he was not touching her anywhere.

She could barely turn to face him, she felt so defenceless. She pulled up her scalloped underpants. By the time she noticed the red on her thighs, the cotton had already absorbed it. She would need to set fire to these drawers. Muireall would know it was not yet time for her period – by now, they all shared a cycle. Fuil mhìosail. For five days Cala turned into a place of disquiet and mystic power, all that iron in the air.

The farmer helped her back into her turtleneck, then gripped her chin lightly. She needed to get out of the hut and back to the farmhouse. Can you give me some prawns? she asked. I can't go home empty-handed.

He kissed her on the cheek. His voice was gentle when he asked, Do you have a few more minutes to spare?

She knew the longer she was gone, the stronger the retribution would be. But the electric cage was lighting up again and so she looked through his eyes at the soft affect behind them and said, Yes.

He rummaged through a suitcase at the head of the bed, eventually retrieving a fawn cardigan. Its arms he held out straight as pegs, waiting for Euna to enter. Then she was warm, warmer than she had been before that first pain of being nude.

Come with me, he said. He led her by the wrist out of the hut. The world was, by any measure, deeply grey. And yet, emerging from that dank and carnal hut, it seemed to flame with colour.

*

The farmer led her to the edge of the sealoch. He had brought a very fine throw net, and he wrapped her fingers around its sanded wooden handle. You could learn to survive here alone, he said. All you need to know is how to catch your own food.

Thank you for your help, she said. But I have true friends, so I don't need to survive alone.

I would like to count myself in that number, he said. I'm Aram.

26

Euna, she said.

And where are you from, Euna?

She felt hot-faced, blasted by his attention. She turned the question quickly around on him.

My father was from Glenfinnan, he said. He died when I was a kid, and since my mother is from Sketimini and they were never married, she wasn't allowed to stay. We lived on a boat in the Atlantic. This is a special secret for a special girl, but my contract finished today, and I'm no longer legally allowed here.

Euna had never heard of Sketimini, but she would not consent to sounding ignorant, so she stayed quiet.

If you're a citizen, he said, consider yourself lucky.

She had never thought of herself as a citizen of anywhere. Nor had she thought of herself as lucky. I suppose so, she said.

On the water she saw a primitive dock and some sharp, impassive rocks. No ships were tethered nearby. The salmon farm, a half kilometre east, was more densely populated with people and their trappings. Two dozen fishermen and seasonal labourers, a supervisor, all manner of heavy machinery, flits of light and activity. Down the sealoch she could see the scene more clearly than she had from Cala. And yet, where she and Aram stood felt so sequestered, the farm could have been a mutual hallucination.

He helped her to cock her arms back, preparing to cast the net. And then they let it fly, the nylon free in the moorland clouds. They found the rhythm that had been absent from their forbidden act. The net broke the water's surface loudly, and Euna felt a slight tug as the weights around its hoop moved deeper into the sea. Aram stood behind her now, clutching her just above the waist, around the middle ribs. He ordered her to drag the net back toward them. He functioned as an anchor. He did not help her do the work, but he made sure she did not lose her footing.

In the net was an algal garland. Wig wrack poked through the nylon; maerl, too, in great red snarls. But not a single fish or crustacean, even on closer inspection. Let's try that again, Aram said.

Euna did not wear a watch, and this drab time of year it was hard to read the sky. She suspected it was late afternoon. Muireall and even Grace would be sitting on the daybed with stingers on their tongues, waiting for her to come back. She did not want to test their mercy any more than she already had. I'm afraid I have to go home, she said to him. I don't really have a choice.

Aram looked surprised. Doesn't sound like much of a home to me, he said. He took his hands back, leaving her alone with the load of the cast net. She stumbled forward before managing to steady herself.

Euna lowered the net to the ground. Though this part of the coast looked less grey than did Cala, she felt guilty for having poached the algae. Surely, unlike Euna, they served a greater purpose. But she was too frazzled to stay and throw them back. And sure, too busy professing with her body not to want Aram. The *Life Grammar* stated that a woman must offer a blessing instead of a goodbye, so she said, Slàinte mhath! *Good health!* She started to walk in the direction of Cala.

She heard the sound of the net entering the water one last time, then Aram's voice calling her back. He held out to her a net of prawns. Trembling, not yet dead. She stretched the belly of her turtleneck in front of her, making a hammock for their small bodies, like a mother entrusted with their survival. She had to get them home. She forced herself to move from Aram, alone on the crushed-rock road they had first walked together.

*

Euna's strategy for coming home was simple. Do not skulk, do not slink, do not try to pass as invisible. Own your badness. So she let the front door of Cala slam behind her and stamped right to the pantry with her boots on to find a jar for the prawns. It was only after she found one and placed them gingerly inside that she noticed they were dead. She had failed to keep them alive. Or worse, she had killed them. She twisted the lid on tightly, then carried the container with her to the library, pausing briefly in the entry to unlace her boots and remove her wool apparel. Cac a' choin. She was still wearing the farmer's cardigan.

In the library, she found Lili reclined on the daybed with a string in her hands. No sign of Grace or Muireall. Oh, Euna, Lili said, sitting up. I was so worried about you. Will you come play Cat's Cradle?

Euna sometimes envied the girl. Her emotions had the depth and span of a crustacean's, coming and going with a nonchalance Euna found incredible. In Euna, feelings took root and remained, sometimes for days, months. The soot of her encounter with Aram was settling in her thoughts and heart. She was replaying her memories from the afternoon, from the time he kissed her to the time she said her blessing, when she noticed that Lili was hanging the string in front of her face.

29

Are you going to play or not? she asked.

Euna's cold fingers had no sense left in them. It was a wonder they were still gripping the jar, but they were, and she managed to offer it to Lili. A distraction. That's all the girl needed. She took that cold smooth and turned it in her hands. On Cairstìne's shelf was a picture book called *Where Do I Find My Kind of Blue?*, in which a bluebird whose home has been destroyed by a forest fire flies from continent to continent, searching for birds who look like her, so she can join their avian family. Lili's eyes were wide as that bird's. They're dead! she said.

Euna reached her hand out to touch the small of Lili's back. The movement was mechanical, at first meaningless. And then, the longer she maintained that contact, the more warmth radiated from it. Lili, too, seemed to temper. The shame that had numbed Euna when she saw the dead prawns started to lift. She at least could care for Lili, simple, sinless girl that she was.

The front door opened. Above its rasp and scrape was a more hostile sound, of Grace yelling. If I have to wear dirty underwear tomorrow because of her, Christ help me.

Grace and Muireall stamped into the library, both red as fescue. Grace cursed at Euna, undressing her for all the Cala hours she had missed, while Muireall stood in a silence that was by its rarity unnerving. Euna's hand was still on Lili's back, and Grace forcibly removed it. You need to do the washing, she said. My clothes smell like the cowshed.

Lili started to cry. This was uncommon in their home, not because they never wanted to, but because the *Life Grammar* dictated that no one in the coven should be *that kind of woman*. The rigour of some of the rules prompted Euna to think of her father, wedded to the Kirk, welded tightly to hard work and prudence. Likewise, here, a person had to steel all feelings.

At first Lili cried in a stylish way, a modest gloss on her eyes. Then the tip of her nose turned pink and Euna knew a great ugliness was coming, just seconds before it did come, in gasps and wails. Lili slid down the daybed and onto her knees, bare beneath her playclothes. She sobbed until Grace struck her, backhanded, on the cheek.

Then came a long silence. A complete lack of action.

After a few minutes, Muireall said, Would anyone like some tea?

The jar had rolled to the edge of their bearskin rug, which lay, lifeless and conquered, in the centre of the library. Euna had been too tired to notice Lili drop the prawns. Harshness was a sort of sedative. After a day of killing beeves, or backbiting townsfolk they had never met, she wanted nothing but to light a fire and recline in front of it, holding broth. Or empty-handed, bound by a flannel pall. Today she had that same sense.

Lili got to her feet, with a hand from Grace. I'll have some tea, she said. Her pigtails were messy, but otherwise she looked unharmed.

The air in the room was gummy. Euna felt the way she sometimes did when reading a text by candlelight – the tide of tiredness dragging her down. She compelled herself to stand and walk up the stairs to the laundry hamper. At least she could do the task she had been assigned, strike it from their list of stresses. She separated the delicate clothes from the hardy ones, making two distinct piles on the sorting table. Through the floorboards she could hear the harsh whistle of the kettle.

She did not, at least, have the impression that anything was lingering. Grace had screamed, and the passion had passed through their home. Nothing was simmering, everything had boiled over, the kettle had shut up and the Earl Grey would be steeping. She put the separated clothes into two reed baskets and, though it was dusk now and she could barely see, carried those out to the washing creek.

In its water, she worked the clothes with her salt and flat-edged stones. She thrashed one jumper so hard its right armpit tore. Everything needed to be immaculate, to look as if it had never been worn by a body. She remembered the blood stains in her underwear, and she yanked off her trousers to remove them. There she crouched on the bank of the creek, naked from the waist down, shaking. She beat and beat and beat the underwear, using most of her store of salt. A thread of red followed the movement of the creek.

She was crying. She must have looked deranged. Or as if she were doing a ritual, skyclad. But no one was there to see it, no mink or marten, even. She cried so dry that her brow pounded, her sinuses seared hard from the inside. She wiped her eyes, forgetting she still had salt in her palm, and then that hurt crept across her corneas.

She stood so the pain would have more room to diffuse. Here she was, as Lot's wife had been after looking at Sodom, turned to a pillar of salt. She should not have peered at that other life – Do not look behind you, nor stop anywhere in the Plain – and for her blunder she was going to burn.

After a few minutes, her tears flushed out the salt. She looked down at the underwear and saw that the stain, though it lingered, had faded significantly. And so she crouched back down. And so she resumed her chore. And so.

*

The next morning, Muireall proposed they make a potion together, since they had not had a chance to properly celebrate Samhain. In her early days in the coven, as a little, excitable, impressionable kid, Euna remembered performing all the rituals they believed good sorceresses should. Divining with incense ash, sacrificing roosters, handfasting. She had been young, but even then she had noticed in Muireall an arcane streak. She seemed to receive a much stronger charge from these rituals than did the other women.

Now they all agreed to make the Samhain potion, because these occasions had become rare. Their herbs were kept in a breakfront cupboard under the stairs, and they watched as Muireall selected them one at a time. Blood leather, bat flower, holy rope. Shameface, snakeweed. These herbs purred to Euna. In her long list of burdens and chores, heaving weeds and peeing in the cold and sweeping stone floors, she had forgotten how deeply these rituals had once affected her. They had spread wide the edges of Cala. With that spreading had come fear, of course. But in response to the fear, she had always grown greater, not shut down.

Lili, Muireall said, heat up the kettle. Bring me some dry smoke and the largest container you can find.

The girl clopped off. What are we making? Euna asked.

Grace was herself again today, or rather, she was the Grace who showed through most often. On her lips was a bright rose tint, and on her high cheeks was a clear mineral powder, most likely crushed quartz. She looked radiant, runic. We'll just have to wait and see, she said to Euna.

No, we won't, Euna said, noticing a pulse in her throat. We used to tell each other everything.

LI. No resident of Cala shall discuss the past. And here was Euna saying *used to*, that criminal phrase. Easy now, Muireall warned her. Lili returned with the dry smoke and an amphora they once kept the oil they pressed in, before their rapeseed crops had withered and died.

Here you go, Lili said brightly, oblivious to the mood that had started to settle in under the stairs.

Thank you, mè bheag, Muireall said. This was another of Euna's favourite endearments, baa lamb, in a kind of baby talk.

She placed the amphora on their dining-room table, removed its heavy lid, and started to pour the herbs liberally into it. Euna wondered why she had asked for such a massive vessel. She could not imagine a need for so much of this mix. In the kitchen, the kettle started to screech again, and Lili ran to silence it, then came back to pour all of its scalding water into the amphora. She offered Muireall a long-handled spoon.

The blend smelled like a goat barn that had gone a long time without being mucked. Theirs, Lili cleaned daily, fluffing the hay beds and forking the cac into a stack by the rockery. Otherwise bacteria could spread, or lice, and a dirty animal was of no use to them. Muireall lowered her face close to the surface and inhaled deeply. Beautiful, she said. Euna wondered if in the years of making perfume Muireall had singed the hairs in her nose.

Grace took four ceramic bowls from the buffet and put them on the table beside Muireall. Instead of getting a ladle, Muireall dipped each bowl into the liquid one at a time, slopping herbs and hot water onto the unstained teak. Lili ran for a rag and cleaned what she could, though part of the wood had already rinsed white.

Shall we drink? Muireall asked. She was holding her bowl to her lips, which had an odd sheen and crack pattern, as if covered in fish scales.

To cleanliness and godliness, Grace said.

Muireall paused. Though she left the troubling words untouched.

The four of them drank. The wet bite was repellent, and immediately Euna started to retch. She held the bile inside. Her body often housed things it should have expelled, hiccoughs and sneezes, so this was not hard for her. The others seemed to be fine with the bitter taste. Lili wiped her mouth with the back of her hand and then took another long pull from the bowl. They had not yet eaten breakfast. Maybe the girl was just famished.

Euna continued to dry heave a few times, her mouth sealed. Had she been alone with any one of them, she would have admitted to the nausea, but in the group she pretended to enjoy the potion.

When they were done drinking, Muireall put the lid back on the amphora. The rest is for the livestock, she said. They had gone from eighty goats when Euna first arrived to twenty; twelve cows to seven; innumerable chickens to a dozen. The broods were not surviving, and no one could say for certain why. Their hogs were long gone, and the stores of fat in their icebox were diminishing, at this point more slice than slab. Muireall had explained that the Cala land was not particularly rich and that growing a sustainable crop would

35

be burdensome, if not impossible, so they routinely ignored the necessity of doing so. Her choice to make this brew today for the benefit of the animals showed prudence. Euna was dubious about its actual effects on the livestock, but the value of the ritual, the intention, she did not question.

Do you want me to take this out to the animals? Lili asked, gesturing to the amphora.

Yes, Muireall said. Make sure each one gets a good, long drink. Okay, my little tattie?

Lili nodded. She ran to put on her rain boots and came back to retrieve the heavy amphora, tracking dried mud into the dining room in the process. Muireall did not seem to notice, and if she did, she stayed quiet about it. Her spirit seemed light, while Grace's was ungainly. Did they carry a set amount of shade between them, and now it was Grace's turn to shoulder it? Lili grunted as she lugged the amphora out of the house. Euna stacked the empty bowls and took them to the kitchen. It was not her duty to wash them this week, so she left them in the soak basin.

She spent the next few hours on the daybed in the library, reading. Her nausea returned with great force and she rushed outside. She did not make it as far as the latrine, heaving instead beside their massive compost drum. She had forgotten to eat before tasting the potion. The vomit was serous, and she was revolted that her body could produce such a colour and consistency.

Kneeling in the dirt, she was reminded of just how non-fish she was. How woman. She had all of these parts, stinking, leaking parts, ruled by inner drives, never by sheer will. She was ashamed to be this creature. Though she had learned to bear the other women's earthiness, hair under their armpits, herb stalks stuck in their teeth, she had been raised by a father obsessed with neatness, restraint. And that had yet to leave her.

Down the flagstones to their door, she heard footsteps. They were too heavy to be Lili's. Euna did not want anyone to see her in this shape, so she crouched low behind the drum. She could not see the person, but she could tell by the sound of their footsteps that they were significant. A congregant from Pullhair had come a few months prior to proselytize, and she wondered if he had returned.

A knock. Some stomping inside, a pot dropping, Muireall's voice hushed by the unopened door. Can I help you? she asked.

I'd like to come in. The voice belonged, unmistakably, to Aram. Euna dry heaved silently. The drum was twenty metres from the door, so she managed to do this without being noticed. A secret, sour taste clung to her tongue. Though she longed to spit it out, instead she swallowed.

Is this a practical joke? Muireall asked. Even when the proselytizer had come, she had treated him delicately, maybe bearing in mind what had happened to Cairstìne. Euna wondered why she was not kid-gloving Aram, if what she recognized in him was essential decency or weakness.

I'm sorry, he said. I need to speak to Euna.

Keep that name out of your damain mouth, Muireall said. The door swung open so hard it slammed against the home's stone exterior. How do you know her?

This was the moment for Euna to reveal herself. She knew her world would be distorted by her failure to intervene, and yet she could not let Aram see her looking so pale, undesirable. She tried to stand. Aram was already speaking with great assurance, not realizing how ruinous his words were. We met a week ago, he was saying. She stopped by the Salmon Company. She was looking for some seafood to share with you all, I think.

Muireall was silent. She was a passive listener, and even after years Euna could not decipher her hush. Sometimes it meant she was heeding the words quite deeply, and other times it meant she was far afield, yielding to some unrelated thought. And then she came back to my hut yesterday, Aram said. I found her sleeping on the cot, poor thing.

What did you just say? Muireall asked.

Lili came skipping back down the flagstones, bless her, little tattie. She was singing to herself an aria, eerie in its creep across the cold noon. *Una macchia è qui tuttora! Via, ti dico, o maledetta!* This was Verdi's version of Lady Macbeth – they had the sheet music in their library. *A stain is still here! Go away, I tell you, or be cursed!* Euna thought of her blood-ied underwear, folded in a careful triangle at the bottom of their communal dresser. She had scrubbed and scrubbed the previous evening, and still.

Oh, no, Lili said. Her footsteps stopped. I didn't see you there, Muireall!

Euna was so sorry for everything. Her heart was begging pardon, her stomach, the branch between her hip and her thigh – she was envious of Lady Macbeth's unruliness, and Lili's, and in her own way Muireall's. Only Euna was bitch enough to succumb to her base self, and then to hide from the consequences. The earth below her was full of ground beetles, godless things. She belonged among them.

Lili, my darling, Muireall said. Do you mind getting me some tea?

It would be my pleasure, she said, curtsying. And then, Hello, I don't believe we've met. My name is Lili.

Aram introduced himself. He asked her, Do you know where I might be able to find Euna?

Lili laughed. She's very sick today, she said. Spewing the way my mam used to before she had my little brother. Then a pause, possibly a look from Muireall. So then, she said, I'm going to put the kettle on.

Euna heard the door close behind Lili. Muireall lowered her voice. You need to tell me why you're here, and then you need to leave.

I came here to warn Euna we have sea-lice on the farm, Aram said. I didn't know, or I would have told her at the time. If she got any of our salmon from the women in town, you shouldn't eat it.

Is that what you came to say?

Well, he told Muireall, I also wanted to see her again.

Muireall said, Leave right now. If you don't, I will get the mattock.

A stand-off, a silence. Then eventually, Aram walked back down the path, and Euna's stomach hardened into a flagstone. He was leaving for good. Muireall would never send her on another seafood errand, not that there were any healthy fish left. And worse, he hadn't given any details about the sea-lice. Could they hop to human hair? Had her afternoon with him threatened her well-being? And that of Cala, so carefully cultivated over the years?

Peeking her head around the drum, she saw that Muireall had gone back into the house. Euna's skin itched. She clawed at her underwear, convinced there were living things inside, certain the infestation had started. Then she stood, shaking the imagined insects from her insides, inseams, making herself feel inferior. She had gone from Mary Magdalene to Jezebel, sorceress to scum-witch. The build had cost her years, the fall no time at all.

She imagined herself at a fork in the sea, currents moving from this pass in several directions. She could go back inside; she could go to the Salmon Company hut; she could leave Pullhair entirely. In her jumper pockets were pest-holes, pieces of dried tissue, but no notes or coins. Indigence had never interested her. Nor had isolation. She was already living with lack. Off-grid, ice-cold. She had already sacrificed soul and body comfort for another kind, a simple sort of oblivion.

She vomited again behind the drum. There was nothing in her belly, so what came out was close to saliva, if a little yellower. She picked a leaf from a nearby alder tree and wiped her mouth clean. She still found nature friendly, despite the dying goats and cattle, the infected seafood.

Euna looked long at the farmhouse, then turned in the direction of the Salmon Company hut, and farther, the ferry. She wavered. Just past noon, the first-quarter moon hovered above her. If Muireall were not ruling Euna, then that heaven-body would. Like the tawny owls and the weasels and the fallen acorns, links in the same long chain, a woman could never truly be free.

II

Six months had passed since Aram came to declare his infestation. Euna had convinced herself the sea-lice were all over her. As keepsake. As relic of the afternoon she upended her simple life. She was certain that Aram had been sent back to Sketimini, or had been scared off permanently by Muireall. Either way she would never see him again, so their afternoon together had blurred into mythology. He had moved softly, soporific with feeling; he had cradled the back of her skull after they made love. He had burned frankincense and myrrh, transforming the hut into a holy place.

At Cala, it was the first day of fuil mhìosail, their communal period. Spring had started to green the heath again, though gradually, and without glory. Usually on this first morning, they congregated in the library to sit in a Tension Line, in which they would give one another neck massages. Euna tended to be on the end, so she rarely received a rub. Today she came downstairs to find the other three women lying on their backs on the bearskin rug, looking in silence at the exposed beams.

She did not say anything. She lay between Lili and Grace, her feet a fourth point in their natal star. Through the bear's skin, she could still feel the cold floor on her back. In another world, the four of them would have been on warm grass instead, just like this, crowns and hands touching, cloud-gazing.

After some time, Muireall said, This is going to be a painful day for all of us.

Because Euna was already feeling the stomach cramps, the pale aura that preceded a migraine, she said, Amen.

She knew as soon as the word slipped that it had been a mistake. Muireall grabbed a handful of the bearskin and pulled its wire-hairs out by the roots. In the last few months, her conduct had grown more and more erratic. She swung from pole to pole, sometimes in a matter of minutes, and not in the charming way Lili sometimes did. If Lili were a goldfish, harmless and distracted, Muireall was a bull shark.

Euna is so special the Lord himself is cupping her blood, she said. She let go of the wire-hairs and ran her palm along the bare patch in the rug. After we're done here, she said, she will come to the greenhouse with me.

Worse than when she gave Euna orders was when she spoke about her as if she were absent. It was hard for Euna to name her emotions lately, and harder still during fuil mhìosail, but she thought of this current one as ouch-ice-vein, or iomagain. I'm not feeling very well, she said. Could we go another time?

Muireall hastened to her knees so she was facing Euna. Her eyesight had got quite poor, but since they could not go to an optometrist, she tended to squint. Now she was narrowing her eyes at Euna in an inscrutable way, maybe because she was angry, maybe because that was the only way she could see her. I happen to know you love the greenhouse, Muireall said. So don't be ungrateful when I try to take you there.

Euna was bound. She regretted telling Muireall how safe and content she felt in the greenhouse. Knowledge in the wrong hands was as risky as a billhook. I'm sorry, she said. Lately Muireall had taken to using low-tech means of surveillance, hiding in the broom cupboard or in the hollyhock beside the latrine, to catch Euna making a wrong – sovereign – decision. And when she did, as she often seemed to, Muireall would tickle the bottoms of Euna's feet with an egg whisk, or braid milk thistles into her hair, or nibble gently, then painfully, on her fingernails until they were torn uneven and close to the flesh. That morning, Euna saw deference as preferable to those pains and indignities.

You must learn to be thankful, Muireall said. Then, Grace, darling, would you do some rearranging for me?

The crests of their heads touching, Euna could feel Grace nod. Yes, she said. What would you like me to do?

The library is getting too cluttered, Muireall said. Move the two wing chairs to the cowshed and all of the tables and magazines to the pantry. If they don't fit there, try your chamber.

Grace asked, Do you want me to do that now?

Yes, dear, Muireall said. Lili, would you be a good girl and go get Euna's riding boots ready?

Euna expected to hear Lili clopping off to the entryway, eagerly cracking open the boot locker. But instead, she stayed where she was. She made a sort of sucking sound with her lips, not a kiss, nor a *tsk-tsk*. I don't want to, she said. Euna will do it on her way out the door.

Just yesterday, obedient Lili had stolen Grace's rose lipstick, the source of her inmost vanity, and spread it across her younger pout. *All the men in the village will bow down to me*, she had said. *I will stun them inarticulate.* Grace now stood and lifted one of the wing chairs, in solidarity with Muireall. She lifted free weights every day, allergic to the notion of getting fat, so her muscles were lean and ready, strong enough to lift the old chair on her own.

Last chance, Lili, Muireall said. She spoke in an indifferent way, as if very tired, over living.

Lili said, If you want me to do you a favour, you have to do one for me. I need some willow bark for my cramps.

Muireall maintained her indifference. Okay, little tattie, she said. Grace will get you some once she is done with the cleaning. Euna, shall we go to the greenhouse now?

Lili's nerve stunned Euna. Though it could have inspired the same sureness in her, it instead bent her to Muireall's will. At Cala, as in any place, there was a tenuous balance. Each of the women had needs, but so too did the group; so too did the rooms they inhabited and the animals they tended to and the plants they turned into tinctures. Euna said, standing, I would like that.

Together they walked to the entry and pulled their riding boots from the locker, then stepped into them. Euna still had Aram's cardigan, though the smell of myrrh had faded from it, and she gladly moved into its familiar warmth. She looked back before going through the door. Grace was rearranging the furniture as instructed, while Lili was lying face down, alone in her defiance.

Muireall took the long way to the greenhouse so they could peek into the outbuildings. Since Lili had given their animals the brew six months before, all of the females had become pregnant. The goats had already given birth, while the cows were a few months from doing so. The chickens had doubled in number. Everyone at Cala was too elated to question what was happening, so instead they ate their eggs and their rugged cheddar and patted their pretty, swollen cows.

Just a few steps into the goatshed, Muireall stopped suddenly. Lili hasn't been mucking their beds, she said. They could get sick. They could get sucking lice.

She was quiet for a moment before starting to cry, which Euna had never seen her do.

Between the stink of shit and the sound of her crying, Euna felt a rare and deep affection for Muireall. Maybe this sadness had been percolating in her all these years, held below the surface by cultivated cruelty. But here, in the goatshed, surrounded by foul aolach? Neither could pretend to be above their nature.

Euna offered the sleeve of the cardigan to Muireall, whose nose had started to drip. She wiped all the wetness onto its knit. The two women were huddled very close together now. The tip of Muireall's nose was pink, childlike, and Euna blew her hot breath onto it. Does that feel nice? she asked.

Muireall smiled in a tense way, unaccustomed to the question. It's just that everything had finally started to go right, she said. We were all here and happy and the animals were giving birth and for once no one saw me as the bidse of the house.

One of the goats, a fine-boned Saanen, trotted over and started to circle their feet. The goats were sage, selective with their affections, and it seemed a compliment to Euna that this one had chosen to join them. There they were, a clan enclosed

45

in the shed, sufficient. A fullness rose in her and dwelled for a long moment, something akin to a sacred experience.

Look at this beautiful doe, Muireall said, leaning down to stroke the animal's muzzle. Look at her winking those pretty eyelashes at us.

The doe made a contented sound, then lifted her tail and started to pee on the ryegrass, soaking both women's boots from tan to brunet. Some of the urine seeped in through Euna's criss-cross laces.

Immediately Muireall struck the doe on the skull, her palm making a loud cracking noise against the bone. Euna cringed. The goat bleated. No blood showed through her fur, though she trotted back to her corner of the shed, where only her left eye shone in the darkness. Muireall seemed shocked by what she had done, as if some irrepressible inner energy had moved her hand. But I love those goats more than anything, she said. She looked at Euna. You know I love those goats, she said.

Euna heard a glass-crash somewhere outside the shed. She pinned it a kilometre away, though it was hard to tell precisely. Sound travelled pure and far in this part of the country, where there were few buildings to break its waves. Euna led Muireall, still crying, or crying again, onto the heath. On the way to the greenhouse, she whispered in the serenest voice she could find, having had few models, You're fine, bana-churaidh.

The greenhouse had gone lush with fresh melons, Hami, Apollo, honeydew, beside vines of crisp English cucumbers. Against their bright spritz was the heavy musk of woodchips. Then Euna noticed that the *musa ornata*, her beloved flowering banana, was covered in shattered glass. Shards shone on its leaves and blushed petals. The fragments made a new beauty of the blooms, though only briefly, until Euna noticed the long rift in one of the greenhouse's panes. All of their careful tending, their songs and hands and water – it would be undone by the cool air seeping inside.

Muireall called out, Who's there?

Euna searched the ground for bricks, blown branches, but she could not even find a rock large enough to have caused the breach. She followed Muireall's lead. Show yourself, she called out.

No one answered. Euna crawled on her hands and knees, searching for the item that had seamed her seamless greenhouse, her one refuge on an acreage of threats. At last, she found something unusual under a floss silk tree, a cold bird, long dead. In its breast was a bullet.

Come here, she said to Muireall.

Muireall obeyed. Is that a crossbill? she asked when she was close enough to see the rigid bird.

Euna spread his breast feathers apart, revealing the bullet with its corona of blood. He was already dead, so she carefully prised out the silver shell and held it close to her face. Steam was forming around her, as the air from outside began to meet the heat that had gathered, and stagnated, inside the sealed greenhouse for years. Euna knew little about guns, had never seen one in real life, but she knew this bullet had come from a rifle. She could hardly breathe. Her windpipe was a gainntir, a narrow place. We should go back to the house now, she managed to say to Muireall.

Through the fracture in the wall came sailing a navel orange, half peeled, then a tangerine and a finger lime. These fruits landed in a pail of garden tools, the lime impaled on a sharp set of pruning shears. Muireall had once mentioned that the minister's wife kept a forcing house beside the church, an orangery.

From outside, someone started to patch the glass using cellophane and clear tape. Euna could see the hands plainly when they touched the window, though the figure, slightly farther away, was indistinct. The person took great care not to stand in front of the break, where they would have been visible. As it was, between the tricks of glass and light – shadows, shifting angles – this person could have had any number of bodies.

Euna was suddenly free from all sensation.

Everything was calm. The flowers. The steam. No one was talking. No one was making mistakes.

She fluttered her eyes and saw Muireall above her, looking flustered. She was straddling Euna so tightly her knees were digging into her high ribs. She was speaking, too, though the sounds had not yet sharpened into words. They were more like rain. But oh – above her friend's face it really was raining, in a grey, unyielding way. The drops cuffing the roof were far louder than Muireall's voice.

As a girl, she had been told faith invoked a sort of emotional stoicism. A devout person is the one who has learned to ask, What does God want from this situation? rather than, What do I want from it? And though she had agreed in her mind, and even, at times, managed dispassion, her gut always had its own loud language.

Euna remembered what had flooded her just before she fainted: void. Detachment. When the figure outside the glass had scared her, maybe she had accepted that she was to die. There wasn't much sense in fussing about what was destined.

Muireall slapped her cheek, not violently, but not tenderly either. Please say something, mè bheag.

Euna tried to speak. She wanted to offer her friend this grace, of reassurance. But her mouth was less hers than it had been when kissing Aram. The muscles around it seemed to have been severed. She managed a cough, through loose, insensitive lips, and that seemed to be all Muireall needed. She shone with delight. The wind lifted, blowing the stony rain sideways, tearing the cellophane patch from the glass.

Around Euna, colours started to saturate, contours to become clear. It was a young woman in a plaid skirt, Muireall said, stroking Euna's forehead with the back of her hand.

Muireall would certainly not have described the minister's wife as young, but Euna happened to know the minister's daughter had recently turned eighteen. The proselytizer had invited the Cala women to attend her coming-of-age ceremony, which he peddled as a garden party with parlour games and fruit juice. After that, he told them, the daughter would travel to the Middle East to do mission work, before returning to marry an older widower from the congregation and settle for good in Pullhair.

Euna said, It might have been the minister's daughter.

What have I always said? They're wicked. I bet she was trying to shoot us instead of the bird.

Euna's cramps were agonizing. She needed to be lying under covers, curtains drawn, a hot water bottle between her legs. Her aura was an aureole around each bloom. Why did you bring me to the greenhouse? she asked Muireall. Were you going to punish me?

Muireall looked hurt. Of course not, she said. She stopped

stroking Euna's forehead, though she did not take her hand away entirely. I noticed the maidenhair ferns were dying, and I needed your help to save them.

The words came out in such a fond, sororal way. Was Euna a béist for always assuming the worst of her friend? With Muireall's help, she gradually stood, then walked down the aisle to the maidenhair. She fingered the nearest fern with care, especially at the ends of its fronds, where the downy leaves had gone brittle. The plant was visibly dying, but Euna did not say that word to Muireall, nor did she despair of their mutual power to restore it to health.

It's just dried out, she told Muireall. Go get the rain barrel and we'll give it a nice, deep soak.

Muireall looked both ways before stepping outside and retrieving their large pail of water. She parted the fern's fronds and poured, the soil absorbing the soak instantly. She poured and poured until the intake was more gradual. The finger lime, the fear lining Euna's throat, the minister's daughter in her plaid skirt – Euna's sin was the dry root of it all. She could no longer stand for Muireall to be the one holding the pail, and she pulled it into her own hands. By then, of course, the plant was overwet, in danger of root rot. Such a fine balance, Euna thought, though she continued to pour.

*

Back at the house that evening, all of the women were suffering from fuil mhìosail pain, in their stiff-lipped, intermittently rude way. Muireall and Euna had not yet told the others what had happened in the greenhouse, in part because they knew it might sound strange, even suspect, and they needed to refine their story first. The four of them had gathered in the living room for their monthly Moog circle, in which Euna played the synthesizer and they performed old standards that Muireall remembered singing with her high school choir, tonight including 'Contented wi' Little and Cantie wi' Mair' and 'Broom of the Cowdenknowes'. They called this kind of therapy ceòl-cluaise, or music for the ears, and it had the same effect hymns were meant to – it opened the women to a world beyond their suffering, or rather, opened them to a world that would not exist without their suffering.

Tonight's session was slightly different. Lili had written an original song she was keen to perform, so Euna was scrambling to learn the chords between more comfortable refrains. It was both moving and unnerving that Lili had chosen to write her own music. Unnerving, perhaps, because Euna had not thought to do it first. And because she had not, for years, considered all the songs they had never heard, in their seclusion. Now this fact struck her as the only great injustice. Of course, so much of that music must be cac, patent and pointless trash, but surely there was also worthy, challenging, near-divine art, which she was worse for never hearing.

Lili stood in front of the women in her pink playclothes, her hair in large, calculated curls. She clasped her hands in front of her chest like a child at a recital and counted Euna in on the keys. Euna played the way she wanted to, and Lili sang the way she wanted to, and though each part was lavish and lovely on its own, together they were dissonant. What are you doing? Lili asked her.

Euna said, I'm just improvising on what's written here.

Lili leaned back sharply, a caesura. Did I tell you to do that? she asked.

Muireall, who had been tolerating Lili's change of character with a mysterious patience, rose to her feet. She whispered something inaudible to Lili, and then the girl said, Do what you need to do, as long as you remember to play my chords.

Grace pretended to twiddle her hair, but Euna could see that she was covering her left ear. She was especially sensitive to sound, as she was to light, and this disharmony clearly troubled her. They never had this issue when they played those songs from Muireall's girlhood, which had prescribed parts, and which, anyway, were familiar to everyone by now. The Moog circle was usually one of their most affirmative activities. They always left feeling restored, tender, eager to warm their pillows and share more earworms.

Are you okay? Euna asked Grace.

Grace straightened her spine, evening her hair waves with both hands. Of course, she said. You sound wonderful.

They had a strange habit, Euna had noticed, of flattering one another when their instinct was to critique. Or on the other hand, of refusing to accept genuine compliments, either because they did not agree or because they did not know how to voice the agreement. If Euna praised Muireall for her precise, effective pruning of their rose bushes, or Grace for her proper seasoning of their pasturer's stew, she often received an eye roll in return, if not an outright insult. She had been told on more than one occasion that her kindness was, in effect, overpowering.

We sounded like cats in heat, Lili said. You know that, Gracie. Why won't you ever just speak your mind?

Grace got decidedly quiet. Euna did not think that Lili had raised her voice, or said anything untoward, but neither did she trust her own judgement. And she knew, if Lili had done either of these things, Grace was unlikely to mention it. She had entered a mood Euna referred to as loch reòite, frozen lake. It was as if Grace were trapped in a thick ice block, an impenetrable slab through which no language could pass. Euna could talk her tongue insensate and still Grace would be in that cold and separate world, no more available or open.

Leave her alone, Euna said. Let's just try again, you and me.

Euna followed the sheet music as it was written, while Lili's voice made waves in the song. Euna waited until after the second verse to improvise, having by then listened more closely to what the girl was singing. This was a loose retelling of 'The Little Mermaid', the dismal Danish fairy tale they used to read nightly when they first moved to Cala. Where the first verse was full of the youngest mermaid's anger at having been left in the underwater kingdom while each of her older sisters explored the world, the second was marked by the mermaid's anxiety at having her turn to see the water's surface, to notice and fall in love with a prince. There, leading into the chorus, Euna let the synth go neon.

Now she understood why the build of sound had to be incremental, and why it had to start with the voice.

Back under water, Lili's heroine was learning that humans live shorter lives than do mermaids, but they may endure after death in soul form, while mermaids turn to sea foam. A water witch offered the mermaid a potion that would let her walk on human legs, though it would also cause her excruciating pain. Lili made her mouth into a wide and unflawed O, and she tried to sing her highest, Yes.

The note she was reaching for was past her cords' capacity, and quite suddenly they broke. So much of the story was still untold. The mermaid marrying the prince; the witch giving her a knife so she might kill him and recover her life under the sea; the mermaid throwing her body into the ocean and becoming foam, only to rise later into the air. But before any of this could happen, Lili sulked down into a wicker chair. She insisted she could not reach that Yes, and that the song could not continue without it.

She started to knead her throat, growling low as she did. We'll finish it during our next circle, she said.

Euna was not so game to give up the song. Heading into that chorus, she had felt airy, immaterial, as if she did not have a body at all. She had been hunting for that feeling a long time without knowing it; the covers they usually played in the Moog circle were fun, occasionally pretty, but this had moved her in a way she had not forecast. For a moment she had been a flawless swimmer, no margin between sea and skin. That's a whole month from now, she said. We'll forget everything we've learned by then.

Grace, still in her loch reòite state, looked at Lili and Lili alone. She asked, Why did you write that?

Lili shook her head from side to side, making a scene of her curls. She seemed angry, on the edge of an outburst. Do you know you've never let me run a single errand? she asked Grace. Euna went twice last year.

This comment caught Euna under the chin. For months she had been behaving well in order to go unnoticed, to hold her name out of the other women's mouths – this, to her, had become the guise of freedom. Now Lili was parading her life in front of their little public, as if it were an idol's, as if it merited envy. She could not just let this happen. She said, You think you know everything.

Muireall came between them. Let's not do this right now, she said, putting her hand on Euna's shoulder.

Why do you act like I'm not even here? Lili asked Muireall.

Muireall had a habit of avoiding conflict unless she, personally, had reason to punish someone. Even those occasions could hardly be called conflicts. The ground between the watcher and the watched was never level. You're imagining things, little tattie, she said.

Lili started to throw candlesticks and novels. She slashed a sack of ashes on a stray nail and smashed firewood against the mantel. At last she punched her hand through the glass face of the grandmother clock, a motion so violent that Grace ran over, ceding the safety of her loch reòite, and slapped the girl. Lili's hand was backstitched with blood, a purl of pure crimson. She sat down in the middle of the bearskin rug, calmly, and drained into its neck fur. Euna went to the kitchen to get a rag, which she dampened in the storage cask. She came back and wrapped Lili's hand tightly, holding the rag in place long enough to feel a peaceful force pass between the two of them.

Tea? Muireall asked.

Lili nodded. Grace straightened her dress and went to the kitchen to boil water.

After the day she had lived through, Euna only wanted to sleep. If one were inclined to believe in omens, which Euna no longer was, the Saanen and the minister's daughter and the synth-induced disturbance might call for a deeper reading. I'm beat, she said to Muireall. Would it be all right with everyone if I went upstairs?

Muireall brightened. She liked when the other women asked for her permission. Go get some rest, she said.

Euna held Lili's rag-wrapped hand to her heart and looked the girl in her eyes. They were soulless, all glass. Then Euna stood and took the stairs two at a time. This month she was sharing the double bed with Grace, and she glowed knowing she might fall asleep alone that night, with her choice of pillow and bed side. Silence other than the voices through the floorboards, the occasional wildcat on the hill.

She stripped naked. Instead of putting on her nightgown she crawled between the sheets as nature had intended her. What a day. She lay nude between the cotton sheets, cold but humming with a kind of stress-heat. Through the window, the moon was no bigger than a slice of finger lime. Or else, right now, she was gigantic. She could reach into the sky and pluck that slice, snack on its arc, let the citrus trickle down her throat. Maybe she would not die bored, after all.

*

A week passed peacefully. The women had started loving each other in a sort of charged, stepping-on-seaglass way, careful not to wake gloom or anxiety in any of the others. Each word was well chosen, each act observed first from at least two angles. And though it took work, and though what they achieved was undoubtedly fragile, they were able to hold

Cala in a state of conscious harmony. They were as safe as they had ever been. Lili's outburst had not broken them, as it might have. What that screaming and smashing had done, at least for the time being, was drain the resentment that had been building like a blister in the house.

Then at once, after that harmonious week had passed, the peace leached away from their home. So quickly and so absolutely did this happen that Euna questioned whether the harmony had ever existed. She understood that those moments had been real, just as in their decade here there had been many spells of comfort and happiness, none of which was erased by the inevitable swings toward fear, frustration, envy. But still, in want of a good witness, she had a quiet suspicion she had imagined all of it.

On that peace-leaching day, a brick came through the kitchen window, as the bird had come through the glasshouse pane.

And then, much worse, much more worrisome, through the brick-hole came a girl in a tartan skirt and pullover slightly too small for her, her lower belly bloated and bare. She flashed her underskirt as she climbed through the glass, scoring her legs. Euna was alone in the kitchen when this happened, burnishing the tiles with a wad of steel wool. She screamed. The girl knelt beside her and stifled the sound with her hand. I need help, she said.

Euna had a chance to look at her face. She had lovely, creamy skin, but each feature set in that base was foul, almost grotesque. Her eyes, far apart, were the colour of bruised apples. Wind had burned a pink ring around her lips, which were pale and faintly downturned, and flaked the broad tip of her nose. Who are you? Euna asked.

My name is Aileen, the girl said, hoarsely. I'm Minister Macbay's daughter.

She lifted her pullover fully and lowered the waistline of her skirt, showing beyond a doubt that she was pregnant. Euna wondered who the father was. And then, though she tried not to, she pictured the finer points of that union, bed, orchid, hand. I want to help, she told the girl, in part to dull her imagination.

Muireall came into the kitchen, likely having heard Euna's scream. And, seeing Aileen, she went stiff. Maybe this was a natural reaction. A stranger had broken the seal of their house, towing bindweed in on her boot treads. But it seemed excessive that Muireall should hold so rigid, and that she, for whom words had such a token weight, flowing with the ease and speed of other people's tap water, could not think of a single thing to say.

I wasn't going to do anything without asking you, Euna said to Muireall, after a long and mutual silence.

Still on her knees, Aileen reached for a rag by the soak basin and started to wipe her legs. She had been roughed not only by the shattered window but by the thorns of a rosebush. Euna had spent years singing to the Cala greens to earn their trust, and, to that end, now they never pricked her skin. But they had clearly been hostile to Aileen. In the webs between her fingers Euna saw burdock spikes and cockleburs. Euna felt a sort of affinity with this stranger, not sympathy, but I-know-how-much-the-brambles-hurt. May I help her? Euna asked Muireall.

Only when she was addressed directly did Muireall move. She walked right in front of Aileen and grabbed her by the chin. The force, again, seemed excessive. You're not welcome here, she said. We've been better than ever lately, and we don't need you walking on our peace. She was chewing and popping a mouthful of gum, a homemade mash of peppermint and beeswax, and with each spoken word flecks of spit flew through the air.

Near the beginning of the *Life Grammar* was a list of values. The women had put their initials beside each point as consent to follow them. *VI. Benevolence. Every person is worthy of our love, attention, and open mind. If someone asks for our help, even if they have personally wronged us, we will hear them out in the spirit of goodwill.* Euna had understood these values to be complete, not to change depending on who they were being applied to, or on which day. And yet, here was Muireall, tall and cruel above Aileen's crawling.

I'm begging you, the girl said.

Get out of my house, Muireall said.

Euna was on the floor, too, still clutching the steel wool. She was closer to Aileen's station than she was to Muireall's.

Muireall put her fingers between Aileen's lips and prised them apart, then hawked her gum into the girl's mouth. Aileen coughed loudly, choking on the hunk, swallowing hard to make room for clean air. Euna was shocked. The poor girl had started to shake. That she would not leave, despite this humiliation, told Euna she truly had nowhere else to go.

And so Muireall had no choice but to switch her approach. Aileen, she asked, do you ever hunt for crossbills?

Aileen covered her face with her hands. These, too, had the same creamy skin, but with flaked red knuckles and patches of ash across their backs. She did not speak. Euna was so tense all of her senses flipped. If it had rained then, the fields would have burned; if the sun had come out, the world would have been obscured.

Mè bheag, Muireall said to Aileen, and her use of the endearment made Euna shiver. Do you ever use a rifle?

Muireall was no longer stiff. She was in the stance she used when she felt impregnable, in total power, one foot slightly in front of the other and both big toes turned outward. Her pelvis was tilted toward the ceiling, her knees with generous give.

I was starving, Aileen said. I left home three weeks ago. I was afraid my parents would notice I was starting to show.

Euna stood and poured a glass of drinking water for Aileen. The girl accepted it with one hand and covered her face with the other.

You're sweet, Euna, but I wouldn't be doing that, Muireall said. Not for her.

Aileen downed the water like a workhorse who has been forced to travel too far. She put the empty glass on the tile beside her and explained to Euna, I met Muireall the other night, after you went to bed.

The Moog circle. Euna had been so grateful to sleep alone, sheathed only by the sheets, at such an early hour. But her gratitude had clearly been misplaced. Nothing in life is free, her mother used to say, or else, Nothing in your life is free – she could not remember, though the distinction now seemed important.

Tell her, slag, Muireall said. Aileen hesitated. Her lips looked wet now, as if she had mostly avoided her sore mouth when slurping the glass of water. Muireall held the girl's chin again, fingertips firm against the bone, forcing words to move through her.

We have something in common, Aileen said. When she then tried to retreat into silence, Muireall tightened her grip. I think we've been with the same man.

Euna started to laugh. Or rather, her body made the sound without her consent or input, the way a stomach sometimes rumbles. You must have the wrong person, she said. I've never been with any man. More laughter, now from Muireall, which startled Euna. They had not talked about the day Aram came to call, and for all she knew, she had been unseen behind the compost drum. Surely if Muireall had believed him she would at some point have exploded at Euna, unable to repress what she knew.

I shouldn't be here, Aileen said, lumbering to her feet. She pulled up her skirt and down her sweater. I'm a damain mess.

Muireall pointed at Aileen and said, She was with your Aram.

Euna closed her eyes. What struck her about this leak was not how much it hurt and humiliated her, but the mundane wash it cast over their lives. They had spent years raising a castle, a stone fort in a forest of gorse, in order to make themselves feel exceptional, Other, even immortal, but it was clear now they were common women. Euna's attraction to Aram was banal, was word-for-word in half the books that bloated the library.

And worse, her perfect pet, whose absence had tortured her, was as cunning and devious as Judas.

Euna opened her eyes and put a hesitant hand on Aileen's abdomen. Is this his? she asked.

Of course, the girl said. Either she was telling the truth, or she would not admit to having had liaisons with two different men. In a house of non-conflict, in a town of confidences, there was no way to know.

She needs to leave right now, Muireall said. She seemed disarmed by Euna's mild reaction to the news. Maybe she had expected, or even secretly wanted, a blowout. She looked at Euna now with a kind of fiery confusion, a face she sometimes made when vermin moved into the silo despite her attempts at perfect sanitation, or when draughts blew through the house despite her weatherproofing.

If she goes, the baby could die, Euna said. She was the same age as Lili, and Euna would not dream of sending that wee girl into the world without someone to buff and file her nails, make her barley pudding, listen to her pulse each morning. Euna realized a moment later she was the same age, too – though life had forced her to grow at a much swifter pace.

I'll find my own way, Aileen said. Supposed to be catching the ferry first thing tomorrow. I'm flying out from Glasgow.

Euna had forgotten about the girl's trip and now, reminded, she felt a heave of envy. She had no sense of Glasgow, how catholic it was, how crowded, whether the streets were full of stray mutts or magi or mermaids rambling on two legs. Do they have hospitals all over the country? she asked.

Muireall laughed at her again. Euna was starting to feel prickly, like a rosebush that has not been sung to in a very long time.

They do, Aileen said. Of course, I wasn't expecting to need a doctor.

The cows in the shed were swelling, and in a few months they would be giving birth. Euna had been so surrounded by their fatty, arable vibes that she was sure she could deliver their calves with her bare hands. The moon had been full ten of the last twenty days, and no one could explain the phenomenon. They just knew some heavy energy was hovering. Maybe driven by this same energy, Euna offered to be Aileen's handmaid.

I don't understand why you're being so nice, Aileen said to Euna. What do you want from me?

She did not know how to answer, mostly because kindness did not, to her, require an explanation. Muireall reached her hands into Euna's hair, first combing it dotingly with her fingers, then pulling harder and harder, until her scalp began to burn white. What are you doing? Muireall asked in her ear.

No one had questioned Muireall when she grabbed Aileen's chin, or when she tried to ensnare the other two women in this charged conversation. And yet Euna was being scolded for her compassion, a value they had all once agreed, in initial and principle, to maintain. I'm just doing what feels right, she said.

Aileen looked moved for a moment, as if ready to accept the offer. She made long eye contact with Muireall. Then her expression changed and she told them she had to leave. She took a handful of peanuts from a bowl on the counter and dropped them into the pocket of her pullover. This time, she didn't climb through the glass. She unlocked the back door, attached to the kitchen, and stepped out onto the softening heath. Euna watched her leave. A wild light, gold, was casting its spirit on the knapweeds. Freckles of white buckwheat spread out across the moor. Here and there a puddle shone like milk.

Muireall whistled, calling the other women into the kitchen. Grace came running down the stairs in distressed, grass-marked moccasins and a velvet evening gown. The effect of the two together was peculiar. She looked stunning but loosely hinged, even more so because this was not a solstice day, and the women were supposed to be in their uniform linen shirts.

I heard sounds, she said, but I thought you might have wanted privacy. The straps of her dress were thin as the edges of peat spades. On either side, her flesh was lush despite the dry weather.

You should have come down, Euna said. We just did something terrible.

Muireall calmly opened the cupboard and took out some oatcakes. She chewed the biscuits in a way that disturbed Euna, letting them go sodden in her mouth, then mashing what was left with her lips. She had powerful, salt-and-soda teeth, and she was refusing to use them, though the sole pleasure of an oatcake was in its crunch. Meanwhile Grace was chewing her middle finger like a mutton bone. Gnawing and gnawing, as if hunting for marrow. What happened? she asked, hangnail in her fangs.

The minister's daughter came here with child, Euna said. She needed help. And this sea monster... Euna noticed little globs of beige on either side of Muireall's mouth from the mashed oatcake. Then she could see nothing else.

Grace said, Oh, that girl. Yeah, she came last week.

Euna's face started to simmer. A hot froth was forming under her skin. Now it was glaring: the *Life Grammar*, which she had taken as gospel, and which she had only violated a few times – shame like a slip noose – meant very little to the other women. She had never read the Scottish constitution, and had, on Muireall's command, forgotten the Holy Writ. In the void that had followed, she had embraced this one code with faith and piety, binding herself to the words.

Oh, that girl.

Piss off, Euna muttered.

Careful, Grace said.

Grace was happy if the raw weather did not give her dandruff. Or if she had a velvet gown to wear. Hers was a selfish existence, and that might have been well had she chosen a wolfier life, but here, where even small acts affected the wealth of flora, fine-tuned salt levels in the sea, it was entirely unjust. Even cruel.

The back door of the kitchen opened and in came Lili, a crow feather in her mouth. Camp and cold-blooded, the Cailleach, she pulled the feather from her teeth and licked its quill. Though windblown, she was in uniform, her hair wiring out from once-deliberate plaits. I was hungry, she said.

Euna stood looking at her world.

Were these women brutal? Worn to the bone? Haunted by devils? Had they simply, over time, turned antisocial?

The constant cold temperature. The years of peeling potatoes.

It was said about Cairstìne Bruce's end that the residents of Pullhair had used spectral evidence against her. Those who suspected her of witchcraft claimed to feel the presence of wicked spirits when they were near her. Euna had pored over the book on witch hunts in the library; the striking part had been about *waking* the witch. Before seventeenth-century trials, suspects were deprived of sleep, so that when they were called to defend themselves, they had started to hallucinate. Even the most refined women would by then have turned feral, telling outlandish stories. They would confess to sins they'd not had the pleasure of committing.

Lili had started to retch into the soak basin, which Euna had spent half an hour filling with well water that morning. Grace went to the cupboard and chose a small bottle of calendula extract, which she made into a tonic for the ill girl. She poured the drink past Lili's loamy teeth, humming a folk song they had once upon a time used to control her night terrors. Hush, sweet baby, she said. It's going to be okay.

Now nothing was rational.

Everything was notional.

Certain things were felt.

Euna could not pinpoint the moment it had happened, but some feature inside her had been recarved. Mountains in the Highlands had been cut when the Cailleach dropped rocks from her wicker basket. So it was natural that over time Euna had lost some of her crags and earned others. She stood in that kitchen cold as a mirror, with the only women who had ever really known her, and felt the light and shade of their presence. In morning light, a mountain may look indestructible, a seat of the ecclesiastic. And in the shade? After years of driving rain, a thicking and riching of the soil, it would not be hard to imagine a landslip.

LATE JUNE, THE mood of summer hung over Cala like a damp comforter. To move through the days took force and time. In the stone house, beside the sealoch, the air was a trial the body could barely stand.

It was in this atmosphere that a postcard arrived, dank, nearly unreadable. The postman came when Euna was alone with the newborn calves, a luck-stroke in a life of only occasional breaks. She did not want to think what would have happened had he come to deliver this postcard when she was in the latrine, or in the cowshed with Muireall. She tucked the postcard into the silk band she had taken, recently, to tying around her breasts. She had spent enough time with the cows and their flooded udders to be bothered by the unused shapes stuck to her own chest. Breasts were for mams. By the end of the year, somewhere far away, Aileen would be free to go silkless.

Euna sneaked into the greenhouse to take the postcard from her silk band. Though humidity had made the pen marks run, she could still fill in the faint words. Aram was being held at Dungavel Castle, a detention centre in South Lanarkshire that he described in the card only as *unspeakable*. She thought of their afternoon on the pier, when he said his life in Scotland was precarious. She had not known how immediate that truth was. On the postcard, there was a smear of brown below his signature, some human yield, cac or fuil. She slid the card back into her band before trimming the maidenhair fern and returning to the farmhouse for dinner.

There she found the other women around a set dining table. She could feel the postcard above her breastbone, a charm, a talisman, as she took her seat beside Grace. Lili served supper, oatmeal potatoes and cold seaweed, and in silence they all began to slurp and chew. Euna could not concentrate. She was wondering what Aram was eating, if he was eating at all. She saw him dipping coarse, black bread into water, licking mushed soy from splits in his palate. She had never been to a prison, or any state building – save the one time, as a young child, she'd accompanied her mother to apply for a passport so she could look for a new life abroad. As soon as they'd stepped inside the government room her mother had started to sweat, to hold Euna's forearm too firmly. Before long she'd declared the line too long and they had gone home to their television trays, never to try again.

After dinner, Euna cleaned everyone's plates, scrubbing until her knuckles were cracked and pale. As she disinfected the dishes, she felt no fear or excitement, only slow, abiding certainty. She could not live here any longer. Knowing that a man, even a duplicitous one, was expecting her; knowing that hundreds of songs, and ripe crops, and fit stock and fauna were living in the greater, greener country. Perhaps this quiet sense of yes, of cool sureness, was what she had heard referred to as faith.

Her chore finished, she massaged Muireall's shoulders and helped Grace into her nightclothes. She wanted her last moments with them to be kind, not for her conscience but for the future trim and humour of the house. To Lili, whose hair she brushed at length, she whispered, There's more life out there. Maybe the girl would decipher the message, or maybe she wouldn't. No one had spoon-fed Euna anything. And though Euna was a good woman, even a good woman could bend back far enough to make herself resentful.

When the others were sleeping, she stepped out onto the heath. In a knapsack she carried the few things she had managed to gather in secret – a sweater, some smoked beef and trout, an extra pair of socks, a few pages from *The Witches Speak* that moved her – and, for safe measure, a letter-knife. Whatever else she needed in order to survive, she could find on her way. She imagined all the women of her lineage had done this, using stones and teeth and sex. She imagined Aram's mother had crossed acres of ocean in a catamaran.

Euna walked overnight to Stornoway, then, having no notes, sneaked on to the early-morning ferry to Ullapool. There, the world seemed huge already, with its fishmonger, its massive, white-painted hotel, its charming bookshop. But she did not have time to linger. She needed to get to Dungavel. Euna walked down the only road she saw, following the Loch Broom, jumping into the ditch each time a car came too close around a hairpin turn. One question roiled in her. Why had she spent a decade referring to herself only as a bana-bhuid-seach, a sorceress, when the self she'd started to know was a redhead, a reader, a lover of goats and greenhouses, among fuller, richer things? Why had she been so willing to take Muireall's word?

The effect of those choices had not been neutral. Whenever she passed a house on her journey south, lit from the inside, she longed to knock on the door. She wanted so badly to talk to somebody that her throat burned, a blazing stake. But even with a body signal so hard to ignore, she could not bear to knock. She was not a witch any more. And not yet a fish. And not near to a real woman. And how could she speak if she did not have a single one of these voices?

For hours, she followed the long arc of the lake. Back at Cala, using the map on the library wall and her rudimentary maths skills, she'd figured it would take her four days of nonstop walking to get to Dungavel. Accounting for sleep and slips from the straight line – she would need to hunt hares, most likely, and bandage her blistered feet – it would take her close to a week. So she would be there in early July, just a few weeks before Lughnasadh, the glad beginning of harvest season. By then each holly tree branch would be clotted, heavily, with berries. By then the tramping and humidity would have made her ugly, too, but this no longer concerned her. She wanted something deeper than to be desired.

*

Two days later, Euna saw the sun rise over a sign for Etteridge. She had not taken a single break to sleep, and she had started to walk the fine edge of delirium. Her thoughts were grazing widely and wildly, her inner drone gone weird and non-linear. She wanted to stop by the side of the road for a few strips of jerky and a nap in the marram grass. Cloud for a pillow, cloud for a duvet. Having moved through two full summer days, she had already proved herself strong as the stock and fauna of Cala.

Oh, then she started to miss them.

She longed to see the two mares running toward her, their manes permed and blown, fresh from the beauty parlour.

Or the cattle in their enclosure, udders swelling with milk, udders swelling with humbugs and Soor plooms.

Or the sheep out on the heath, their bubble-coats so pretty and white, gathering sticks to play games of shinty.

She welcomed these hallucinations. They were company, after all, and she was alone on the road. The morning was foggy and grey, though at the moment she did not trust her distinction between eye and air. Maybe the day was rainy, or maybe she had started to cry. Maybe she was a sheep with silver sad all down its face wool. Or a dark morning of some war size. Or all the longing in the world, long johns, long and longer eyelashes, long and longer and longest memories, maybe this had all poured in when her sleepless body opened.

Well, she thought, I've woken the witch.

A man passed her on the road, wearing glasses with drops of condensation on them. Euna was grateful for this sign that it was, after all, raining. She had passed many cars and few pedestrians, so she had not yet spoken to a soul. This man said, Guid morn.

She tried to speak but could not. She was too uncomfortable to make a sound, as if her tongue were coated in a fur that she could not remove with her fingers.

Ur ye okay? he asked. Een a bit bloodshot. He pulled a flask from his jacket and offered it to her. He looked quite young and then quite old, first ten, then seventy-five, a schoolboy then a grandpa, then a schoolboy again.

She shook her head. He took her hand. Can ah offer a warm nest tae sleep in? he asked.

This grandpa child wanted to be sweet to her and that was a very, very welcome thing after two days and at least ten years of loneliness. She could not use her fur-tongue, so she let herself go limp and pleasant, hoping he took that as assent. It seemed to work. He helped her climb over a fence and then led her down a little stream a few feet, or maybe a few miles, to a blackhouse.

He had a cot in one corner and a cat in another. A Bunsen burner and a few flannel shirts. He told her to rest in the cot while he boiled water for tea. The cat's coat changed from pink to sparkling silver so fast Euna felt sick. The blackhouse reeked of rum and currants. She struggled to stay awake, to drink this warm offering, but she was so feverish she was going blind. Then her exhaustion pulled her down completely, like a weighted throw net.

*

Euna woke to the sound of a hatchet being whetted. The sun was just starting to set, its soft rose giving way to a stone shade. It must have been close to nine o'clock. Sleep had renewed her body, but more so her mind, which now felt sharp and percipient. She looked down the length of herself, and other than the abrasions on her feet, she had not been physically harmed since leaving the coven. This affirmed for her, temporarily, that she had made the right choice.

She drew the curtain beside the cot and looked through the window at the man who had invited her in. He was pale and middle-aged, a wee bit scraggy, drenched in sweat. She watched him sharpen the blade for a few minutes before darkness, a drop cloth, obscured him. All she could see then were the sparks that flew as he ran a coarse file along the axe's head. Maybe she should have found this threatening. But Euna had only been alive, truly alive, for two days, and so instead she watched him as an anthropologist might, with care and curiosity, taking inventory of his movements.

Shit! he said.

She was startled. She had not heard anyone curse in English for years, not since she was young and her mother would do something like burn the eggs, or catch her finger in the hand-loom. Though Muireall had allowed them to speak English most of the time, she had made sure that in their heated moments they switched to Gaelic, the home-soil language. She did not want their reflexes tied to the Church or to Britain. This man, oddly, seemed conditioned to do the opposite. Goddamn, he said.

Then she heard him stomp across the crunchy, sundried grass and open the door to the blackhouse. It was completely dim inside, and he fumbled around until he found a torch, which he turned on and pointed toward the cot. Euna hauled the lambswool blanket over her body, then peeled it back far enough that she could see him. The fur no longer on her tongue, she managed to say, Evening.

He bumbled to her, bumping a still life from the wall. Awright? he said, sweat in pellets on his brow and hairline. Ah hiner it's okay ah took ye haur. Ah didne want ye tae gie burst by a motur. He spoke eagerly and with overwhelming speed.

Everything is fine, she said, slowly, aware of her peculiar way of saying vowels. She had grown accustomed to being understood at Cala. Whatever else had partitioned the women, words had been their accord.

Whaur ur ye frae? he asked.

Her nightmare: a question. She could no longer simply nod and pretend to understand him. Pullhair, she said, cautiously.

She had guessed right, or at least had avoided saying anything to embarrass either of them. Pullhair? Wa ur ye sae far frae haem?

I'm sorry, she said. I don't follow. It had never been this difficult to connect with Aram, though he had presumably learned to speak from his Sketiminian mother. If anything, Euna's own speech had seemed tattered. Aram, on the other hand, had cut his words cleanly.

The man knelt on the cement-and-dirt floor beside Euna. The upward glare of the torch made him look worn and whey-faced. Ah am wondering hoo ye got sae lost. And if ah can help ye.

This she heard, but did not entirely understand. Were people kind? Her experiences were adding up to a sort of surreal earth-model, one that failed to prove their morals or their malice. Her childhood had been marked by cruelty and neglect, as had moments at Cala and in Aram's hut – but then, there had been moments of just the opposite weave, of complete well-being, even splendour.

Now he had his hand on her hand, in a paternal way.

She softened. She had not realized how deeply she craved this contact, but now that she had it, she could feel the veins in her arm rafting pure, red light. I'm going to visit a true friend at the detention centre in Dungavel, she said.

Then at once his face was full of hard edges. His lips, already thin, vanished inside his mouth. Euna could not imagine what she had done to upset him, but she did not have much confidence in her ability to read others. He stood and walked to the opposite corner of the blackhouse, where hours before he had been boiling the water for tea. He took the butt of the torch between his teeth and lit the gas flame. I'll make ye some scran, he said.

When he turned his back to her, the move had a forever feel. He would never put his hand on her hand again. And there was something dire about love being offered and then taken away. If she had not first known the effects of that affection, she would never have missed them.

Thank you, she said. I'm quite hungry.

She heard him muttering as he clanged a string of cast-iron pans. Criminals, he said. Takin' aw uir jobs.

He started to fry some kind of stink-fish. Its funk made her homesick, both for Cala and for Aram's hut, and she felt then that she had made a great mistake in leaving. She nestled into the lambswool. Back at home, Lili would be turning down everyone's sheets for sleep – one woman would be climbing into bed alone, which now seemed less like a pleasure than it did a punishment. How nice it would be to sleep beside someone now.

Fesh is ready, the man said.

Thank you, she said. She sat up cross-legged, causing the middle of the cot to sink as she accepted the plate. She heard something mewling below her. The cat. She had not imagined him. She pinched a hint of fish between her fingers and held it over the side of the bed. A rough tongue took the scrap.

Sae, the man said. Ur ye trying tae gang marry some Ukrainian? Keep heem frae leaving ye?

She did not know what this meant, but she had spent years tuning her ear to the fine turns in Muireall's voice that suggested ease, angst, anger, pleasure, grief, and the hairs on the back of her neck went erect when she heard the way he said that particular word. *Ukrainian*. Prickles. She knew, too, that she had not walked two days in the danger domain of strangers and feral animals just to play the role of diffident, countrified girl. She would not let him push that character on her.

I'm not trying to marry anyone, she said, between bites of fish. I told you, I'm going to see a true friend.

The man blinked. He took the cat into his arms, snuggling the creature tightly. The cat watched her with auger eyes, licking his little teeth. Though his breath was pleasant and his nails had recently been trimmed, he looked starved, thus unloved. His coat was skinnish, his skull flyspeck. He was no goat or stallion, of course, but Euna now saw him in a more tender light, having known his hunger. Less so the man holding him, who may have been just as unloved, just as hungry.

Euna scarfed the rest of the fish. When she was finished, the man said, Thaur is a blanket oan the green. He used the cat as a riot shield, clearing Euna from the cot with its taut body. Guid nicht.

She stood. Her feet were swollen and scored, and as soon as she rested her weight on them she wanted to scream. But she was determined not to be seen as weak or needy, so she stood straight against that stooping pain. She walked to the threshold, where she found her boots, although she did not remember removing them earlier that day. Good night, she said, mostly to the cat. Both faces, stacked, one stubbled and the other furred, watched her as she walked outside.

She found the blanket in the hair-grass, rumpled and damp with humidity. Still she stretched out on the wet wool, her face aimed moonward.

Slowly she was gumming together an image of the world.

In this corner, here, a man in pain and his ratty cat, alone, spiteful, but outwardly sweet, in certain ways caring. If she hadn't met the two of them, she would still have found a way to rest and recover, though she had been on the brink of blackout, and that link had at first done her good. Despite its stench, the fish had refreshed her, and the hours in that dry cot had been a mercy. In this corner, here, some complicated shading.

*

Euna was back on the road just past dawn, having eaten two strips of jerky and treated her feet with torn tormentil leaves. Briefly she had considered going into the blackhouse to thank the man and his cat for their help, but instead of taking a chance on his reaction, which could have been warm or murderous, she had headed back to the road. One fine point she had learned the day before: insecurity made a person unpredictable. Though she no longer wanted her life to be ruled by sure outcomes, she knew this was not the time to test her new-found nerve.

And so she followed the road in one steady direction for hours, her pain a certainty, her thirst a certainty.

The day was deceptively mild. Through a cloud canopy the sun looked pale, but by mid-afternoon the back of her neck was burning, the rim of her lips brambled. Every so often a chough would come low and track her for a kilometre, then skim the tree-line on its course back to the mountains. Or a truck would pass, casing her in its exhaust. The way was otherwise long and monotonous, and by dusk she had started to hallucinate again, assigning texture and colour where they did not belong – silk bark on silver birches, hot pink over painted road markings. All she had was her walking, so even this lick of brainsickness couldn't slow her down. She carried on despite her blisters and her delusions. She carried on through the still summer evening and then, without lull, through the long, chilled night.

Early the next morning, the rising sun cast diamonds on a stream ten metres from the road. It was marked by a plaque: *Loch Tummel*. The ache in Euna's joints was so acute by then that, without stopping or stripping any clothes, she submerged herself in the water. Below the surface, she cooled. For a perfect moment, she lived in that complete, bodiless void, floating, freshening, until she ran out of breath. When she rose into the air again, though she could not see herself, she believed it was with mermaid grace. She drank from the stream and it seemed her skin did the same, absorbing the moisture through its scorched pores. Everywhere, a pale blue glimmer – in her hair, on her fingernails, in the folds of her now wet, now weighty tunic.

She tried to sing the song Lili had written, but she could not remember the lyrics, and her attempts to do so were frustrating. Had it been about vanilla planifolia, or astral travel, or stovies and love apple soup? Euna could so viscerally remember what it had felt like to score the song, and yet she could not remember a single line from it. Splashing in the river, she sang any word and non-word that came to her, the way a child does, unafraid of slipping up, and for the first time since leaving Cala she felt a sensation she did not hesitate to call joy.

After some time, a woman in a green tartan dress came to the riverside. She looked like a moving spread of moss, her hair downy and short and her movements so natural they were nearly impossible to detect. She seemed to be in her mid-thirties. When she reached the brim of the waterbody, she lay down on her stomach and, propping herself upright with her elbows, dreamed one hand through the river. As she parted the current, the pale blue glimmer moved onto her wrist, then downstream to a set of standing stones. I hope you didn't loo, she said.

Euna laughed. The moss woman pressed herself right down into the soil, and Euna wondered whether that hurt her breasts, or if she, too, had banded them. She did not know if that was a standard thing to do or a strange one, a world thing or a Euna thing.

Do you live around here? Euna asked.

The woman was now resting her cheek against the earth, ready to vegetate. Not really, she said. I drive my camper around until I find a place to stay the night. Bitch to park, I promise you that.

Euna leaned back into the water. She was at ease with this odd, primordial woman, and she did not need to know why. She floated, her mind free of questions. They lived there together, in and by the river, until Euna pruned and the sun turned orange enough to announce noon. Then she clambered onto the bank, where the woman was still breast-pressed, and sat beside her. Where are you headed? Euna asked.

The woman rolled onto her back and shaded her eyes with a flattened hand. Anywhere you want, she said. With her backhand visor she could not block the sun entirely, and a speck of it fell, sparkling, on the inside of her tear duct. The twinkle made the woman look punch-drunk, possibly wicked.

After the bad juju in the blackhouse, Euna was too frightened to tell the woman where she was headed. She loved the verve they were now sharing, and she could not bear for another person to approach and then ditch her. To protect herself, she stayed vague. South, she said.

The woman smiled. Several of her teeth were edged with gold and silver veins. Then we'll head down south, she said, brightly. And my radio is broken, so you can make our soundtrack. You're a good singer.

Sounds like fun, Euna said. She flashed a rare smile. One of her own teeth had rotted while she was at Cala, and she had pulled it with a pair of slip-joint pliers. Unlike this woman, who had mended her tooth defects with delicate ore, she simply had a hole where the molar should have been. So she tended not to show it to anyone.

The woman winked at her. See that you don't burn, she said, pointing to the sky.

Euna stood and moved into the shade of a hawthorn tree. The woman wandered here and there, foraging, mining the earth for roots and mushrooms. When she returned to Euna, it was with arms of sweet clover, Scots lovage, scarlet elf cup. She ironed her skirt across the grass and laid this lunch spread on top of the tartan. Let's eat, she said.

How do you know none of this is poisonous?

I've gotten by on my own for a long time, the woman said.

Euna, having walked a full day past her last meal, took from the spread a handful of fungus. Wind had hacked her lips, so she ran the soft caps across them. The stroke was of velvet shank. She remembered eating these many times when she was younger, as supplement to the one-item suppers she was given at home – a drumstick, a roll, a chunk of cheddar. And so, sidetracked by that memory, she ate all the mushrooms before the woman could try one herself. Euna looked down.

Daing ort! The shame of her empty palm.

The woman said, You must have been hungry, dear one.

This moss woman had been so generous and, as she had with the stink-fish, Euna had gorged on that generosity without offering any in return. She belonged deep in the mud. The mushrooms should have eaten her instead.

I'm so sorry, she said. I can't believe I didn't save any for you. She saw a hollow in the hawthorn, large enough for her to curl inside, and she thought how nice it would be to slide into that narrowed world, the narrowest one she had seen yet. At Cala, once, they had found a roaming lamb and had eased her into life on their farm, space by slightly larger space – first a coop, then a pen, then a cowshed, then the moor and all the commons. Euna craved a smaller cavity.

Don't worry about it, the woman said. There's plenty more where that came from. Now, want to see my camper?

Euna nodded. She could not believe her good fortune to have met a woman like this, one who could sense things and who, without being ordered to, treated others with tact. If this were its own kind of bewitchment, Euna would choose it over Muireall's black magic any day.

Euna followed the woman for a time across the meadowgrass. When they reached the vehicle, Euna was struck by its misplacement. Parked beneath a young elm it seemed colossal, if not aggressive. Beside the tree's fine foliage, its mural of beefy men and blazing cigarettes looked entirely urban, curious.

The woman unlocked the camper door for Euna, and then helped her to mount the two steps by grasping her, firmly but not forcefully, by the waist. They entered together. The interior was warm and smelled of simmered cloves, here and there a note of nutmeg. At the rear was a full oven and stove outfit, and near the heart a breakfast nook and a well-worn pullout couch. Velvet curtains concealed the half dozen windows, and leopard-print shells covered the driver and passenger seats. Euna was surprised to see that this interior was larger and more comfortable than that of the blackhouse.

Euna reclined on the couch and the woman knelt beside her, feeding her sprigs of sweet clover. This, even more than her songplay in the river, was a moment of supreme bliss. This camper may well have been the throne of God. Ready? the woman asked, when she had no more clover in her hands. Euna grinned broadly enough to reveal her missing molar.

Yes, mè bheag, Euna said. The woman scrunched her nose as if that were a funny thing to call someone, though at Cala, of course, Euna had grown to think of it as a common term of endearment.

Was that Gaelic?

Euna was surprised and a little unsettled by the question. Of course, she said.

How lovely, the woman said. Haven't heard a word of it since my nana died. She kissed Euna on the forehead, lips soft as the velvet shanks, and then took her seat behind the wheel. The last time Euna had driven down the road was ten years prior, when she had run into the estate car Muireall had hired to take them to Pullhair. Once the adrenaline had worn off, she had grown timid – the whole time she had pretended to sleep in the back seat, too cowed to look through the window. Now she stood and drew the velvet curtains, diffusing the day's gold around her.

Onward, she said.

She had promised the woman a soundtrack, so she sang and sang. The words came as they had in the river, as vibrations and not as thoughts, above and beyond appraisal. The woman stroked the ignition. In the sun that was now glinting through the windows, Euna caught the steel wink of a mattock, inclined against the kitchen counter. I'm Muireall, by the way, the woman said over her shoulder. She yanked the gear stick down and started to drive.

*

A few hours later, they reached Drumclog, a town in screaming distance of the detention centre. Having carefully studied the map on the Cala library wall, Euna had committed this name to her memory, impressed by its primitive, cramped sound. When they arrived, Euna saw that Drumclog did not align at all with the image she had invented in her mind – the panorama was huge and damp, a long, boggy mire with rampant scum. She had expected something smaller, drier, maybe something more like a prison cell.

Muireall parked the camper with its front wheels in the swamp and its back on a level plot of grass. She turned around and announced, in a kind of ancient twang, Ye have got the theory, now for the practice.

Euna felt like the camper: partly immersed in mulch, partly parked on firm ground. I'm not sure what you mean, she said.

The Reverend Thomas Douglas, Muireall said. We all learned about him in school. Don't tell me you've never heard of the Covenanters. The word sounded vaguely familiar to Euna, as an ancestral surname sometimes can, or for that matter, anything inherited: in a floaty, feathery way, untethered to any real meaning. Muireall asked, Little Gaelic-speaking, loch-bathing lady, what stone have you been living under?

The day-gold was at once too vivid, and Euna closed her eyes. Even so, she could hear Muireall climbing to the middle of the vehicle and kneeling again beside the couch, menace around her like musk. Where are you going? she asked, wedging a hand into the bend of Euna's elbow. Of all the places to touch her, this one was odd, her hand lodged there so snugly. And yet her voice was airy and spacious, reassuring. Half mulch, half firm ground.

Euna wondered if the name Muireall and the mattock inclined against the counter had been flukes, not grounds for fear. In the years since childhood, she had only met a few people, and just because a central one had been called Muireall did not mean she owned the name. Euna had no way to know what was true. And even if she did know, beyond a shadow, she would still struggle to accept it. The original Muireall's authority had, quietly and completely, erased that capacity of hers. I'm going – she was slow with this, soft with this, step-by-step with all of this – to Dungavel.

Muireall asked, Do you know someone there? Euna could not see her face, but her voice, at least, had remained steady.

Yes, Euna said. A fish farmer I met up north.

He must be special, Muireall said, a little lift in her pitch. No one goes to visit that place on a whim.

When Aileen had come to Cala, breasts and belly swollen, Euna's tenderness had not been an act. She really had felt that charitable toward the girl, had wanted to house her even, or especially, in her heifer condition. Hearing Muireall call Aram special, though, she felt newly possessive. All her blood pooled in her legs. The triangle between them, where thigh met private arch, began to tingle.

But she was not spiteful like the man in the blackhouse. When Aileen had come to Cala, breasts and belly swollen, Euna's tenderness had not been an act. When the crops at Cala had mysteriously started to fail, she had always been eager to share what could be salvaged of the harvest.

What she wanted: to tell Muireall to stay parked for a day, so Euna could explore, sieve her sensitivities, and then appear as saviour to Aram, all the while knowing a good and guarded world was waiting for her inside the camper.

Euna opened her eyes. She asked, though her body told her not to, Will you come with me?

Of course, Muireall said, without pausing to think. It would be my pleasure.

85

Cac, Euna thought. A chaca. A yes.

Well, that's wonderful, she said.

Sure, no one was holding a gun to her head or a mattock to her throat. But if she always did what she wanted to do, she would be no better than Grace, with her senseless vanity and her lens of self-interest. If Euna could not be a good Euna yet, she at least could be an impeccable Grace.

Is he expecting us at any particular time? Muireall asked.

No, Euna said, he's not expecting us.

We can spend the night here and go to Dungavel tomorrow, then, Muireall said. You rest up, darling. Meanwhile I'll get us some dinner.

Need any help scavenging?

Muireall smiled. She stroked Euna's hair in a way that milked all the tension from her body. We're not in the barrens any more, weirdo, she said. There's a commercial farm nearby.

You have money? Euna asked. Muireall nodded, and this fixed in Euna a funny kind of reverence. How do you make it?

Muireall flattened her lips. She remained pleasant and natural, soft as moss, but she said, That is not a polite question. No woman should have to justify her capital.

I'm sorry, Euna said. My manners are sickening. Do you have a ruler?

Muireall looked confused. I don't see why you would need a ruler, she said. Are you hiding some maths homework somewhere?

To have your péire slapped with a ruler was perhaps peculiar here, especially by a stranger, and at your own request. Was this true in all of Scotland, every suburb and borough?

And in England, and Wales, and in Aram's home country of Sketimini, wherever in the world that was?

Just wanted to scratch my back with it, Euna said.

Muireall smiled. Let me find us some food, she said. You deserve a quiet moment.

Euna sat up and faced Muireall. Thank you, she said.

My pleasure, Muireall said. Be back in a shake. She walked to a pair of boots left salt-stained and rigid by the door.

Once Muireall was outside, Euna felt stoned by her sudden freedom. All she had was time. All she had was permission. She unbuttoned her trousers, which she had wanted to do for hours but had not, for fear of being seen as too coarse and country. It was a treat to finally let go of that tension. And for once she was in charge of meting out that treat. Now, waistband loose, she wanted to pray, so she knelt on the laminate and knitted her fingers together. She addressed the prayer to God, and then to Aram, and then to the original Muireall. None felt right. Dear Euna, she tried.

*

Early the next morning, still full of the turnips and red pudding that Muireall had made on her return, Euna set off on foot. Muireall was snoring, having finished a few drams of Dalwhinnie, post-neeps, pre-sleep. Sneaking out before the folks around her were awake: this was exactly what Euna had done at Cala, and at the blackhouse. She was not proud to find herself again on this path of no resistance. She wanted to be calm and mettlesome, even when in conflict, even when being untrue to her given word. But for now, here she was.

She had left her belongings in the camper, sure she would be barred from bringing them into Dungavel, and hopeful that Muireall would wait for her if she had all her effects. Free of her property, this was the most pleasant walk she had taken since leaving Pullhair. It was also the briefest, and in under an hour she found herself on the Dungavel grounds. Around an imperious, turreted castle had been erected a barbed-wire fence, and in front of the fence stood a half dozen guards in bright orange jackets, carrying billy clubs and massive guns Euna could not identify. Each guard seemed to live in his own province, surrounded by an invisible border. No one exchanged a word or a look. Could she have made a wrong turn? This place seemed suited to the dangerous and deranged. As far as she knew, Aram was a migrant, not a murderer.

Though she sensed the guards' intent was to scare her, she had no direct experience with them, scary or otherwise. So she walked up to one, a young, turbaned man with a finely flecked grey beard. She stood seventeen hands high, and he could not have been any taller than that, because she looked him in the eye. She asked, Can I go in to see my husband?

The guard looked back at her. Visits start at seven in the evening, he said. No entry until then.

Glancing sidelong at his watch, Euna saw it was only eight in the morning. Her throat tightened. She had hiked so far, scraping the skin from her ankles, flaking the burned rind from the back of her neck, and after all that she was no closer to the man she thought she needed. She was as alone here as she had been on her worst days at Cala, when Muireall had tongue-lashed her but refused to use the school ruler. She did not deserve that release, Muireall would say, or she was too filthy to touch.

Thank you, master, she said to the guard. He gave her a strange look.

She crouched on the tarmac, hands graceless by her crotch. She missed Muireall's sternness, which at least she had come to understand. These guards had never saved her from the humiliation of an egged house or a burned effigy, nor had they, for that matter, offered her neeps and a pullout. And worse, they had in all likelihood hurt Aram.

Crouched on the tarmac, confused and nostalgic, she knew only one thing. She could not leave now without seeing him, her incongruous love, two-faced and tender-hearted, grating and enchanting. She needed to reach him in this quiet, tortured place. No one had ever made her feel that worthy. Leaving without seeing her brightness reflected in his eyes might have dimmed her for good.

*

Midway through the day, men and women came in a tour bus to rally on the free side of the fence. They all carried signs, written in marker on hand-cut cardboard. These could well have been a craft of Lili's, had the words been less charged: *No one is illegal. We stand with the dirty strikers.* Together, they read out a long list of names. Near the end of the list, they lowered their heads together for a moment of silence, then, eyes skyward, said one final name. It was not Aram's, and Euna felt a flare of relief, though she knew her response was self-centred, Gracelike. An older woman in a veil – not quite a nun's habit, but one as long, as black – started to howl.

The guards moved all of the protestors into a precise formation, much like a bell, bottom-heavy. This they did not resist. Their bodies were being ordered, but their voices were no less heard. They did not stop chanting their practised mantras.

After an hour or so, they put down their signs, and each took a candle from their rucksack. A woman flicked a flame onto each wick, and though bright sun subdued the effect, the pack watched the smoke with awe, as if in pitch dark. Euna knew instinctively that someone had died. She had never seen a gathering like this one, but she felt the blood inside of her turn ice cold, holding her erect from the inside. The woman began an aiste-mholaidh, like the ones Muireall used to deliver before butchering a cow at Cala. As the woman spoke, the reason for the vigil became clear: a man, routinely denied access to a doctor, had hanged himself with a rope of braided hair.

Couldn't someone in another cell have played medic, made a little clinic for the man? Euna had filled and pulled Grace's teeth, had snapped Lili's shoulder back into place when she fell off a galloping stallion and dislocated the bone. She could not imagine pain that would merit a slow hanging.

The woman Euna had seen earlier was on her knees, wailing. The guards had by now forced the crowd into such a small area that her face was pressed into a man's overcoat, which deadened the sound. She was speaking a language Euna did not understand. It could well have been English, given Euna's clear ignorance of its ins and outs.

Euna stayed crouched by the fence, a riskless distance from the guards and the crowd. Her waistband was too tight again, but here she was not in a position to unbutton it. She watched as one of the guards used his club on the woman's back, three times, with great precision.

In her little patch of hogweed, Euna sat cross-legged and closed her eyes. She wanted to conduct an Open Forum to see if they could all, for a while, just sit quietly together, but she sensed it would be high-handed to ask this woman to stop howling. Or rather, it would make of Euna a tyrant, dictating how this woman was allowed to express pain. So she focused on two hums under the woman's words – a pair of horseflies and the electric gate. Into her nose came sea-blue light, a rinse right through her heart and chest.

My son, the woman was now saying to the guard, who had for the moment stopped striking her.

Relax, the guard said.

Take it easy, another said.

Euna thought about her mam in Bucksburn, blind eye to all manner of evil. And still. It was unbearable that even a slipshod mother should create a life and have no power over its ending.

She felt a strong pull toward the crowd. Hadn't she loved it when her true friends called her bana-churaidh, heroine? A woman needed to be brave to deserve that name. As she stood to join them, one of the guards noticed her. In her silence she had enjoyed a kind of invisibility. Now, seen, she could no longer be a bloom of hogweed. He stood with feet spread and fingered his baton.

Euna thought about running back down the road to the camper, begging for safety and forgiveness from Moss Muireall. But there was a fullness here she rarely felt. Despite the guards' pressure. Despite the group's distress. This was bigger than mucking the goat stalls and cooking mutton and killing wild buckwheat with white vinegar. In the standing, or in the intent behind it – there was a vital, holy swell she had long been searching for. Silently, she named this feeling làn. And as she continued to stand, that beautiful làn filled her whole, unsheltered body.

*

Shortly past seven, after the tour buses had taken the protestors back to the place, if anywhere, they belonged, a guard directed Euna into the visits room. There she found a range of wing chairs, their white leather flawless, and a pair of well-polished drinking fountains. She was astonished. From Aram's postcard, she had expected excrement on the walls, an amphora of urine in each corner. But here she was in a rather open room, recently painted, or repainted, a muted blond. She would invite her own guests here for pekoe and oatcakes, had she anyone to entertain.

There were three other visitors waiting to talk to their loved ones, but Euna won the draw – Aram was the first to come. He looked strained, his bones made plain by his time inside. She remembered him having thick, black eyebrows and curls streaked with silver, but now he was uniformly grey, from his own hair to the jumper and trousers he had been assigned. The odd adornment he had worn before, the block of driftwood, was still around his neck. But he had since whittled it into a kind of crucifix.

When he saw Euna his eyes shone in the same boyish way they had when she'd first entered his hut, wind blown, dressed in her loose tweed. My happiness, he said, shuffling on worn sandals toward her, I'm so glad you found me. His boy-shine turned swiftly to a stony kind of absence. He embraced her with stiff and flexed arms, pressing her against his ribs with excessive force. Euna was relieved when, a moment later, the guard came to shunt his baton between them. No touching, he said.

Sorry, guv, Aram said.

Euna walked a few steps to the fountains and filled a paper cone with water, then offered it to Aram. His lips were marred by dryness and filth, a broth, a red sauce. His was the face of someone who had gone a long time without being noticed. He gulped the water, but it did nothing to wash his mouth clean. Clear beads clung to his bushy beard.

They sat down in two opposing chairs, about a metre apart. You've got a spot of... he said to her. He gestured toward her nose, but with a side glance to the guard stopped short of actual contact.

Of what?

A spot of green, he said.

Euna touched her nostril and felt a hard wad, which she hauled away, ashamed. The last time she'd seen her reflection was in the river, and then she had been afloat, washed fresh. Now she was a worse form of herself, both snotty and on land. He looked worse, too, of course, but she was fixed on her own failings. How long do we have for this visit? she asked him.

I'm not sure, he said. Truth be told, no one else has come to see me.

Not even Aileen? Euna asked.

Aram avoided her eyes, as a child does when caught in the act of doing harm. He was in no way the person she remembered, the irrepressible, robust man who had made her feel like a neach air leth, an exception to every strict rule. How did you get here, my beauty? he asked quietly, making her feel exceptional again.

By ferry, she said. On foot. Near the end I got a ride from a stranger.

Aram leaned in, focusing on the tip of her left ear. From his lips came a reek, the kind of dank breath all the Cala women had when their crops failed and for months they had to eat slop and scrapings. A stranger? he asked, clearly shaken. But you're mine.

Euna absently braided her hair.

An emaciated silence. My happiness, I'm so glad you're safe, Aram said at last. Did anyone follow you?

At times on her trip, slipping through Slochd and Sluggan, breaking by Kincraig, Euna had felt hunted in a way she could not voice or reason. But she would not admit this to her man, for whom she was the only porter of the outside. Despite his duplicity, she wanted to be his little champion, to give him at least one reason to feel safe. Of course not, she said. I was very careful.

Good girl, he said. This is why I sent for you.

Euna walked back to the fountain and this time filled a paper cone for herself. Having sipped the cone halfway empty, she filled it again, watching him over the rigid rim. He was watching her, too, his knuckles locked tightly in his lap. From this distance, her body remembered it: the drama and cabala that had circled him in the hut. This is why I sent for you. His words disturbed her. But his look wakened something else, the flickering current. The sort of pop and snap.

When she sat back down, Euna said, Well, you're a bit of a mess. But underneath that you're the same good farmer.

He smiled for the first time since she'd arrived, or maybe much longer. He looked in her eyes now, as if her flirtation had erased all prior offence. And, he said, you're the same bad ban-Leòdhasach.

At this, the guard dragged a metal stool across the room, the sound so loud and aluminous it stopped their conversation entirely. He placed the seat between Euna's and Aram's chairs and perched on it, not turning to either of them, not speaking. Where Muireall's surveillance had relied on the element of surprise, on her hiding in the broom closet and the hollyhock, this relied only on the guard's conviction that he had the power to do what he wanted, with little consequence.

Sorry, guv, Aram said.

He did not acknowledge that Aram had spoken.

Now a man wearing a brimless, rounded cap entered the visits room. He was reunited with another man in the same cap and a linen body shirt with toning trousers. Though Aram had seemed handsome compared to the scraggy man in the blackhouse, compared to these men he was gaunt, unremarkable. The two men engaged in an intricate handshake, hovering just beyond the point of contact. As this happened, Euna watched Aram in her periphery. He seemed slowly to wilt, his brow bowed toward the linoleum.

What's wrong? she asked.

His response came straight away, as if he had been holding the words for months, waiting for someone to give him the occasion to speak. I'm the only one from Sketimini, he said. There's a block of Afghan guys, for instance. They speak Pashto to each other all day, and even though they get treated like trash – he paused to look at the guard, who did not react – they don't give a meall cac because they're here together.

Her lust for him was resurrected when he used his foul Gaelic. Her body had been trained to respond to those sounds, as to the dong-dong of the Cala dinner bell, or the ding-ding of the Cala cowbell.

You're from Pullhair, too, she said. And Glenfinnan. Maybe there's someone like you, if you think a bit more broadly?

The guard moved his chair closer to hers so he could hear what she was saying. And just as the guard became more attentive to her, Aram's face went stony again. His lust was lost behind that flint. Smothering her with that aolach breath, he said, Euna, you wouldn't understand.

This shocked her. She had walked a week to be with him, maybe hexing her whole existence. Worse, he was now a disappointed daddy, calling her by her Christian name. The room felt newly small, cell-like. Why are you pushing me away? she asked. Her mind had started to heat, as if her skull were full of coal, smouldering.

As if mirroring the guard, Aram did not acknowledge that she had spoken.

I came so far to see you, she said. I blistered my feet for you.

And still he held his silence, stayed locked inside. It was only months later that Euna realized he had been protecting her, that the guard's sudden interest was tied to her threat and to his authority to deal with threats.

She tried to jolt Aram one last time. I starved myself for you, she said.

Aram did not break. She could not be ignored by the one man who was supposed to make her feel seen. So she grabbed him by the chin, as she had seen Muireall do to his precious Aileen. You know what, Aram? she said, forcing him to look at her. You don't know anything about me, or what I understand. Rach thusa.

Now the guard leaned forward on his stool. She thought he was going to bracelet her, force her out of the facility, but instead he put his hand on her knee. Whatever heat was rising from her was hypnotic to him. He made his pleasure apparent, flashing his teeth, massaging his thighs with long, deep-tissue caresses. As soon as she saw this approval, a cold black came over the coals. His respect, his clear and sinister respect, raked out her inner fire. She let go of Aram. She was disturbed by whatever hag had just emerged from her hollows. This prison pulled something delirious and illogical from inside her. She needed to leave.

I'm tired, she said. And I have a true friend who may still be waiting for me. For the record, I don't regret seeing you.

Aram did not appear to be shaken by what had just happened, and this distressed her more than her sudden break had. Her anger had moved over, not through, him, and so he had in his soundless way denied it. Whether he'd done this intentionally or instinctively, having been inured to anger after many months here, she did not know. He said, simply, Thank you for coming, my happiness. He did not ask when she would return, nor did he seem eager to stall until she could leave on a more loving note. For all she knew, he had another visitor on the way.

Euna waved to him as the man down the sealoch had waved to her, plainly. Slàinte mhath, she said.

She asked the guard to escort her out, and he did, through a metal detector and past some mastiffs with dense, muscular haunches, to the other side of the barbed-wire fence. She started back down the road, heart stark, as the wind worked into her nerves. This was not the first time in her life she had been bereaved, but nothing had ever carved her this wide open. The night air moved through her as through a cave.

Occasional headlights cast shadows onto the road, which stretched in front of her, infinite and hostile. The landscape was fictive. The bell heather and hazel could well have been made by Lili's hands, special effects of sgàilich. Euna had nothing, trusted nothing, was nothing. As the headlights of a juggernaut approached, she drifted into the vehicle's path. It would have been so simple.

The driver swerved and she found her way back to the road's shoulder. Her walking was a task like any other, bleak, weak of spirit, and with this in mind, she forced her way through the kilometres of null. Head down and braids back, she parted the void. This was not death. This was the first breath after death. She kept moving, for the second time, away from Aram. On a crushed-rock shoulder she had long dreamed of walking together.

*

In a long hour, she was by the mire at Drumclog. To her relief, to her profound relief, she saw that the camper was parked in precisely the same place as it had been before. The curtains were drawn, the lights at their full brilliance. Euna could see Muireall clearly, back hooked over her crocheting. She had waited, despite Euna's inability to do the same. She had not assented to eye-for-an-eye. Euna had to plant herself in the wet peat and breathe, so sudden and dense was her gratitude.

Muireall missed a stitch and cursed. Then quite calmly she held her effort to the light, fixed the stitch, and kept on crocheting. Euna smiled. She walked to the camper, stopping to scrape her boots clean on the stairs. Inside, Muireall glanced up at her with the warmth of Christ and then looked back at her craft. I left baked beans for you on the stove, she said, and a tin of Irn-Bru in the fridge.

She may as well have told Euna a pair of sheepskin slippers and a gilded copy of *The Witches Speak* were in the inglenook. She had so quickly secured a world that seemed to Euna today, for the first time, gimcrack.

Euna filled a bowl with beans and a stein with the Irn-Bru. She settled herself onto the couch cushion beside Muireall's and set her stein on the armrest. Unhooking her back, Muireall looked at Euna. Next time, just be honest with me, she said. It would save me some worrying. Why did you go alone?

Euna took a moment to adjust, as a person's eyes do when exposed to a new and brighter light. At Cala it had been a guessing game. Locking up and choking off and archiving for later. Or never. Or straining to read shifts in energy. Steeping. Creeping around the cause of whatever discord, refusing to look right at it, choosing instead to let the thing ingrow, like a bad hair.

I just wanted to see him on my own first, Euna said. And then, tentatively, Are you mad at me?

Muireall put down her crocheting so her attention was entirely on Euna. When she spoke, her voice was placid and sincere. I was disappointed when I saw you were gone, she said.

And now?

Now we've chatted about it. She kissed her fingertips and then touched them to Euna's forehead. If it had been bigger, we may have taken longer to move on. But this is just minor. Have some supper and try not to fret.

Euna could not believe this: the passing dissonance had been just that, passing, as opposed to a noiseless, days- or weeks-long build that would end either in catharsis or lasting bile. Muireall, she said, thank you. She forked into the beans, still warm, spiked with pecks of white pepper. Muireall had reduced the tomatoes they were immersed in, which had clearly taken patience.

How did it go, anyway? Muireall asked.

Euna hesitated. It certainly had its good moments, she said.

And your man?

Let's not talk about him.

Muireall wrapped her arm around Euna's shoulders. Days can be kind of shitty, can't they, she said.

Really, Euna said. Measgachadh caca.

Muireall clapped her hands together. There's that lovely Gaelic again, she said. You're such a special girl. Muireall's use of the word had a different feel than Aram's. Muireall seemed unmoved by whether Euna believed her or returned the sentiment. In her *special* there was no sale.

I can teach you some time, Euna said.

Muireall glimmered. Oh, I'd love to hire you, she said. Always thought it a shame that it should die off with my nana.

Euna had never dreamed she could make a coinage of her language. At Cala, her words had seemed routine, similar as they were to all the other sounds around her. But now they were a means. Now *airgead* was actual silver.

So listen, Muireall said, I rang a few of my friends in Glasgow.

In her head, Euna finished the sentence: ... *and I am going to see them without you.* The shift was quick and instinctive, and as ever, ended in her exclusion. I've been thinking all of this was too good to last, Euna said. I've had a wonderful time here with you. And I thank you for everything you've done.

Muireall, her arm still around Euna, began to knead her friend's shoulder. I'm inviting you to come, goofball, she said.

The whole heavy day came down on Euna's head. Her eyes were suddenly full of tears. She didn't care if she was *that kind of woman*, now that she was here in this little, well-lit interior, now that she was no longer bound in leather to the *Life Grammar*. Muireall, she said, when she could. 'S toil leam gu mòr thu.

What's that mean, hen?

I like you very much.

Then I suppose, Muireall said, we have a mutual admiration society.

Euna nuzzled into her friend's shoulder. She felt Muireall's breath, soft as cushion pink, on her cheek.

This band I used to roadie for is playing in Glasgow, Muireall said. Kind of Celtic punk. Good show of pride. Will you come with me?

Pride was a thing to be ashamed of, to spurn at all personal cost. To Euna's family, as to the women at Cala, it was a sin worse than sloth. And yet she trusted Muireall deeply, and if Muireall said pride had its place, then Euna would follow her there. She told her, Yes I said yes I will Yes.

Joyce, Muireall said, smiling. My favourite, back when I was a hell-raising teen.

That brick from Cairstìne's bookshelf, someone else had read it? The odd thing about her *Ulysses* was that half the words had been darkened with lampblack, presumably by Cairstìne. Sentences would dangle, thoughts would hang. All questions – What in the water did Bloom, waterlover, drawer of water, watercarrier, returning to the range, admire? – would end in blank space. At least as far as Euna could tell, with her stunted reading skills. Now she knew a woman who could tackle those troubling blanks. We have so much to talk about, Euna said.

We sure do, hen. But for now you should sleep. You'll want to be rested for this show, trust me.

Euna nodded. She finished her beans and rinsed the plate under a stream of running water, which, after years of the latrine and well, was all but numinous. She removed her tunic without embarrassment.

Another sip of the Irn-Bru and she was lying down, teeth a bit woolly, but soul full. Muireall wrapped Euna in a downy throw and dimmed all the camper lights. In the near dark Euna's heart pumped, as she conjured the concert in Glasgow. Men with glittering guitars, a glorious crush of dancers; the images dimmed and became dreams. But unlike the cranachan and the burning church, these held her in a safe and soothed place. A real cala. These were dreams she would have, given control, chosen.

Euna woke to the violent sound of someone vomiting. The curtains were still drawn, and through the windows she could see a city, steep and monolithic, lit by a sullen sun. Muireall must have driven to Glasgow while Euna was sleeping. She looked down. On the cobbled street was a young man, head between his knees, pants low enough to show half of his péire. She did not have any artichoke tincture or lemon balm on hand, but she would comb this unfamiliar place as if it were her mission. The man needed a nurse, and who was she to neglect another's needs?

Muireall, bent at the dinette over a cryptic crossword, must have noticed Euna's interest. He's drunk, she said.

What time is it? Euna asked. She had seen folks malkied a few times in her life, mainly her mam, but those moments had mostly happened in the guest room after lights-out, with the requisite sum of shame. Now Euna was appalled, though Muireall seemed calm about the man's immorality.

Eight in the morning, Muireall said. Why, are you hungry?

I mean, yes, Euna said. Then she gestured to the man. But I was mostly asking because of him.

Muireall put her pen down and came to perch on the couch beside Euna. You've never seen a man out his nut? I must ask again, little Gaelic-speaking, loch-bathing lady, what stone have you been living under?

The last time Muireall asked, Euna had been too reticent to tell the truth, and for good reason. No one wants to be abandoned in random woodland. But now she was in a city and, having survived acreages of Highland and bog, every home and museum seemed to gleam with promise. The people may have been bare-péired and moonshined too early in the morning, but among them must have been at least one true friend. Besides, Euna had a sense that Muireall was with her for the long haul.

So, she revealed to Muireall a small part of her story, a few scenes from Cala. She turned from charm and glamour. She used her plainest tongue. Still she held back all that would make her sweat or suffer from an overbeating heart – the church, her family, Muireall's worst abuses, Grace's suspicion, Aram's sex. When she was finished, Muireall embraced her. Swatch at you, she said. You're a fecking badass.

Despite her kind sentiment, Euna bristled against the embrace. She had said so much, while Muireall had offered nothing in return. With all that rambling, Euna had dug herself down to a new level of unlovable. Muireall was only pretending to be supportive. Before long Euna would reveal her real self not through word but through deed, and then Muireall would heave her onto the street.

Euna detected on her own bare shoulders and her trousers and even on her downy throw a scent, a kind of gritrock, linked closely to Dungavel. She longed for the perfumes she used to wear at Cala, big and bloomy as they were, unbecoming as they often were. At least they had covered her.

Awright? Muireall asked.

Euna said, I need a wash. A smell keeps clinging.

Muireall did not press on this. She said, Sure thing. There's the tap in the corner, and I can get you a fresh sponge. Or if you want a real bath, I'll go and bat my lashes inside one of the hotels.

A hotel sounded immoderate. Euna said, A sponge is fine.

Okay, hen, Muireall said. She fished a clean sponge from a sideboard and threw it into Euna's lap. I've a few errands to run, and I'm sure you'd like some privacy. I'll be back in a while. If it suits you then, we can go to the show. She put on sunglasses and some busted-in combat boots, which gave her an unruffled affect, and blew air kisses from the doorway. Euna felt little heat streaks run down her cheeks.

This time when Muireall left, Euna did not feel stoned by her freedom. In this camper, even with Muireall around, she was free to romp and move as she pleased. If she wanted to pray, she knew she could do that at any time. After years of pining for these precise comforts – running water, a private space with a locked door, a forbearing friend – she now found them, bird in hand, a bit intimidating. The man on the cobblestone retched again, and she felt a stitch of envy that he was in such discomfort, which, at least, was familiar to her.

She tried to open the window but found that it was fixed. So she rapped on the glass and hollered in her highest register, Hello. Good morning. I see you there, sir.

The man looked up with his eyes half closed, the world for him surely blurred. He yelled, Taigh na galla leat.

Euna was more thrilled than she should have been that a kerbside arse was telling her to piss off. But his Gaelic was perfect, his filthy mouth alluring. She grinned. A thrustair nan seachd sitigean! she called – *you rotten piece of shit!* She gave him a thumbs-up through the glass. He burped and passed out.

Hey, wee willie, she yelled. She banged on the window, but he seemed to be impervious to all sound. Beyond his wilting body, she could see a few other people – a woman arranging finger limes outside of a greengrocer, a man and child farther down the street, carrying glitter-filled balloons. She considered going out to whack the man awake, as she refused to be neglected any longer, but she felt safer on this side of the glass.

She took the sponge to the corner and saturated it under the tap, then removed her clothes. She scrubbed herself until she turned real bright, the colour of an uncooked steak at Cala. She liked it this bit rough, this bit skin-peeling. That little bugger, she repeated as she scrubbed, until it became a mantra.

After a long bout of polishing, she ended up pink as a baby and just as pure. Only then did she stop washing. As she beat her tunic with a backhand, trying to smack out the Dungavel stink, she looked down at the man lying on his bile pillow. She fixated on how clean she was, how alone and superior in her sealed motorhome. And, though she knew the feeling would at some point fleet, it did make her feel fitter to be so far above this man. If she was a mess, at least she was less of one. If she was sad and aimless, at least she was strong enough to face that darkness with a clear head.

*

Euna stayed in the camper all day, waiting for Muireall, who returned around dinnertime with whisky, an eccentric set of canned foods, and a few hardbacks she had borrowed from a place she called the Women's Library. To Euna it sounded so charmed, so full of tall shelves and yellowing novels and tender, feminine guardians, that she almost forgot how lonely she had been all afternoon. Her imagination started to rewrite that real experience. But she put a quick stop to that. She wanted to be like Muireall, who spoke directly, who refused to let hairy feelings ingrow. I didn't think you were going to come back, she said. I got worried.

Muireall laughed. You think I'd part with this camper? she asked.

Euna laughed, too, because it seemed like she was supposed to. Muireall pulled a large platter from the kitchen cabinet and opened all her wee wartime tins, then arranged brined gourds and oily fish on the platter, a limit of pear quarters around its rim. Bon appetit, she said, and they sat at the dinette together.

Now Euna felt like the man out his nut, ready to vomit. Maybe Muireall had spoiled her so far, but this meal did not compare well to what she had been eating. Even the suppers at Cala, once the livestock had started to sicken, had kept to a higher standard. She wondered if she could tell Muireall that she—

Hey there, hen, eat up, Muireall said. Someone gives you a meal, you down it. Don't just sit there aff in dreamlain.

Euna was embarrassed. She took some of the oily fish, so unlike the catches she had eaten in Pullhair, save the toy-sized eyes and scales. Muireall poured two tumblers of whisky, drank one down, and placed the other on the dinette in front of Euna. Euna thought of the man on the cobblestone, who had, mid-afternoon, pulled himself upright and stumbled into the sun, whistling 'Will Ye Go, Lassie, Go' as if nothing at all had happened. As if one could trundle on without repenting. She was nothing if not greater than him.

Still, she drank the whisky down. It had a heavy bite, bitter and almost hostile, like that of horehound. Her throat burned.

Muireall pulled a leather jacket similar to her own from the camper closet and pitched it at Euna. Put that on over your tunic, she said. Then we'll go. Euna did as she was told. She was thrown by the whisky, a bit angry, a bit lusty, a lot ready to fight. She followed Muireall out of the camper and through the city, taking the flask from Muireall's back pocket now and again, drinking a few mouthfuls as fuel. The walk was short and the night dark, and all she saw of Glasgow was its thick and central waterway, lights imaged in it as scrabbles and scrawls.

Euna was crocked but still standing when they got to the venue, a warehouse with smashed windows and walls burned into skewbald. Out front dozens of kids in joggers and crop tops, or short plaid dresses and studded trainers, were smoking and cussing blue streaks. She mumbled to a girl with a septum ring, Bum one? With one last sip of the whisky, Euna was suddenly jaked, too tanked to stand or think sharp thoughts.

Cigarette in hand, she smoked and coughed lung up and puked. Disgraced. Kid beside her hideous and trying to neck. Up the oil and tinned fish again. Muireall laughed so Euna laughed. But her mood was choppy loch. Muireall met friends, five or six of them. Suddenly she was speaking like the blackhouse man. Canty tae meet ye, she said. And then, Let's hae some fin.

Inside, the room was spinning. Each was in their body, flawless, swimming. Then came music, bigger than Moog, madder, all around her and in'er heart. Grime, Muireall called it. Faces like at Dungavel, all kinds of pale and melanin. Anyone from Sketimini? Euna screamed. The room was really rolling. That heavy beat. She felt nil. She felt all.

Front row. Muireall's friend had his hand on Euna's péire. Too sluggish to struggle against him. So she huffed a bit in his blond hair. He ruffed it out. Whit is wrang wi' ye? he asked.

I wish I knew.

He laughed. Weel, be cannie in haur, ye slag.

Her skin was vibrating with the song. She saw other kids shoving so she shoved the guy who'd called her a slag. He shoved back. It was not like punishment, a cold shoulder or a ruler. Power moved between them. The man on stage said his name, Deliverance, and shouted out Aberdeen.

Room spinning.

Bodies swimming.

A decade since anyone had mentioned her hometown.

Then the punk band was playing, Deliverance on stage with them. Five of them jumping, wumping the whole warehouse. We're Firth of Forth, the péire-toucher said.

Next song was in Gaelic, Deliverance coming in with his Aberdeen slang. The sound meld. The hash of high and low, wild and slow, so grand. This was làn. Muireall held her hand all the way onto the stage, then, Sing. Little Gaelic ting. Sing. Euna did not know the wording. But she was grinning and eager and Yes I said yes I will Yes. She took a mic and blacked her brain out while her mouth worked. Crowd so loud her ears turned inward. A Gàidhealtachd, a kid called, elated. Muireall yelled, There's yer pride!

On the ground again, still full of làn. The world so damain beautiful. The room jammed with family, a fresh homeland.

Her face would not stop smiling. Nothing would bring her down from this high, this shimmer, summit of glam and music. Then she puked by the subwoofer.

From behind, someone held her red hair. Euna went unbent, wiped the spew from her lips, looked at the freckled hands. But no. But not possible. Aileen? And so pregnant. Her face different, fed in good fettle, full of light.

How are you here?

Aileen snorted. Had to back out of my mission work. I got scared. You know, it's dangerous over there.

Over there. Yes, it did sound distant and dangerous. Euna was thrilled the girl had stayed. Kept her face so golden, glowed by one growing inside. And nearer, the clear eyes, the queer way her lips curled, the sheer allure of her being there. She wore a fine necklace. Euna reined her in by its chain. Àillidh. Aileen. This was the first night of a life.

IV

BY THE MIDDLE of August, Aileen had left the boarding house in Possilpark where she had been renting a tiny, tick-ridden room. She had been sharing a low-income unit with a couple who would inject a drug Euna had not heard of, and then shriek at one another, make loud love, rake their hands over a guitar at four in the morning. All in the great, hanging heat of summer. All in the gloom and smother of Aileen's new solitude. She described the place only as *unspeakable*. When she moved into the camper, which Muireall and Euna had parked semi-permanently in Castlemilk, it was only natural that Aileen and Euna would share a bed. After all, there was limited space, and necessity is the mother of affection.

Castlemilk was not by any means a beautiful place, but Euna had learned that in the uniformly grey tenements and the uniformly grey faces there was a particular kind of comfort, if not actual kindness. She found the size of the district familiar, charming, and every time she passed the same dishevelled woman with her five kids in tow, or even the same ned in his red sportclothes, it would give her a kind of pleasure. Not to see them stuck, as some were, in poverty amber, but to know that in a world with such fogged edges there were sharp and constant points: red hoodie, child with snotty nose, grocery bag ripped at bottom, crappy old aerials on each building.

She would have been rather happy, she thought, to stay within those frontiers entirely. She could have made quite a go of that. Mornings reading in the camper, afternoons buying groceries or doing the washing, evenings having a drink with her friends, every so often going to a concert. Only hitch was that Muireall frequently sent her and Aileen to do chores – walking all the way to the suburbs to pick up a particular kind of cake flour, or researching arcana at the library, despite how hard it was for Euna to read at a high level. One time Muireall even packed the two young women a picnic and rented them road bikes, although neither ban-Leòdhasach had learned to ride anything but a mare. Muireall never offered them a reason, nor a choice. On those near-daily occasions Euna felt that, for reasons obscure to her, she and Aileen were not welcome in the camper, and that did not sit well in her gut.

It was a grey, faded day, and Muireall had just finished her crossword. Though she had been awake for several hours, Euna was pretending to sleep, so she could stay with Aileen in dreamlain. When they were awake together, Aileen was fitfully distant. Euna felt desperate each time she read aloud a paragraph about first love, almond blooms, linen canopies, hoping to receive affection and instead earning a laugh, or worse, radio silence. But when they were asleep, the small bed pressed their bodies together. All the warmth she had dreamed possible with Aram, or with any other person, moved over and through their two sleeping forms.

Aileen bolted upright. Looks like mid-fecking-morning! she said. Ye can wake me up next time, ye ken.

Euna sat up then, too, and perched on the edge of the bed beside Aileen. Her back was stiff from lying for so long. Good morning.

Morning, hens, Muireall said. She straightened up from the dinette and went to start her daily pot of stout, hard-wearing coffee. You're in for a treat today. We're going on a field trip to the library.

The library – as far as Euna was concerned, one of Earth's sacred scenes – was an hour and a half away by foot. A field trip meant a ride in the camper, and that was fine news. Euna started to sing a random soundtrack, hoping that by doing so she would subliminally move Muireall to start driving. Now that she knew they were going to the library, had selected its interior from her mind's image archive, she could hardly stay still. When she was very young, this had been the trial of every Christmas morning: having pictured the roast in the oven, with its crest of thyme and moat of fat, she would feel as if a smaller version of herself were running around inside, in circles, restless, unable to unsee that one image. Each bided moment had felt then, as it did now, like a life sentence.

I get your hint, Muireall said. She went to the driver's seat and started the engine. Buckle up, loves, she said over her shoulder.

On the drive, Euna watched the city through the fixed window. They followed the A730, a monotonous, single-veined road, its only grace a casing of wild cherry. Then as they came closer to the city centre, the road widened, leaving space for signs announcing barbers, pubs, surgeons, cemeteries.

Muireall flew so swiftly past them that Euna, who wanted so badly to read every word, began to get aggravated. But then the steadiness of the non-colours, the sky and road and stoic buildings, pacified her.

They turned onto Shawfield Road, bounded by a squat brick fence and immense streetlamps, all azoic and industrial – then, round the bend, the primitive river. It reached into the adolescent parts of her heart. The camper coasted over the river smoothly, on a bridge that was, though man-made, as mesmeric as the water. On the far side, again, grey bricks were only outnumbered by clouds, sandstone by wild drivers.

She knew they were nearing the library when the business signs turned from cracked and peeling to freshly painted, revitalized. The city core was comelier than Castlemilk, where Euna had seen two menfolk running around with harpoon guns, and many others getting jumped and gashed and harassed, or else swigging from flagons in broad daylight. The only way she could understand the difference was this: thick of winter at Cala, her belly used to stay warm, while her hands and feet would go numb. When there was not enough blood to keep her whole body hot, it would pool in the centre.

Muireall parked around the corner from the library and helped Aileen and Euna down the stairs. They reeled a bit, stepping onto solid ground after the feverish ride. Together they all turned the corner. Each time Euna saw among the many outdated buildings that single modern one, its face etched with the names of eminent novels, she brightened. For years she had believed herself to be the only reader on earth, the only creature strange or dissocial enough to need life support from lifeless things. And now a whole building had been raised to prove her wrong.

Euna moved behind Aileen and put one hand on her love's waist, the other on Aram's child. Pretty magical, isn't it? she asked.

Waste ay fecking money, Aileen said.

Hey there, quacking ducks, Muireall said with a laugh. Stop bickering. Play nice for the dead poets.

Sorry, Aileen said, with an exaggerated curtsy. I'm going to blame my hormones. I'm glad you've finally found a welcoming place. You really went through hell back then.

And what was that supposed to mean? Neck prickles. Sure, Aileen had seen Cala, on one of its most suffocating days. But she did not know the place at all, not the intimate way Euna knew it, not well enough to pass such casual judgement. They had been a family, and only someone on the inside of a family can salt and beat its laundry. So she entered the library feeling guarded, and miffed, and a bit homesick. But if she could weather this mood anywhere in the world, it was here, where in this massive archive there were bound to be a few books that spoke to her.

The library's smell calmed her. It was not musty, as she remembered, but sweet and lightly floral. She knew as soon as she came inside that she was safe. Muireall drifted to the poetry stacks – she lived for landscape verses, reading Li Po, Christina Rossetti to the younger women, which thrilled Euna no end – while Aileen grabbed a stack of comics and dumped herself, spread-legged, onto the middle of the hard-wood. Euna knew a person was only allowed to read in a wing chair or else reclined on a daybed, but the librarian did not seem bothered by Aileen's dumping. Euna stood in front of a random shelf and ran her finger along each spine, unable to read the words without also touching them. Her finger stopped suddenly on a paperback she must have overlooked on her previous outings.

The Witches Speak. She had not seen it in its entirety since leaving the north, and now here was a worn copy, smudged by others' thumbs. She stretched the belly of her tunic in front of her, making a hammock for the book, as she had for the prawns some months before. Farther down the shelf she found a volume called *Malleus Maleficarum*, subtitled *The Hammer of Witches which destroyeth Witches and their heresy as with a two-edged sword*. This one weighed down the tunic-hammock too much. Once it was in there, she barely had room for one more.

She was attracted to a book with a title she could not understand, *Le miroir des âmes simples*. Were those words in a different language, or were they simply beyond her narrow English window? For once, the Bad Witch Muireall wasn't there to help her read the big-girl parts. Still Euna was drawn to the book by a sort of magnetic pull, a heavy aura she could not ignore. So she took it into the hammock and then, having considered a wing chair, she splayed on the floor as she had seen Aileen do. The librarian looked at her longer than she had at Aileen, perhaps because her plopping down now seemed to be part of a trend, one of young people plopping, but she let Euna's oddness breathe.

Ploughing through *The Witches Speak*, she found that, in this new setting, the words she had once taken to be sacred were in fact fairly dull, full of holes. They failed to strike awe into her, and more importantly, they were not the divine truths they were masquerading as. They were just something a person had come up with and then written down. Anyone could have done it, even Euna, had she the assurance that people would read it.

Before long she was on *Malleus Maleficarum*, which scared the cac out of her. Witches should be made extinct, it said, in essence. Over hundreds of pages he advocated for torture, for tying witches to pickets and burning them alive, in view of the public. Euna thought of Cairstìne, stalked and sunk to the bottom of the loch, and her cheeks started to bake. Near the back of the book she found an historical note. The treatise had been written by a German clergyman in the fifteenth century, after his sexual obsessions with an alleged witch caused him to be expelled from his home. A bit angry, a bit lusty, a lot ready to fight. Theologians called the work immoral, counter to demonology, but among the public at the time its sales were second only to the Bible.

So it was written by a nutter, yes, but one who had appealed to, or at least intrigued, a whole nutter segment of the public. A significant one, it seemed.

Hey, hen, Muireall said, snapping her fingers in front of Euna's face. How's the air in dreamlain?

I'm sorry, Euna said, eyes still down. This book was taking me somewhere strange.

Don't read that shite, Muireall said. I mean, you're an adult and you can read whatever you want and blah blah. But I'm telling you that book is torrid, blistering garbage, and a non-garbage person like you shouldn't be wasting your time in the pish and tush.

Now Euna looked up. You have a way of putting things...

There was the twinkle in Muireall's eye again, punch-drunk, wicked. Here lies Muireall, she said. She had a way of putting things.

Euna laughed and snapped the book in her lap closed. Still she held its great leather weight there as a kind of mooring.

Anyway, Muireall said, your girlfriend has somehow managed to fall asleep reading about mutant massacres. She pointed to Aileen, who was lying on the floor, an issue of *X-Men* tented over her. You should take her for a coffee or something, eh, pet?

Come with us? Euna regretted asking as soon as she had done it. She knew the answer was going to be no; she had that unnerving and unnamed sense that Muireall was trying to get rid of her.

I need to give the camper a bit of a tune-up, Muireall said. Take her for a cup at Papertrail and I'll collect you both in a couple hours.

Yes, ma'am. Should we pick up something sweet for you? I've seen how much you like black buns.

Whoa, mistress of surveillance! Muireall said. It's nice and weird that you know that. But nobody serves black buns outside of Hogmanay. I'd love some cranachan.

Cranachan. The word ignited an ache in her. But Muireall was already trying to get rid of Euna, and she could not stand to push her friend farther away by telling that horrid truth. So she held the story of her childhood and the burning church. She held it like pee all night at Cala with Lili beside her, held it within her four walls, like Aram in the nearby castle. I'll do what I can, she said.

Muireall pulled a few banknotes from her jacket pocket and tucked them into Euna's tight grip. Buy her a drink, okay? Something fancy with whipped cream. Gotta be nice to our loved ones so they don't split.

She winked and was off, leaving Euna on her own, anchored by the leather. She hesitated, then carefully moved it from her lap and onto the library floor, before going to kneel beside Aileen. She stroked the girl's temples until she wiggled her nose in a charming and even tempting way, slowly waking up. What had made her seem grotesque in the pinched atmosphere of Cala, the far-apart eyes, the broad nose, now made her seem rare. And rareness, in this room, was something to be celebrated.

Ìosa Crìost. Was I really just sleeping on the floor of the library? This baby's an energy leech.

Euna stroked Aileen's temples again, this time beaming. It had not occurred to her before Muireall said it, since Euna had always been the one to split, but it was true that Aileen had made no promises, nor had she ever seemed smitten in the same way Euna was. Euna had to accept that, as Samhain gives way to Nollaig, then Eanáir, people follow their own seasons, and between them the climate can change. Let's get you the tidiest coffee in Glasgow, she said.

Aileen seemed eager to do that, tramping to her feet and leading the way outside. Euna had not had a chance to read the final book with the inscrutable name, the one she had initially been so drawn to. So, with her heart hammering and her conscience a two-edged sword, she hid it in the folds of her tunic, then followed Aileen into the dowdy day. Though she had stolen the book, the dust around her did not turn suddenly to lice, nor did frogs begin to fall from the sky or boils to cover the intimate parts of her body. She puffed out her relief and took Aileen's hand. To steal and not be caught or punished, it turned out, was pretty fun.

So they went on their way to the cafe, as if they were two normal women, not rank ones from a cocked-up little village, troubled ones with DAMAGED GOODS signs around their necks. Not saints or whores. Not sorceresses or scum-witches. Just two ordinary, coffee-drinking women on an ordinary, coffee-drinking date. As they moved down the street, Euna smiled and smiled at all the people who hardly seemed to notice them. It was wonderful to walk and not be looked at.

In the pale white cafe were a handful of people wearing headphones, absorbed in the still life of their notebooks. Euna was struck by the handsome plants in every corner, a fiddle fig, a maidenhair fern, well and bright as anything in the Cala greenhouse. And then, she was struck again: from sleek speakers around the cafe came a song she had heard first in the Moog circle, 'Nothing Compares 2 U'. Until now it had been immobile in time, held in that stone room full of women and synthesizers. She had only heard Lili singing the words in her motley, overly emotive way – and now, to have a woman singing them beautifully, her voice both sensitive and assertive, Euna was entranced. She led Aileen as far as the cash register but then stood there mute, held hostage by the single. Aileen seemed to have no such problem. Biggest mug you've got, she said. Full of hot and sweet.

Euna pointed at the chalkboard behind the barista to order a coffee and cranachan. She had spent the past weeks studying the way Muireall and Aileen spoke, trying in turn to mimic their lilts and diction. But she was not ready to test herself in public yet, especially not while surrounded by this exquisite song.

Drinks in hand, they tucked themselves into a booth across from a pair of strangers who were clearly besotted with one another. Euna felt a need to outperform them. Especially after what Muireall had said, about the whipped cream and the splitting. So she played with Aileen's tangled red hair, lifted the mug to her lips and tipped the coffee down her throat. Aileen coughed. What the hell! she cried.

Euna felt terrible for spilling such a hot mess on Aileen's chin and tartan. But she ignored her instinct to say sorry, and as soon as she did, the whole thing took on a fresh absurdity. She laughed. A big, bubbling, dumpling-in-a-pot laugh. Whoops, she said. That was really weird of me.

Aileen looked pissed off, briefly, before her expression eased and she started to laugh, too. For the first time with real intention, she leaned in and kissed Euna. The electric cage around Euna began to light up again. The pleasure was so fast and frantic she was afraid to lose herself in it. She pulled back. The voice she had lost by the chalkboard now came out without strain. I love you, it said to Aileen.

You're a fecking nut, Aileen said.

The song changed. This next track sounded more like Deliverance, though it was likely a different artist. Euna drank her coffee, and under the bitterness was a sweet trace, of blackberry, or syrup from a silk tree. Aileen kissed her again, this time with less passion and more care. Euna was wary of that warmth, having just had her feelings scorned.

Aileen looked at Euna. Her expression was blunt. My life was rubbish before I met you, she said.

And now?

I mean, honestly, she said, it's still not great. I'm as big as Castlemilk and I'm carrying a random man's baby. Sometimes when I'm hanging out with you I forget that.

Euna felt as if she had just eaten henbane, the way her arms roasted and reddened, her body clammed and clotted. She could not stop showing Aileen her missing molar.

I'm not such a sap about it, she said. But you took me in at my worst and didn't want anything in return. Do you know how uncommon that makes you?

I don't see why that would be uncommon, Euna said. You needed help.

You haven't met enough people yet, I guess.

Euna drank the rest of her sweetbitter coffee with one neat little finger pointing all the way to the sky. She could not look Aileen in the eyes. And if you haven't noticed, Aileen said, pinching Euna's little finger, you're quite pretty.

She had, of course, never noticed that. Grace was the attractive one, and she had made sure everyone knew that undeniable fact. Euna tried to peek at herself in an upside-down teaspoon, but the reflection was distorted. Instead she pulled the stolen hardcover from her tunic and turned it over, to see herself in its shiny laminate.

See what I mean? Aileen asked. She traced the reflected features, which did look quite pleasant now, at least as long as Aileen was touching them.

Aileen picked up *Le miroir des âmes simples* from the table. She started to flip through the book, and as she did Euna tried to read it over her shoulder. Euna struggled with the obscure words, some of which she had never seen in her life, maybe because they were old and out of fashion. Aileen pointed to a passage partway through the book. Hey, wee tutor, what does that say?

The first part was easy enough to read – *I am God, says Love, for Love is God and God is Love* – but Euna had to wrestle with the rest of the passage. *Thus this precious beloved of mine is taught and guided by me, without herself, for she is transformed into me, and such a perfect one, says Love, takes my nourishment.*

Euna turned to Aileen. The couple across the table paled in her periphery. The two women were alone in the white room. Euna played with Aileen's hair not because anyone was watching, but because she wanted to. Bliss was not possible outside of the red tangle, the two inches Aileen's head tilted when touched. To stroke that surface, alive with kinks and knots, was to rocket very close to heaven.

Mid-touch, Aileen spotted a stain on her blouse. Oh, fur fuck's sake, you've spilled coffee aw ower me.

Well then. This particular heaven had fences. This particular heaven had sea-lice. This particular heaven had curfews, rules regarding speech and touch, prison guards to keep folks under control – and yes, blouse stains and romance slanted to the left, so that love tended to roll in one direction.

Aileen went to the bathroom to wash herself off. As she was walking away, Euna had a double sense, grief on the one side and relief on the other. While Aileen was gone, Muireall, as promised, came to find them. She had something in her hand, a large, hard case curved like a waterbody.

I got you something, she said.

There was that Christmas morning feeling again. Euna

started running around inside of herself. She took the case and cracked it open, and in it was something she had fantasized about, though she had been too afraid to give voice to that vision – a guitar, a gorgeous, polished bass guitar. Ink black, with humbucking pickups and a lean neck. She touched the object and was shocked.

Euna wanted to show her gratitude but did not know how. She had never seen anyone perform that act. Then Aileen came back from the bathroom with her shirt doused in water and partway see-through, and started to jaw at Muireall for taking so long. She did not seem to notice the guitar, warm, no, aflame, in Euna's hands. She did not seem to notice that in the time it had taken her to scrub one shirt clean, Euna had grown a new set of veins, made only for rafting pure, red light.

Let's get out of here, Muireall said. I left the motor running. We don't want some numpty making off with the camper. The three women left together, Muireall winking at Euna as thanks for the cranachan.

Back in the camper, Euna started to finger the fretboard. She did not know, at all, what she was doing. And though these first notes were ugly, what they aroused in her was not. She spent the rest of the day doing this, playing without an amp, making small and half-formed sounds, while her friends rested and stewed mutton and scoured their summer shoes until they shone.

It was in this afternoon of half-formed sounds, of humdrum chores, that Euna found her *âmes simples*. She could do her lyric work while a few paces away someone puttered, someone ran the tap – not speaking, of course, just making those soft hums of *I'm here*. This sense was different from làn but no less vital. She decided this was beathachadh, benefice, nutrition, living. Here, after all, was her heaven without fences.

V

Two months passed with their requisite ups and downs. The ratio of làn to beathachadh to assorted bad-sad feelings was comfortable enough. Làn was exceedingly rare, but when it did happen, its effects flowed deep and far. The rest was fundamental in building her being-house. Foundation, grouting.

When, two months after she got her guitar, Euna woke in the middle of the night completely soaked, she could not have known she was headed toward the highest moment of làn her life had, to that point, offered. Aileen's péire was in her lap, and, pulling back and flipping on the overhead lamp, she saw that Aileen's striped nightshirt was wet. Euna poked her awake. Mè bheag, she said, I think it's happening.

Aileen reached a hand back to feel her nightshirt. Well, shite, she said. I need to get to a hospital.

Euna helped Aileen to sit upright, no simple task, given how swollen and top-heavy she had become. Muireall straightened up from her cot, where she had been sleeping before Euna turned on the overhead lamp, and came to sit between the two women. She clapped her hand onto Aileen's far shoulder. Hey, kiddo, she said. This is why some civilized folks go for check-ups when they're pregnant. To avoid nasty surprises.

Shut up, you stupid bawbag, Aileen snapped. Euna felt a bit of a chill. For a minister's daughter, the girl sure had a filthy mouth.

Muireall stroked Aileen's cheeks. They were at this point in the pregnancy dappled with acne, and Muireall was careful as she touched each pink mark. She said, You know what, I was asking for that. Euna, make sure she's comfortable. I'll get us to the hospital.

She went to the driver's seat and buckled herself in tightly. The radio was still broken, so Muireall started to sing her favourite driving tune, 'Flower of Scotland'. She had taught it to Euna, who joined in, though this earned her a bladed glare from Aileen. Muireall pulled out of the greengrocer's car park, where they had established for themselves a pleasant little setting – a lawn of primroses poking through the concrete, a few blue tits as pets – and burned down a series of roads en route to the university hospital. She parked illegally across two doctors' spots and, with a twinkle over her shoulder, said, Off with you. Aileen, do you have identification?

Yes'm, she said. But aren't you coming with us?

Oh no. I don't do well in these places.

I need you, Aileen said. I'm scared.

Muireall paused to consider the girl's plea. Something was clearly drawing her away from the hospital, while Aileen's call for help was binding her. Euna could not bear to see that tension. Muireall needed to know she could come and go as she pleased; that anyone should hold her against her will, even Aileen, was too much for Euna to tolerate. So, against her nature, Euna interfered. Don't go too far, hey, she said. We'll look for you here when we have a happy baby in tow.

Okay, Muireall said. She sounded relieved. You know, one of these days I'm going to buy you a phone.

As long as you pay for it, Euna said. Which was not actually much of a joke, considering Muireall paid for all they did, going to museums, eating chips and cod, with her furtive cash-stream.

You know I will, you cheeky brat, Muireall said.

Aileen was by then gritting her teeth, so Euna gripped her waist and helped her down the high camper stairs. She strapped her guitar onto her own back, sure she would have some downtime to practise while Aileen was birthing the child. She said a rushed blessing to Muireall and closed the door. Outside it was raining, romantic. Euna longed for string music. She helped Aileen into the hospital, a tall, four-winged erection, all colourful and modern. Where Cala had been full of cobwebs, literal and figurative, of stinky books and knick-knacks and vintage tincture bottles, everything here was minimal and new, chosen partly for its clean aesthetic. Get me some fecking painkillers, Aileen barked.

Euna took her by the crook of her arm to a reception desk and, drawing great attention to Aileen's belly and damp nightshirt, had her transferred straight away to a bed in the maternity wing. Euna asked the nurse for painkillers, flat ginger ale, gossip magazines. She knew what she had witnessed in the passion and dissolution of Grace and Muireall's relationship – from that she had tried to collage an image of loving: tea, touch, bounty, stories, then potions, silence, abstention. So she helped Aileen to fluff her pillows and braid her hair, and then, fearing she had made herself a wee bit too available, reclined in a chair on the far side of the room's gossamer screen.

On that far side was another woman set to enter into

labour. She was nearing middle age, and she looked like some of the troubled residents of Castlemilk, anaemic, malnourished. The nurse came back to deal Aileen her magazines and soda, and to sedate her, as she had demanded they do. On his beeline to Aileen, he slighted the other woman. She did not cry out to him, nor did she press her call button after he had left. And so she stayed where she was in bed, sweating like a kettle about to shrill, invisible.

She gave Euna a look she could not quite parse. She sensed this woman was being judicious with her silence. At times when Muireall was clutching the ruler back at Cala, Euna would latch her lips, locking the voice inside. She had not started off doing that. But after a while she had learned.

The woman refused to break her look. It was awful to have those eyes on her, as if Euna were complicit in something monstrous that she could not possibly understand. Or worse, that she could understand if she risked burning down the life she had just started to build. There was something under the woman's irises, imprecise and prickly, and it linked to the lack Euna had seen in Possilpark, and before that to the kids running around in Bucksburn, mucky and scraped, knees too large for their skinny, unfed legs, and for that matter, to the desperate mam at Dungavel.

After a while of being watched, Euna went back to Aileen, who was young, and moneyed, and beautifully drugged. She was sleeping deeply on the white sheets, bleached as they had been to hide other patients' stains. Euna curled up beside her and laced their fingers together, singing a lullaby into her creamy ear. When she was ready to join Aileen in dreamlain, she pulled the shared blanket over their bodies.

There they were warm and far from harm. There they were insulated from the things they did not understand.

*

A full day later, on the first of October, Aileen gave birth to a tiny blue thing, a ghoulish boy. Euna counted back the months to when the girl had first climbed through the Cala window, showing her swell, and gathered that the child was premature by about two weeks. This seemed significant. This seemed like something Euna could have helped to prevent, had she nourished Aileen properly. But there was no room for shame now. The boy deserved a better welcome.

Aileen was recovering in the maternity wing. Euna did not want to be there any longer, not as long as that distressing woman was sharing Aileen's room and the baby, so small and so blue, was in an incubator nearby. She went outside. She sat on a bench in front of the hospital with her guitar on her back and waited for Muireall to return. It was still raining, and Euna only had on her tunic, her plain, cotton trousers, and a pair of slip-ons Muireall had bought her on a solo jaunt downtown. Euna was getting soaked, her collarbones cold, nearly iced. And yet there was a looseness in her not fussing, in her simply sitting there and letting the clouds clean house. She held her tongue flat and took in a mouthful of the water. She had been too tuned to Aileen's needs to ask the nurse for a drink for herself, and besides, she had got quite good at standing thirst.

By some miracle, Muireall did show up, some time later. Her face was noticeably bruised. She started at every sound, starling or car alarm, and her eyes darted from place to place.

Aileen's newborn baby had that same energy, raw-nerved, verging on panicky. What happened? Euna asked.

Muireall said, Some caveman just robbed me at work.

Rain filled in the frown lines of her face. Red lipstick was caked across her cupid's bow. It was only in seeing this compromised version of her that Euna understood how much she had come to rely on Muireall's starch and stability. She was an adult in a world of halted children. Euna put her hand on her friend's shoulder and rubbed it gently. I know first aid, she said, if that would help.

You don't understand, Muireall said. He's taken the camper.

She was right that Euna did not understand. You told me it happened at work, she said.

Muireall lifted her nose in order to look down it. I don't know why you're so thick, she said. But since you don't seem to have it figured out yet, I work in the camper. I sleep with men for money.

Euna had learned to sort intent, as a way to maintain faith, and Muireall's intent had never been to hurt her. Right now, she was just scared, and so she was using the mouth of her worst self. Euna did not want to do the same, so she stayed quiet.

Remember the drunk when we first got to Glasgow? Muireall asked. He's a client. He's the one who took the camper.

You left me alone with him that first day.

I had to go out. I locked the door. Better that you knew the threat, or better that you took your shower in peace?

Euna considered the question.

Anyway, you had the mattock, Muireall said. I've chopped off a wandering finger or two.

One thing had just become clear to Euna. Muireall worked,

day after day, to be as poised as she was, to build a loving and lived-in camper realm, and to fill it with food and kin. It was not some act of magic. It had taken sweat and forfeit, and now blood. Euna wanted to ease Muireall's burden, even as she wanted everything to go back to how it had been, before this man had stolen their home.

Aileen had our baby, Euna said. He's not looking too hot yet, but I think he'll fill out nicely.

Muireall inhaled. She seemed to be straining to contain a whole mess of sentiments, or sounds, or tensions. Surely a person could not hold all that inside without becoming a cloud eventually, dimming, dumping down a skyful of rain. She took Euna's hands into hers, which were cold and quivering. I'm so happy to hear that, lamb, she said, word by pinched word. How's Aileen doing?

She's tired, Euna said. Like, tired as hell. But you know her. She's been insisting on the best pillows and painkillers.

Muireall clutched Euna's hands more forcefully now, crushing their finest bones. Where are we going to take them? she asked. She sounded desperate.

Anyone else would abandon us now, Muireall. You said it yourself, people split all the time. You don't have to make this your problem.

I never told you this, Muireall said, because I wanted you to like me. But I lost a child years ago at this same hospital.

Why would that have made me dislike her? Euna wondered. But then, Euna had withheld her own story for the same reason. She approached Muireall, very slowly, as she used to approach the most skittish horses. I can't imagine how much you've suffered, Euna said.

Muireall was crying now. I was eighteen and out on a long tour, she said. I never slept. Drank too much. The boy would have been your age by now.

I see why you didn't want to come in with us, Euna said.

You girls deserve a good life, Muireall said. As does the child.

Euna stood with the cold wind mincing her skin. The way ahead looked sick and dark. I have no idea how to make that happen, she said.

Nothing in my life is free, Euna's mother used to say. That must have been it. Maybe she had reasons to get rubbered. She used to throw things at Euna's father, New Testaments, collection plates. Maybe he had reasons to moor their lives with scripture. Euna was a mother now, a kind of mother, anyway, and though she could not redo her own childhood, she could do everything in and out of her control to make the newborn's right the first time around.

She held Muireall close, while the woman cried from some ancient place inside. Euna plumbed her own body to that same depth, to find the place from which courage would certainly come. And between her ribs she did find the muck, the heartbreak. Let that be the origin, she thought. Let that be the aolach, the rain the rain, and let a new, young world sprout from so much shit and hardship. In the middle distance, Euna saw a nurse wheel Aileen to the hospital exit, a snugly wrapped infant in her lap. The parcel was hardly larger than her two hands. She looked flyblown, her skin blotched and her hair dirtied, but her air was rather serene.

Euna waved. The nurse rolled Aileen over to them and helped her to stand before heading back into the hospital.

Isn't he a bit small to be sent out already? Euna asked, once the nurse had gone. Surely he'd do well with a few more days in the incubator.

Aileen said, There's no space for us. If he were sicker, they'd make room for him.

So they're sending him out before he's fully cooked? Muireall asked.

Aileen laughed. Then she noticed the tears on Muireall's face. Awright? she asked.

Awright, Muireall said.

Euna put her arm around Muireall's shoulders and gestured to Aileen with a wink of the neck. Euna started to walk north, in the direction of the River Clyde, and the other women followed her.

Hey, Aileen said a few minutes later, why'd you park the camper so far? You have no idea how much my tits weigh.

Here's the thing, Muireall said.

Euna said, We've had a bit of misfortune.

Aileen rolled her eyes. You've got to be feckin' kidding.

Their squad pushed ahead through a miserable airstream. Euna dreamed they were back in the Hebrides, where such foul weather could be mythicized, spun into song and story. Head in the mist, she whistled a tune that came to her, an abstract one full of sharps and flats. She knew their route was both far and uncertain. She knew, likewise, they could survive an epic trek. They were too odd and obstinate to give in to despair. And besides, when Aileen grew tired, Euna would take the baby into her own arms.

PART 2

I

THE DAY ARAM was released from Dungavel, after nearly five years without counsel or trial, he walked ten kilometres to get a milkshake. For weeks he had been thinking only of that thick dairy, the suck it took to earn the drink. He supposed it was a kind of perverse reach back to childhood, a substitute for a mother's comfort. His own mother was in Sketimini, wherever that was – she had once pointed to it on a map, vaguely, and brushed him off when he'd asked her to point again – if she was still living at all. He had not heard. Anyway, she had never fed him from her breast. When he was very young, she had diluted the milk of their Highland goats with saltwater, while his father was at sea, shackled in the hold of some trawler.

Aram had not had many visitors to the castle. Only Euna, chaste and handsome Euna, and two or three of his other womenfolk. Though she had only visited once, a disastrous scene, Euna had never drifted far from his thoughts. He hallowed her. He wanted her. Even after she sent him that shocking postcard, a sketch of his own son with the note: *Lachlan Iain Macbay. Born the first of October. Mother and mother and baby healthy.*

In the first restaurant he found by the road, dingy but gen-erously dotted with booths and tables, he chose a cramped stool at the counter. The stool was directly beside that of the only other patron, an older woman with a cherubic face, wiry, retreating hair, a lower half spilling well over the stool's rim. On the sandwich board was a single flavour of milk-shake, malted. A repulsive vinegar, the only condiment to be offered in the detention centre. But his craving was such that want trumped reason, and he ordered the shake. The woman slapped a few pounds onto the counter before he could pull out his slim money clip. Looks like you could use it, she said, with a smoker's chuckle.

What a gift from a princess like you, Aram said.

The woman propped herself on an elbow and leaned in so that when she spoke, she grazed his stubble. Having double-and triple-bunked in the castle, he was most comfortable this close to others. Pressed like domestic creatures. No room for the holy ghost. You in a rough spot, sailor? the woman asked.

You could say that, he said, with a little grin. He knew he was a bit unkempt, not having showered or shaved in weeks, but he was sure his allure ran deeper than hair grease and grey sideburns.

I'm Fenella, she said. We've never met, which means you're not from around here. And I like that. You haven't seen my laundry on the line.

I like a bit of dirt every now and then, he said.

She flushed red. Though the years of being held without trial had been dismal, soul-dimming, they now offered him one advantage. He was not on parole. He was free without condition, and he could roam from home to home. He would

138

call his womenfolk soon, at least those whose numbers he could remember, but in the meantime, it would do no harm to milk a few pounds from a kind stranger.

A television in the corner was showing a broadcast split into quarters, each with a splinter of the news. It seemed a new world had been forged in the five years he'd spent inside. The United Kingdom had been tabled and redrawn. His first thought was of Gainntir, of Muireall's face the time he came to see Euna and she instead opened the door. The face had been stiff. So full of fear the actual skin had hardened, as in a mask.

His shake came, and he drank it down without pause. When he was finished, Fenella asked, Shall we go back to my shack?

He hoped she was ribbing him. But he had learned in this charming part of the country never to assume. By all means, he said.

I'll get my mare, she said, as she went out the door. Again, he could not read her deadpan.

But indeed, as he gathered his trousers around him, which had become loose and unsuitable during his time at the castle, he heard the whinnying of a horse. Before heading out, he palmed some sachets of syrup and a set of cutlery. He was obeying his father's adage: only a fool goes off on a stranger's horse without some syrup in his pocket. Or some slight variation. The sachets and utensils went into a rucksack he had been awarded on his way out of Dungavel, though, with its blue tint, red stripe, and star, it clearly belonged to one of the men from the DRC. The guards had not seemed bothered.

Out front Aram was gratified to see, in newly pouring rain, his new friend Fenella. She sat on the grey mare with her head dramatically thrown back, looking as if she were going to erupt into an aria. With his waistband in one hand, he climbed onto the horse behind her. She smacked the horse's flank and together they cantered down the road.

*

She had not been joking about the shack. Fenella lived in one room, without plumbing, and with only an occasional lurch of electricity from a small windmill. Her place was no larger than the Salmon Company hut had been, and it was certainly far more crammed. Inside were at least five hundred books, stacked to the ceiling in pilasters. The shack, not far from the shoulder of the road, was bounded by rows of wych elms. A single wildfire would have razed her whole realm.

So, she said. I like a man to cook for me and then read one of these books out loud in one sitting. I like when a voice gets hoarse from too much reading. So you must keep going, no matter what. I'll pay you.

And sex?

Not really my thing, she said.

He had never cooked, and though he would never admit it to any of his womenfolk, he could only read at a rudimentary level. In the castle he had learned by reading the Bible, both in the worship group he had joined and on his own. That book had kept him sensible. If only he had discovered it before Euna came, maybe he could have shown her a forgivable version of himself.

There was a scratching at the shack door, a small set of claws raking up and down the wood. I have a pet, she said. Are you allergic?

He shook his head. He had never met anyone with a pet. Farm animals, of course, but never an impractical thing, kept as a companion. Fenella opened the door and in came a little mutt, no higher than Aram's knee. The dog had a bird in his mouth that looked to be a crow, and he whiffed of the wet. Aram kept his distance from the dirty creature. He had grown too thin to get sick.

What's your name, then? she asked.

Aram.

I like to change his all the time, she said, to keep him on his paws. Do you mind if I call him Aram for a while?

Aram had lost sight of the world for half a decade, sure, but this particular favour did not seem polite. Anyway, it didn't matter whether it was polite, because he did not like it. He simply said no.

She happily accepted his no. And the rest of what I said? she asked.

He had ten pounds in his pocket and a mental Rolodex, but nothing more. He wanted the woman's money. Yes, princess, I'll read to you. But you'll have to pay me a hundred pounds a day.

Seriously? Get over yourself, Aram.

I'm a man with needs.

She thought about it for a while, absently petting the mutt's head as she did. I'll name him New Covenant, she said. You'll take fifty pounds a day, no more, and I'll teach you how to improve your reading.

How'd you get so rich? he thought to ask. And then, How'd you know I have trouble reading?

Inventor, she said. And you are a completely transparent man. You may as well have glass for skin.

And so it was that Aram found himself, a few hours later, peppering a pot of baked beans while Fenella reclined on a deeply grooved armchair, book in lap, waiting for him to finish. The woman had little in her fridge and pantry, and all he could find to supplement the beans was some tinned salmon. Now the sight of that pink tint disgusted him, having been linked to it for so many working years. But he wanted to do right by Fenella, who, for all her peculiarities, seemed genuinely to care for him. Baked beans alone made for a sad supper. They'd been given better meals in the castle.

So he prepared the dish as beautifully as he could, in her choice rice bowl. It was hand-painted with the likeness of her dog, in the manner of a royal portrait, the mutt even wearing a bustier. Aram's mother had taught him to paint when he was young, and together they had mixed the dyes using iris root, sundew, peat soot, all collected on strolls through the Highlands, mother and son, preparing to make potions. His favourite part had been peeing in a jar, or collecting the goats' pee in one, so they could use the urine as a fixative.

After they had been displaced by his father's death from Scotland, and created a life for themselves on the sea – his mother insisted no country would welcome her, and she refused for obscure reasons to return to Sketimini – she had become creative with her tints. Ultimately she'd settled on red algae, maerl, salmon skin. But being forced from the Highlands, after the sacrifices she had made to get there as a young woman, truly washed her out. Her paintings were bad from then on, made as they were by insecure hands.

He brought the dish to Fenella, who slurped her tongue across her lips to show her appreciation. Where's yours? she asked.

Oh, he said, I didn't know that was part of the deal. I just wanted to make sure you were fed.

She rolled her eyes. You fancy yourself some kind of hero, don't you, she said. Real rough-and-rugged Caledonian. It's romantic, and it's nonsense.

Awright, awright, he said, laughing. I'll have a damn bowl of beans.

They ate together in amicable silence, while the dog licked the salmon tin clean. The beans were rubbish, but at least they were warm. You're a pretty bad cook, she said, when they were done eating. I should probably have checked before I hired you.

If you think I'm a bad cook, wait 'til you hear me read.

Her laugh turned into a cough. We'll start out easy, she said, and threw a thick work into his lap. *The Hammer of Witches which destroyeth Witches and their heresy as with a two-edged sword.*

Are you serious?

I told you I would help. And I will. I love to teach old dogs new tricks.

He opened the book, and already in the first sentence he found two words he could not understand. They seemed old and mouldy, and besides, he did not know any that were not in the Bible. Fenella patted the arm of her chair and he sat there, close to her, while she spoke the words he did not know and waited for him to repeat them several times, until he was comfortable recognizing them. For many hours and pages they followed this routine, until his voice was, as she had desired, hoarse. She did not forbid him to drink water, but he knew how to decipher the wants of womenfolk, so he kept his throat dry.

Very late at night, after hours of this exercise, she said, That's plenty.

She went to feed and groom her horse while he brushed his teeth with a finger dipped in baking soda, using water from a bucket by the sink. There were separate cots in the shack, each with pillows and a duvet, and he curled into the smaller of them. He had never felt a more comfortable embrace. He listened to Fenella rustling around outside while he drifted toward sleep. He was happy here, in an odd way, and he knew he could hold on to that happiness for a while. But even with his every need met, some part of him remained phantom. *Mother and mother and baby healthy.* He hid the postcard under his pillow, hoping, as he slept, it would bring dreams of his son.

*

The weeks passed quickly as Aram and Fenella followed this same routine, riding around on her horse during the day, coming home so he could cook and read to her at night, all the while building his nest egg. The books she chose were many and varied: novels of Mishima, Müller, Mahfouz, memoirs of architects, office-bearers, old-world warriors, transcripts of important political meetings, translated screenplays, classical sheet music. Her tastes reflected a woman separate from the world but in love with its every nook and fork, and anything she had, he read. He felt he was receiving some kind of private tutorship, and though Fenella had the diction of a piece of fried cod, she was smart and thoughtful.

Aram found that when he flirted with her, in a way that worked on most women, even chaste and handsome Euna, he was chastised. Playfully, but still. Despite their first encounter, she did not seem interested in his magnetism or his advances. And so he had to find a way to relate to her that did not involve sex or any of its attendant tensions, and in so doing, he felt himself struggling, asking questions of himself that he had never asked.

One evening, as he was closing their novel for the night, he made the mistake of using the sketch of Lachlan Iain as his bookmark.

Who's that? Fenella asked.

Just a dumb drawing I did, Aram said.

No, she said. That's a real person.

How did she perceive so much? It was eerie, though mostly annoying. He dog-eared the page they were on and tucked the postcard into his breast pocket, where it belonged. He tried to put the book back into its pilaster, but by driving the spine too hard he caused the whole carefully erected tower to fall.

I'm going to sleep, he said.

Good luck with that, Fenella said.

The cot that had so comfortably embraced him before was oppressive that night, the pillows too full of down, the duvet stale and fusty. He did not dream of Lachlan Iain, as he sometimes did, but of his father. The conditions at sea had been dire, he knew, because his father would return from each fishing mission with gashes and infections, which his mother would clean as best she could with witch hazel and shredded potatoes. The trawler hold was said to be so fetid that fishermen, locked down there as punishment, would often suffocate.

When Aram's father did not come home, rumours went round that his wounds had gone septic and, to avoid the same fate, the others had thrown him overboard. This was gossip, of course, but still Aram's mother blamed herself. She had not cleaned the wounds properly. She had let him carry something foul and contagious to sea, where he had died for her sin.

Aram dreamed about his father's last goodbye. He saw the man's face in the night, on the deck of the trawler, windblown and brave. Disfigured by a brutal life, but not ill. His father waved from the growing distance and was gone. Aram woke with stunted breath.

You okay, sailor? Fenella asked from across the shack. Sounded like you were choking there.

I'm fine, he said. Then, after a bit more thought, I may need to borrow your horse.

We'll talk about it in the morning, she said.

He found it hard to believe there would be a morning on the other end of this night. He heard the mutt walking around, and though it normally slept at Fenella's feet, now the creature came to lick Aram's fingers. He leaned over the side of the cot and picked up the dog, then let him lie down on the duvet. He climbed under the blanket beside Aram, and though he still reeked, his warm body was a kindness.

In the morning, Fenella made some cowboy coffee and said, without hesitation, This is the part where you leave me.

He had expected her to be forward when she, inevitably, asked him to move on, and she was. Consistency was a gift she had given him. Harder than the loneliness at Dungavel was the arbitrary way rules were applied. You never knew how your actions would be rewarded or punished – the same thing could get you released or sent to ad seg, depending on what the guard had to eat that morning.

Was I that obvious? he asked.

You want to borrow the horse. They always want to borrow the horse when they're ready to go.

You're right, of course.

That bookmark. I want you to find your kid. But I can't give you my mare. I'd be stranded and dead here if I gave her to every man I cared about.

His throat felt tight again. It bothered him that he should have trouble breathing here when he had been fine through five years of inferior air, especially during the dirty protests, during which the other men in his block refused to use the latrine, instead rubbing their excretions on the walls.

If you want, I have an old tricycle. Thought I should pick it up in case a man tried to steal my horse one day.

He smiled. I'll have to swallow some amount of pride. But I'll try the damn trike, why not.

Sadness passed briefly across her face. You've been my favourite one, she said.

Tug in the gut. He asked for her address. She looked as if he were a bampot for thinking a shack would have a postcode. If it's all right with you, she said, maybe we can leave this as it was – a lovely episode.

She unlocked the shed for him and produced from it a

rusted red tricycle. It was adult-sized, with a wide basket between the back wheels. He did not have enough gear to fill the basket, but he put his rucksack in there, and the syrup, and a few more snacks that Fenella provided for him: salted crisps, gourds in brine, strips of beef jerky. She peeled off many pound notes and tucked them securely into his waistband. Then, maybe most importantly, she put in the basket a feedbag of books.

He gave the horse and the mutt a thumbs-up. These farewells were wearing on him. He had left everyone at the castle without fanfare; that was just how it was done. Now he sat on the saddle of the tricycle and started to ride toward the road. When he reached the shoulder, he heard Fenella call out, Your trousers fit much better now.

The wind picked up and he had to pick up with it. He did not turn. He could not see her charming smile, or the gloam of lamplight through the shack window. He would then have stayed forever. And his child could not be raised by women alone. He knew too well how that went.

*

On the long ride north, Aram kept his mind occupied. He had become remarkably good at that. At Dungavel he had studied Gaelic with one of the dirty protestors, holding his nose as he learned words for flowers, lus-taghte, cuiseag rosan. Now he cycled through all the man had taught him. He would be fluent by the time he reached the Highlands. It was, after all, Euna's chosen language.

Any time he stopped to rest or ask for help – which he did

often, as a man who valued comfort – he tried to use this Gaelic first. To pass as a son of native soil, more Scottish than the Scottish. He was still not a citizen, but if he tried hard to disappear, maybe he could avoid being outed.

He went into a corner shop to ask for a toilet instead of going by the road. Lots of cock's-foot to piss in, but he was too good for that grass. If a mutt would water it, he would not. Inside the store, he noticed a telephone behind the counter and asked in Gaelic if he could make a few calls. The cashier said, Whit the buck ur ye sayin'?

Aram asked again, this time in English. The man lifted the receiver and hand-dragged it across the counter. Aram turned his back on the man and phoned his womenfolk one at a time. A half dozen picked up. Only a few were happy to hear his voice. With the cashier on the other side of the counter, he could not seduce the cranky ones as he normally would have. He couldn't recite poetry, or say with gravitas how much he'd missed them, how long his lonely nights had been. He wondered, if the cashier had not been standing there, if God's presence alone would have stopped him.

Eventually the cashier put a hand on Aram's shoulder and whipped him around. What's wi' aw the callin'? Ye jist gie it ay jail?

Aram had been dialling the church in Pullhair, where he had last seen Aileen, but now he put the phone back into its cradle. You'd think so, he said. I lost my power for a few days and needed to let some friends know I'm doing fine.

Ur ye gonnae buy anythin'?

Not today, Aram said. I just want to use the toilet.

The cashier pointed to a door behind a rack of magazines

and a chiller cabinet of drinks. Ower thaur, he said. Dornt flush anythin' weird doon th' lavvy.

Aram stopped briefly to thumb through the magazines on his way into the toilet. He had a satisfying piss and rinsed his hands with water. He stepped out of the little room still buttoning his trousers, which did, as Fenella had said, fit him more tightly now. He could barely tuck his clag all the way inside. While he had his head down, a group of teenaged boys hurried up and surrounded him.

There were five in total, four white and one black. They stank and had pocked skin. They punched Aram in the jaw. One kicked him in the back of the head, then struck his right kidney. The clerk stood silently outside the circle, looking a bit shaken. No one at the castle had ever tried to beat Aram, despite his fears of that happening. He would have fought men, but these were not men. He protected the organs he needed and waited for the boys to get tired. They were riled that they couldn't get a rise from him. Witless fucking cocksplat. Shitgibbon. They spat on his sweater, now sullied with blood. Shunted him onto his knees, knocked a tooth clean from the gum.

One smashed his hand through the chiller cabinet and took out a few cans for his friends. The cashier said, Cannie noo. That's mah merchandise.

The store went blank. A minute later, the scene appeared again to Aram, but without any depth. When he was these boys' age he used to fight for money, and it was common for an eye to swell shut like this. Above his one seeing eye were Catherine wheels, a few clear floaters. These kids had hazed his brain and halved his sight. They could have killed him.

Isaiah 56:10. Israel's watchmen are blind, they all lack knowledge; they are all mute dogs, they cannot bark; they lie around and dream, they love to sleep.

The cashier got a broom from the toilet and swept up the broken glass, then with a wet mop cleaned the gore and drool. The boys seemed to be in light spirits, laughing and grabbing magazines from the rack, saying obscene things about a singer on one of the covers whose name Aram knew well: Euna. He stayed on the ground.

The boys, bored, turned to leave. At no point did they break from jeering and hollering, calling each other worse names than they had called Aram. Everything to them was a put-on, a prank, a future story. On the way out the door, one of them turned back to look at Aram, still on the ground, heavy as a buck carcass. The boy did not say anything. But no divine witness could deny. He, at least, had looked back.

*

That night, Aram slept twenty paces from the road in a little copse of gorse trees, with a rock thick enough to crack a skull beside his head. Even perfect Gaelic, it seemed, would not be enough to protect him. Words would only hold weight if he were precise in his use of them. If he could politic his language, sharpen it into a fillet knife. And not just with women who already wanted him.

Isaiah 42:16. I will lead the blind by ways they have not known, along unfamiliar paths I will guide them; I will turn the darkness into light before them and make the rough places smooth.

His eye was still swollen shut. He needed to get his vision back before he could lead others, or else they would all fall into a proverbial pit. So he went to sleep praying his sight would restore itself, and swiftly. When he woke up, as the morning came coursing through the gorse trees, he saw its bands with a clear eye. No wheels or floaters. Just pure and faithful sunlight. This was enough to bolster his belief that someone was watching over him. And that called into him a fullness he rarely felt. Only in moments of physical pleasure had he known this vital, holy swell. Silently, he named the feeling sàimh.

He rolled up the pullover he had been using as a pillow and put it into the tricycle basket. He was still a few days south of the Hebrides, but he had the strong and sudden sense of being close to his destination. He could smell the grouse the women in town used to roast on certain Sundays, feel the moor cold as a witch's tit under his feet. In the saddle now he pedalled hard and merged onto the empty road.

Nice day. Pretty birds. A bit of fear buzzed in him from the night before, but not much. He trusted something. And that something was slowly taking shape. It was not a person; or at least, it did not have a body. It was more like the sea, essential, merciless. And no injustice, no deportation or death, would go unseen by it. Nice day. Pretty birds. On that fair morning, the road ahead was clear.

*

In Moneydie, in Perthshire, he chose a house at random and stopped by for tea. It had started to rain again, and Aram was cold, his sweater a dead weight. A man with outdated hearing aids answered the door. Aram knew he looked a little unkempt, now with bruises and abrasions on his face. But his charm ran deeper than all that. He asked, Can I trouble you for a cup?

Miserable out there, the man said. Come in.

Aram gladly obliged. The house had just a few rooms, one each for eating, sleeping, reading, and peeing. The old man had unwashed dishes on his dining table, and more in a corner sink. In the bedroom, which Aram glimpsed on his way to the toilet, were great tangles of clothing, bunched bedsheets, plants knocked out of their pots. Something wretched about seeing soil indoors, on carpet, no less. The place looked as if an intruder had come in and rummaged, but Aram had a hunch this was not so.

With the toilet door closed, he took off his dirty sweater and wrung it out, working to get the red down the drain. With soap, he scrubbed and scrubbed, and still a faint spot remained. He hung his sweater over the shower rod and came back to the eating room in his undershirt. The old man was fretting over a hotplate, muttering about boiling water, babbling water, always too hot, never quite hot enough. He didn't want to put his finger in and burn it, but he couldn't see any bubbles on the surface, and she always used to do this for him, where was that little tin of tea leaves anyway, and it's been raining so much but the bloody holly hasn't bloomed.

Are you okay? Aram asked.

The man looked up. Put a shirt on, he said. I've got loads.

Aram noticed a bandage around the man's hand. A burn

on his palm was clearly visible outside of the binding. Why don't you get me a shirt and I'll make the tea?

This seemed to suit the man. Aram waited until he had left the room to turn on the hotplate. While the water warmed, he fumbled in the cupboards for the tin of tea, which he found behind a hoard of expired crackers. He wondered how many people in this country were living like this, with burned hands and soil on the carpet, no one coming to visit or brew tea. From the kerb this place had looked lovely, blackthorn bushes and a rock garden in front. Inside was a whole other earth. Aram looked in the fridge for milk and instead found greening cheese and some jars of mint jelly.

The man came back carrying a lovely cable-knit sweater and pulled it down over Aram's head. The fit was snug, but not suffocating. My gift to you, he said. You can't be going around in a dirty shirt.

The water had boiled. Aram poured it into a pot with two bags of Assam and let the drink steep. He wanted to lift the man from this sad condition, but without the man knowing. It would take some sleight of hand. Where are you headed? the man asked.

Up north. I'm going to see my girlfriend.

In that case, you should probably wash first.

Aram laughed. If you're offering to let me use your shower, I'm game. It's been a while since I've had hot water.

Help yourself, the man said. He took two cups from the sideboard, one that said Alban and one that said Jane. I know you think it's untidy in here. I don't entertain much. I watch the six o'clock news and I do puzzles and that's plenty. Brings a certain peace to know the end is coming.

Come now, Aram said. That's a bit morbid.

When I watch the news I don't have to stew too much about it. You worry about the rising sea levels and failing crops and all that. I've already got one foot in another place.

Aren't you lonely?

I wasn't unhappy to see you. But this is how I live. No need to get precious.

I've always liked having people around, Aram said. Actually, I kind of wilt without them. I was just in a spot without friends for quite a long time, and it made me crazy.

So you'd be lonely in my place. Good thing that I'm in my place, then, and you're in yours.

The tea was sufficiently strong. Aram filled both cups and took a drink from Jane's. I'll be honest, he said. My girlfriend doesn't know I'm coming. Actually, I'll be meeting my first child, whose mother is another woman.

Oh hush, the man said. I'm not interested in you young people and your sex triangles.

Nobody mentioned sex.

I worked forty years, he said. Earned a little privacy.

You see worse things on the news every night.

That, I can turn off.

Aram drank the rest of his tea in silence. He had expected some sage advice from the old man, some reassurance on his long journey. Instead he had received judgement. The tea, at least, was good. He fixed on that. By the time he reached the bottom of the cup, he was less upset. The insult had after all been minor.

The man went to find a towel in his bedroom and came back to give it to Aram. It was a plush bath towel, neatly folded. I have limited hot water, the man said. Enjoy your shower, but bear that in mind.

Aram nodded. In the shower he was careful to turn off the tap while he lathered his hair, angled his hands into his recesses. The old man had set out a razor in its original packaging, so Aram got to shaving. He ignored the pain that came from grazing his bruises and bumps with the fresh edge. Discipline, he knew, led to righteousness. He shaved his shoulders and the back of his neck best he could.

When he was presentable, he put on the cable-knit sweater and his own trousers and returned to the room intended for reading. The old man was there in a rocking chair, an afghan around his shoulders, halfway through *Macbeth*. In the corner a small television was showing the news. He asked if Aram would like him to read the play out loud. Aram reclined on a sofa beside the rocker, his feet hanging over the armrest as if he were a gangly teenager. Yes, he said. I love it when people read to me.

The old man stood and went to mute the television. He sat back down and carefully arranged the afghan about himself. Will all great Neptune's ocean wash this blood/Clean from my hand? No, this my hand will rather/The multitudinous seas incarnadine,/Making the green one red.

When he read, he affected a deeper voice, a lovely, resonant tone. Aram watched the images on screen while he listened to the script. A woman in a headscarf, a man with Odin's Cross tattoos and a finger in her face, a police officer. The words of the play went a bit foggy, difficult to understand. Maybe Aram was getting sleepy. He forced himself into the room, into his body, again.

Lamentings heard i' th' air, strange screams of death,/And prophesying with accents terrible/Of dire combustion and confused events/New hatched to the woeful time.

On the back of the sofa was a tartan blanket, and Aram covered his body with its welcome weight. The man kept reading, and the news kept reeling on, until it was finished and deposed by a gardening show. A nice nannyish type, pulling hemlock by its roots. Aram was sure now that he was drowsy, and that was why he was feeling overwhelmed. That had to be why. He was a man of God and men of God did not worry that evil had prevailed; they trusted that there was a greater plan. He asked the old man if it would be all right for him to turn the lights off and get some rest.

The man shelved the play and said, You can stay the night. Happy to help a tired traveller back onto his feet. But just the night. I like my solitude.

Perfectly fair, Aram said.

The man stood and turned off the television, tucked the tartan more tightly around Aram's shoulders. If you get hungry, he said, leaning toward him tenderly, toughen up and go back to sleep.

Aram laughed. Get to bed, you old dingleberry, he said. The man flashed his teeth and turned off the floor lamp. In the near dark, Aram could hear him shuffling out of the room and into the next, knocking some furniture over in the process. He felt, briefly, sad, or maybe guilty. Then he remembered what the man had said, about not needing to get precious. And so a certain peace came over Aram.

He dreamed that night of Euna. He was in a boneyard with her, boiling over with great and unutterable anger. He knew why he was mad, though he couldn't make his mouth say it: Euna and Aileen had named the kid Lachlan Iain, set him up to be more Scottish than the Scottish. The child was all them and only partly Aram. It was clear now in the dream that his mother had died – Euna was putting myrtle on her grave, reading a eulogy. He still couldn't find his voice so he kicked Euna in the throat to stop hers from coming out. In the dream it was all he could do.

When he woke up in the morning, he felt terrible about being so violent with his love, even if it had only been a dream. He'd kicked her just like those kids in the corner shop had kicked him. He lay on the sofa and let himself suffer from the guilt for a while. He tried to shift the fault to Aileen, for getting pregnant, trapping him, but he could not. So he bottled the feeling up and sent it to sea, like any good fisherman.

*

He made a crock of oatmeal for the old man, flecked it with the only dried fruit he could find in the cupboards, redcurrants. He had become a decent cook while living with Fenella, and that was a good thing. It increased the value of his stock, made him welcome in more places. Better, food offered him another source of physical pleasure, helpful for a man with such strong appetites.

The old man was still in his room with the door closed when Aram left the house. Either he was sleeping or he was avoiding idle chatter. This suited Aram just fine. He took a spoonful of oatmeal from the crock and left the rest for the old man to enjoy whenever he chose to wake up.

Back on the road he felt invigorated. The rest had been lovely, even vital, but he was energized now in a way he hadn't been then. The biting air. The scenes of crimson leaves and common oaks with their necks gone stark. He pedalled out the bad spell that had controlled him the night before. He pedalled, in fact, for a full day, until suddenly the muscles in his legs cramped. They got hot and tight so fast he had to pull over, stretch in a patch of marram grass.

He had almost resisted visiting any of his womenfolk, as a way of proving to himself his devotion to Euna. That had been fairly easy, since most of them had sounded pretty pissed off with him, and he had never been one to beg. But need had a way of warping one's character. Now Aram was in pain on the roadside grass, in front of a sign for Inverness, where Effie the Embalmer lived.

She had never been his favourite woman. He had met her at a pub in town, where he had gone on a weekend trip. They had got sloshed and messed around in the bathroom, then her flat. She had caked on makeup, foundation, false lashes – even drunk, this had embarrassed him, to see how hard she was trying. But he was dog-tired in front of that divine sign for Inverness, and crisps weren't going to make for much of a supper, not now that he was in touch with his deeper appetite. He had worked to put his weight back on, to get his clothes to fit him nicely, and he refused to sacrifice those gains so gamely.

He punched his quads to get the blood pumping again and forced himself back into the saddle. Before long he was in town. He had been to Effie's flat just that once, though they had since spoken on the phone, and now he strained to remember where it was. He knew the name of the street,

Douglas Row, and the colour of the door, emerald. Her place was right beside the river, and he remembered her walking to the window after they'd slept together. Thank ye, she had said, with too much breath, to the water. Then she'd turned to him and said, Isn't it enchanted?

Well, no, he did not think water was romantic. Actually, it was a murderer and a lunatic. If he could drink milk and whisky alone for the rest of his life, he gladly would. To Effie he had said, It pales beside you.

He found Douglas Row without much trouble, and on the street there was only one emerald door, so he knocked on it. Bless her, Effie stomped down the stairs in a terry bathrobe, and when she saw him she yelled, You bassa!

Forgive me, he said.

She looked furious. But her flat smelled of meatballs and masala, and he knew already she was going to invite him in. He waited while she unleashed a tirade of insults, knowing she would tire herself. It did not take long. When she stopped cursing, he told her she looked pretty, which she did, probably because she hadn't known he was coming.

My face is naked, she said. You don't give me any warning, and you expect me to be beautiful?

I just said you were.

She slammed the door. She opened it. Is that a tricycle?

He nodded. I'll let you ride on the handlebars.

She rolled her eyes. Still, she moved aside so he could enter the small, vaguely familiar foyer. You look like horse testicles, she said.

They ate curry and rice while they watched the water through her one window, rain-streaked and marked by dead insects. He asked insignificant questions and she offered brief and guarded answers. After dinner, he rinsed the dishes and thanked her for sharing her food. She cast a slanted look at him. Trying to be a hero now? she asked.

He began to knead her shoulders while he whispered sweetnesses into her ear, more of habit than desire. As he massaged her, she stiffened. After a moment she breathed out and her shoulders, rigid buds, went loose as blooms.

You can't do this to me, she said.

Do what? he asked. He was not playing innocent. He said what he meant.

Pretend to care about me. I cried over you, you tit. You can't come back and erase all that.

He turned her so she was facing him and then let go of her shoulders. He had been thinking of himself as a found man, but it was plain she was blind to the change. Either he had deluded himself into believing a person of flesh could become one of spirit, or, likely, she had been licking her wounds all these years to keep them moist. It was such a brief encounter, he said. I didn't know you were still raw about it.

So now it's my fault, innit. You're an animal. You must have kids all over the goddamn country.

Effie had stumbled on the one put-down that actually had power over him. He was filled with a bitter ire he held tightly behind his teeth. He felt the sudden and strong need to be alone. He went into the other room and lay face down on the couch, muttering his mood into a tweed cushion. When Effie came into the room a while later, he was punching that same cushion with two precise fists. In between, he was not sure what had happened. He had sort of lost focus.

The hell is going on in here? That's an heirloom pillow.

Aram calmed, came back into his charm. He sat upright on the couch. Nothing at all, my treasure, he said.

Something wrong with ye, she said, snatching the cushion from beside him and cocooning it as if it were an infant. It's time ye went home.

I will, he said. But I need to sleep here for one night. I promise I'll be good. He knew this would work. If he could rely on anything in the world, it was that lonesome women lived for promises.

She tapped a finger on her cheek, as if thinking. But she proved that to be fake when she soured her expression suddenly and said, Get the hell out.

Aram saw that she was serious. He had no choice but to limp down the stairs, his legs even tauter than before, and lace his boots. He looked up with his eyes wide and childlike in a last effort to convert Effie. She stepped over him and opened the door, revealing the river, silent and snakeblack. For a second, she seemed to reconsider the send-off. Then she took him by the neck of his cable-knit sweater and hauled him into the street. Good luck with yourself, she said, and locked the emerald door.

*

Aram slept on a bench beside the river that night, too tired to ride his tricycle any farther and too stunned by Effie's tantrum to think of another plan. For the first time in his life he, having tried in earnest, had failed to seduce a woman. Whatever charm, whatever – to quote one of Fenella's esoteric books – *furor poeticus* had led to his perfect track record seemed now to be gone. He suspected he had wanted to fail, and only in part to please the Almighty.

He woke to rain barraging a bare part of his body, near the notch of his collarbone. Effie had torn the neck of his sweater when she had thrown him into the street, leaving this small place exposed. But one person's spite did not undo another's kindness. The old man had still given Aram a sweater. Just then he saw Effie leaving her house in her embalming uniform, clutching a large cosmetics bag. She saw him, too, and started to hurry down the road without looking first, narrowly missing the grille of an oncoming car. Once she had disappeared, he wanted her as he had not before. She was the fish just past the hook. Though he wanted to, wanted her, Aram resisted following Effie down the street to her funeral home.

I John 2:16. For all that is in the world – the desires of the flesh and the desires of the eyes and pride in possessions – is not from the Father but is from the world.

He was single-minded about forgetting her. And then, after a few minutes focused on the badness of his lust, his body distracted him: his lower back hurt from sleeping on the hard bench all night. So he stood and stretched, and when he was looser, found the groove in his tricycle seat.

If he rode hard, he would make it to the Ullapool ferry by mid-afternoon, and depending on the boat schedule, he could be in Pullhair by night-time. He pedalled off into a sudden downpour. From the dirty striker, Aram had learned the word *baisteadh*, both rain and baptism. With this term in mind, the rain went from a discomfort to a kind of ceremony.

What had been odourless before now smelled floral, like a spray of daylilies, or like Euna, nude, in his fishing hut.

By noon, the *baisteadh* did not seem all that benign. It came down to this: he did not know much about Sketimini, except that its official language, according to his mother, was Assyrian Neo-Aramaic. And, though he could have surely found a way to explore that obscure tongue, he had chosen Gaelic. Had he wanted to impress Euna? to cross out his mother and the thorny feelings he fastened to her? to disappear in a country that sometimes needed, and other times shunned, imprisoned, him?

Yes he had yes he had Yes.

In Fenella's shack he had noticed a heavy university text, *Neo-Aramaic Grammar.* He had picked the book up and set it down immediately, as if it were made of white flame – he found it both compelling and repellant, in a way he could not begin to explain. Now he remembered that Fenella had left a feedbag of books in the tricycle basket, which he had covered with the clothes those boys had savaged. He pulled onto the side of the road and scrambled in the bag to find the book that would spark when he held it in his hands. Fenella, who noticed everything, must have seen his unusual connection to the text, because there was her frayed copy.

He knew what the disciple John had said. The book was not from the Father but from the world. And yet, when Aram held it, something eternal firmed in him.

He made the ferry with minutes to spare, which was fortunate. In autumn the boat only crossed the water once a day, and it was now the end of October, five weeks past the equinox. As he used his last pounds to pay his fare, he imagined what might be waiting for him in town. He hoped there would be fishing work and a hut with room enough for him, so he could stay to raise his boy. He hoped that Euna still lived there, and that she would agree to see him despite the way their visit at Dungavel had gone. Mostly he expected to find the same place he had left, a conservative town of eighty well-meaning people, deeply enmeshed in one another's lives.

The wind on the ferry deck was harder than it had been on land, and it nipped through his cable knit. Aram crossed his arms tightly over his chest. The warmth he had earned on his long trip north – he would not let it leach out so easily.

*

All through Pullhair the land looked burned. Beauty bushes were bowed, barberry trees short and scarred. Each yard Aram passed was clogged, the post office's with creeping thistle, the guest house's with selfheal. He did not hear or see a single animal. He had stayed in Stornoway overnight so he would first see Pullhair in morning sun. Truth was it would have been finer in full shade.

While in Stornoway, at a folk museum, he had read a plaque about the history of Pullhair. A century before, its population had been close to a thousand. After the First World War, the herring fishing industry lost certain European markets, so many of Pullhair's residents found themselves stripped of their livelihood. They lived in overcrowded crofts, or they had no land at all, and over time the population dissolved as folks left to find work farther south. Having read this, Aram rode through Pullhair with a feeling of grief, latent sorrow.

It was curious he had never heard anyone talk about that culling. The town had a history they held in grieving silence, and so it lived under the moors and blunted every grass blade.

He rode down the one paved road looking for abandoned houses or farms, fragments of that time long gone. When he lived here five years before, he had never seen crosses marking sea graves, or tablets paying tribute to the people who had settled then left the town. Books had been written of lesser exoduses. He found it hard to believe that so many people could suddenly migrate, with no one to tell their stories.

During his time inside, he had craved the quiet of this island. And now that he was here, it did not seem quiet at all; rather, it emitted a strange white noise. At least in the castle pain had not been held in confidence. Wrath had been rewarded, just as aggression had been aired. Here the earth hummed with a kind of tacit sadness, a note pitched so only dogs could hear it, if there were any dogs left.

Aram went first to what had been his fishing hut. He wanted to root himself there before going to the church or to Gainntir. He wanted to know if he would have work and a home before he presented himself to his family, so he could be precise in what he promised them. From the outside, the hut looked the same as it had then. Built of stone on a concrete foundation, not even a gale storm could stir it.

Rucksack in hand, he opened the front door and found an animal had taken over the space. A small, furred marten, with one lost eye. Aram remembered something clawing at the door when he and Euna were in there together. Though they'd shielded themselves from it then, the creimeach had since got in. Aram caught it by the tail, and it snarled at him, clearly alarmed. He opened the hut door and threw the creature as far as he could, into a spread of charred heather. Only after he had done this did he remember wild animals, increasingly rare here, held a new place in the order of things. Anyway, this one was a living tie to his day with Euna. He squinted into the heather, trying to recoup what he had lost, but the lapse had cost him – the bush was flush with the ground, free of any creimeach.

With his old broom, Aram swept up the dung and prey bones the animal had left behind. Then he stopped to look at his digs. Whitish light fell through holes in the door, revealing a few familiar details. Aram's cot was still there, and even his thin blanket, though now it was in utter tatters.

He took the postcard of Lachlan Iain from his sack and ironed its edges. He had no pillow to slip the card under, so he put it directly onto the cot, facing down. From the tricycle basket outside he gathered his other effects, his books and snacks and syrup, and established in the hut a library, a pantry. It had been simple before for him to live here without trim or ornament. He had never felt the need to mark out rooms, to establish that particular level of comfort. But since then the world had tugged at his red nerves and caused a swerve in him. He could no longer live as a simple organism, surrounded by plain stone walls.

*

An hour later, Aram walked to the edge of the sealoch. He was thrilled to see, down the shore, equipment still standing where the farm had been: automatic feeders, mechanical filters, scareherons. A half dozen men were in the loch, wet as high as their thighs, casting fly lines. Whatever had spoiled the earth had mostly spared the water, and to Aram this was a miracle. He did not care if the bog cotton rotted, the harebells turned amber and fell from their stems, as long as nothing harmed his beloved salmon.

He walked to the farm. He did not recognize any of the fishermen, but that was not a surprise to him, since they were presumably only there for the season. Most were in the loch, but there was one younger man standing on land, with his line cast into the water from that dry distance. He was wearing a cap with a white eagle. In the castle, Aram had learned this was Poland's coat of arms. He asked the man where his supervisor was.

She's at home today, he said.

She?

Yes, he said. Why, you some kind of chauvinist?

This town really had been turned over. He thought of all the things he used to say to his friends about women, right here, on the bank of this lake, while they smoked and took their brief lunch breaks. No one had tried to shame him for speaking freely. Not in the slightest, he said.

You looking for work?

That I am.

Bad timing, the man said. Season's already over. Most people have gone home already. We're just here catching some of the escaped fish for our families.

Shite, Aram said. How had he forgotten such an obvious detail? His life for so many years had submitted to these seasons – hard work until Samhain, hibernation, then, till

Earrach – that they had once been ingrained in him. Now he had fallen out of touch with all nature, and that, for a man who had come of age at sea, was a deeply disorienting thought. Of course, he said.

Grab a few fish for yourself, if you want.

The water would be bitter, and Aram's boots were not weatherproof. But crisps and brined gourds would not carry him through the winter. He walked into the loch, already starting to clot with frost. He did not have a net any more, and he knew better than to draw attention to himself by asking to borrow one, so he looked in the cold, clear water for a smudge of orange. Seeing colour, he reached under the surface. He was out of the habit, his impulses dimmer now than they had ever been, and he came up empty.

From some distance away, he heard a fisherman call, Trying to bare-hand your dinner?

A few others laughed. The young man in the Polish eagle hat told Aram to come back to the shore, and once he had done that, he offered Aram his rod. I'm freezing, he said. Use this and split your catch with me fifty-fifty.

Aram did not like to share his catch, but he would not snag a single fish without a line. He nodded, and with this new means hauled a huge sum of salmon. They were more abundant than he remembered them being in the wild – nearly as abundant as they'd been on the farm, where they had been forced to spawn.

Each time he caught one he threw it to the fisherman whose rod he was borrowing. The man was waiting by the lochside to pack the pink slipperies into a cooler. By the time the sun started to sink, just past four in the afternoon, Aram was frozen up to his taigeis. In a strange way the sting delighted him, as a token of his long commune with the elements. Better still, he had filled four coolers, and two of them were his to take to the hut and eventually to the church. He was connected, proud.

You've done this before, the fisherman said, when Aram was beside him on land.

A few times.

I wish you had come sooner. It's been a bizarre year. Feast and famine.

Why's that?

No idea. I swear the salmon are demented. You'd think on the farm, at least, we could regulate them. That's why we have a farm in the first place, so we can control the conditions.

But your supervisor should have sorted all that out, no?

Moody bitch. Some days she'd come and scream at us, tell us we were worthless and she was going to ship us home. Other days she'd bring us bowls of boiled sea lettuce and fawn over what a brilliant job we were doing.

On the horizon Aram saw a pelican, a bird he had never noticed in the Outer Hebrides. Growing up at sea, he'd seen them routinely. They would then appear to him in dreams, while he was huddled beside his mother in the boat hold, always opening their bills to swallow him, or using their sharp tips to drill his eyes deep into his skull. Bed-wetting nights, crying-dry nights. This pelican loomed over the water until it dropped, spurring only a faint splash, and came back into the air with its beak bloated.

Anyway, the other fisherman said, good riddance to her. I'm heading to Lisbon for the winter. I can work at a call centre there.

Aram nodded. If it weren't for his family, he might have asked to come along. Instead he asked if the other fisherman could show him the supervisor's house. He could not explain her strong lure, but he felt it, in his pulse and his damp palms he felt it.

Sure, he said. She's home for some creep holiday, though, and she'll poison me if she finds out I brought you there. So keep my name out of your mouth.

That'll be easy, since I don't intend to know your name.

They set off together toward the hut with their arms laden with fish. They dropped the coolers in the pantry area, and once they had left, Aram secured the door tightly so the marten could not steal this hard-earned fare. After a brief stop at the other man's boat – a bowrider with five on board, shouting at the man in an unknown tongue – they followed the loch toward a headland, an isolated cut of the coast. All at once Aram's skin itched, and he tried to tear his sweater from his body. He was sure the shirt was infested, that there were living things crawling inside. He had been this way before.

II

GAINNTIR HAD CHANGED. The latrine was tarnished with blood and carved with profanities; the goatshed had been torched and the cowshed stripped of half its siding. The silo looked strangely pristine, covered as it was with a gleaming coat of white paint. Where before there had been chirping and crowing, the sound of that young girl singing her aria, now there was silence. Aram waved his hand to dismiss the other fisherman, who seemed anyway to sense he was not welcome on these grounds. He shook Aram's hand and returned the way he'd come. By then the sun had set completely, and it was a clear and brittle night, somehow void of both cloud and moon.

With the other man gone, Aram stole to the dining-room window. On his way he bumped into a compost drum. His boots were still wet and so the sound fell dully. In the dining room were a dozen lit pillar candles, and in their intense glow he saw a seated figure, erect in a bishop's throne, with her back to the window. Around the table were four complete place settings and in the centre a charcuterie board piled with all manner of fruit and meat, terrines, rhubarb preserves, sausages, cured garlic, loaves of bannock, mustard. Above the unset fire was a banner that read, in a childish scrawl, WELCOME TO THE DARKER HALF OF THE YEAR.

Aram knew by the long torso and the cropped black hair that this was not Euna. He was scared, but in a larger sense sad, seeing this woman alone at her abundant table. Then the singing girl, who had introduced herself those years ago as Lili, came tramping down the stairs. She was wearing a one-piece playsuit and a paper mask over her lips, which by its flaws looked homemade.

The two sat on opposite ends of the table, facing one another. Lili pulled off her mask and Aram was surprised to see her lips were perfectly normal, not disfigured, meaning the mask served a function other than concealment. The two women filled their own plates, then filled those in front of the two empty chairs. Until these ghost meals were piled and pretty, they did not say a word. Then Lili closed her eyes and recited a prayer Aram could hear only in part through the glass: *Ancestors... veins... home of autumn... remembrance. The restful haven of the waveless sea.* When she was finished, both women ate the feast with their hands, preserves and mustard staining their fair skin. The one whose back was to him uncorked a bottle of red and poured a glass for each place setting. When she stood to fill Lili's he recognized her body – she had answered the door when he came to Gainntir looking for Euna, and within a few minutes had threatened to hack him with a mattock. It was not entirely sage to be hiding, uninvited, under her window.

As Lili lifted her wine glass to toast, she caught sight of him. Her eyes went wide and girlish, as if she had discovered a secret trove of Samhain presents. The other woman must have

noticed this, too, because she whipped her head in his direction. Aram was too slow to sink himself into the burdock; the
torso woman looked at him and cocked her shoulder back.
She shattered her glass against the window so wine attainted
it, forced red through new fractures. Oddly his instinct was
not to run. He stared through the split and tint at the woman.
She was gruesome, even sourer than he remembered, with a
severe and uneven haircut and a sunken, sallow look to her
cheekbones. She wore a strange pair of spectacles, ones that
hooked around the backs of her ears and looked antique.

He gestured toward the door. She came close to the window
so that when she spoke her lips grazed the broken glass. We
haven't finished eating. Stand there and watch. When we are
done I may open the door for you.

Who is it, Muireall? he heard Lili call.

So that was her name. He nodded. Lili reached under the
table and put a different mask on, this one with two painted
cat eyes covering her own. They ate what remained on their
plates, Lili, blinded by her mask, overreaching her dish a few
times. After they finished, Muireall stood, and on the outside
of the farmhouse Aram ambled to the front door, hoping
she was mirroring his movement on the inside. To his relief,
she opened the door. Her energy was spidery and obscure –
when he first came, at least, she had been outwardly hostile.
Now she took him by his wrist, firmly, with a taut smile,
and brought him into their dining room. She pulled back
one of the chairs, a campstool, really, and pressured him to
sit. Famished, and assuming her seating of him was a kind
of invitation, he reached out to pick up a link. The woman
slapped the sausage from his hand so it fell on the table linen,

and then she arranged it with care on the plate again. She seemed more scared than she did cross.

That's not for you, she said.

Understood, he said. I don't want to interrupt your feast, but if you don't mind, I have a few questions.

Lili started to hum at a high volume, until abruptly she clapped her hands and flung the cat eyes from her face. Muireall's hands were moved by tremors, faint ones, but visible no less. Otherwise she was stolid, a stone wall.

Hello, he said to Lili, my name is Aram.

As he spoke, Lili creased her forehead. Wait, she said. I know you.

Yes, we've met, he said. I'm a friend of Euna's.

Euna, she repeated, fear and reverence in her voice. Is she alive? She pinched Aram's forearm with her nails. Wait... are you alive?

Muireall was still standing immobile, her mouth gently agape. Now tears were teeming in her eyes. She was completely cleft from the act, as if she were not even aware she was about to cry. Aram said, I haven't seen her in a few years. But yes, sweet girl, I'm fairly sure she's alive.

From upstairs, Aram heard the ringing of a hollow-sounding bell. Instinctively, Lili straightened, lifted the only plate that remained untouched, and ran up the steps. Muireall looked through her tears at Aram. We lost a huge part of our family, she said when Lili was out of sight. Our cridhe. Our shared heart.

She sat down stiffly on her throne. We haven't heard a word from her, she said, wiping mustard smut from her fingers. Not a single postcard.

Aram had relied on his lost love being in Gainntir now, as she had been then, hoarding her virtue for him. He had no back-up plan. He withered, knowing his faith would, for now, go unrewarded. So she's not in Pullhair? he asked.

Muireall sucked her breath in, clearly bothered by his interest. Of course she's not here. If she were here, she'd be in our home, I promise you that.

That was enough. He stood up from the campstool, ready to rush back to the bowrider, cross the ocean to Portugal with the men talking foreign tongues. At least he could work in the call centre and scrape together a bit of tender, live a humble, righteous life. Then he stopped. He had forgotten his son entirely.

The whole ride north, the old man's house, the ferry, Aram had deceived himself. His was not some divine quest. He had only been looking for her, earthy, embodied her.

Why are you even here? Muireall asked him. She was happy before she met you, old man. You infected her with all your dirty ideas and made sure she was miserable.

She was the one who came to see me, Aram said. She chose to come.

You don't know her the way I do. She's fragile. She's not suited for the brutal world outside.

In that moment, Aram loved Euna so much he could not dream of another timeline, one in which they had never met. But he was ashamed he had embraced her overtures, made her carnal, rushed what had so clearly demanded slower, more careful judgement. She had been a rose in a greenhouse, and he had fissured the glass. You're not wrong, he said.

Muireall drank right from the wine bottle. You don't get to

come here and atone, she said. I lost my baby. My heart will never unbreak.

I understand, he said. I'll go.

It was plain in her face that she wanted to throw him out, as Effie had, tearing his sweater. And yet she seemed reluctant to let him leave. Come to the library, she said, picking up one of the pillar candles. That's where we go after dinner.

He followed her past the stairs and front entryway into an airy, book-lined room. The space felt icy, grades colder than the grass outside, and despite the furnishings and the softcovers, rather vast. She led him to a corner nook, and with the held flame she showed him a kind of sanctum. On hooks hung Euna's tweed trousers and linen shirt, as well as a nightgown he did not know as intimately. The one shelf in the alcove had been carefully adorned with a hardback, *The Witches Speak*, a laundry stone, and a dried salmon sliced lengthwise, eyes and teeth intact.

Muireall said, This is our seomra thiar. Our room to the west.

He reached out to touch the tweed, remembering the chill it had carried that autumn day, Euna's warmth beneath the cloth. Muireall grabbed him by the wrist again and forced his arm back to his side.

He asked, What do you want me to do?

She let go of his wrist and took the laundry stone into her free hand, turning it over, making even its slight weight menacing. Men are all the same, she said. You just want an answer. You want us to do the work of thinking for you.

I want to do right by you, Muireall, he said. But I can't possibly guess what you're thinking.

Muireall turned from him, taking with her the room's only source of light. He could no longer see the seomra thiar, not the dried fish or the dull linen. The nightgown, white and fluted, held its shape even in that new pitch, a phantom frame. Muireall lay on a bearskin rug in the centre of the library, the candle close to her and the bear's hair. She had Aram all muddled. He missed Fenella, her constancy, her straight bent. Muireall was more like the guards, and her vagary gave him the same feeling theirs had – of being bound to someone's impulses, of desperately wanting to submit to their rules, but not knowing how, fickle and formless as they were.

He heard Lili darting back down the stairs. She rushed to the bearskin rug and lay down so the crown of her head was touching Muireall's. She's not doing very well today, she said, winded. I could only get her to eat a tangerine.

Aram came to join them. He could not lie with his crown touching theirs, not without feeling unseemly and out of place. Instead he sat cross-legged at the rug's edge. Who are you talking about?

Lili said, Grace. Our other bana-churaidh. She's not doing very well.

What's wrong? Aram asked, gently. I used to treat my mam when she was seasick. Maybe I can help.

It's not like that. She's sad and it's making her do things. She tried to... Lili paused for a long time, then took one of her plaits and wrapped it around her throat, mimicking a hanging motion.

Aram remembered. A man in a neighbouring cell had hanged himself. He had asked to see a doctor so many times – until, finally, he had chosen a sure end over that purgatory.

Aram had been forced to listen through the night, through pillow fillings, finger earplugs. He had stifled those sounds a long time. In the hush of Gainntir, they came to him again.

Lili was tapping his knee to get his notice. Was your mam ever that kind of sick? she asked, when he finally looked at her.

He said, No, thankfully not. She was only ever sick in the physical way. But I did know someone who did what Grace tried.

You did? Lili asked. I read about a girl doing it in one of the library books. But I didn't know real people could.

Yes, he said. Real people can. Grace might want to see a doctor, or at least get outside a bit more. What she needs isn't here, and it might be somewhere else.

Muireall, still lying down, rolled her eyes so they were on Aram. My Gracie, she said, my beloved Gracie, was perfect before you came along and stole our cridhe from us. Don't you see, Euna was the anchor who held this all in place?

Aram said, Euna must have felt a lot of pressure.

I can't believe you touched her, Muireall said. Her words were pointed and meticulous, as if she had gone from simply speaking to reciting an invocation. And then you had the gall to sleep with that filthy Aileen.

Aram felt as if he had been collared. The room's temper had turned. Aram couldn't stand it, not after the castle, after years slowed by that same musty air. He stood up, brushed his trousers clean of the dust and ash that had amassed on the bearskin. Ladies, he said. If only you could know how sorry I am.

You can't leave just like that, Muireall said.

Psalm 118:5. When hard pressed, I cried to the Lord; he brought me into a spacious place.

Keep an eye on Grace, he said to Lili. She needs you.

Lili nodded dutifully. To Muireall, he said, Oidhche mhath leat, *good night to you.* Though she tried to hide it, he could see she was impressed by his Gaelic. He left the house and headed out onto the heath, stopping by the dining room to steal a few sausages on the way.

It was a bitter night, the wind as wide and cold as an ice sheet. And yet the air was tropical against the lasting bite of the library. When he made it to the dock he found that, of course, the bowrider was already gone. His new life had tipped before it left the shore. He sat on the dock, where he had gathered splinters in his péire so many times, listing his womenfolk for parties of amused fish farmers, and looked out over the loch.

Everything was still and sullen. Then in the darkness he saw an outline, akin to the nightgown in the nook. The shape was so vague he could not be sure what he had seen. Like Muireall's rules, it was all but formless. He looked down for a while at the concrete dock, its shape constant. When he lifted his head again, the water was just water.

In the off-season, when he was home from the trawler, Aram's father used to tell him stories of the blue men of the Minch, small creatures that lived between the Outer Hebrides and the mainland. They would swim with their torsos above the sea, dancing, playing shinty. They recited poems and chatted with mariners, and sometimes the cruel ones waited for sailors to drown so they could drag them down to the loch-bottom. They looked remarkably like waves. Aram's father claimed to have seen many, and at the time Aram had not questioned him. He had loved the story.

Aram minded the peaceful scene and tried to forget the course his night had taken. But he still heard the man hanging himself. He still saw Euna, pulling her underclothes up hastily to hide the blood.

He had gone to Gainntir inflated, airy with anticipation. He had held something close to the feeling of fullness, of vital, holy swell – sàimh. And he had left, just a few hours later, feeling that he was at best unimportant. At worst, he was a caustic force, and the town would be finer had he never lived there. No wonder Grace was laid up in bed. No wonder Euna had cut from this part of the country and Lili seemed stuck in her girlhood.

He wished he could slip now into the water and forget all he had heard and done. He would live in that complete, bodiless void, floating, feeling only the pain of purification.

*

At first Aram stayed in the hut because he didn't want to cart his catch around. Had he hauled those coolers too far, the fish might have lost their flush and flavour. Or so he told himself. Mostly they were heavy, and he avoided hassle as he did sealice. He worked hard when he needed to, but when he had the time to unwind, he would never deny himself that pleasure. And now he had nothing if not time.

So he stayed in Pullhair, making, actually, a kind of replica of Fenella's magical shack. He invited the marten inside as she had the mutt; he cooked salmon nightly; he read her books end to end. When his supplies of food and novels ran out, he vowed, he would look for other pastures. He dried some of the salmon into leather, so it would keep longer, and he read the books deliberately, letting each word hold its long haunt. He resigned himself to this sheltered life, though he drew energy from talking to other people, and in that matter his needle had started to dip low.

Eventually, Aram started to get lonely. Head in those vapours, he considered going back to Gainntir, if only to have one good conversation. In the castle he had been denied two vital things, freedom and company. Had he gone to the farmhouse, he would have gained the second and lost the first, and after much deliberation he decided that was, at this point, a poor bargain.

There were other houses salted around Pullhair, of course, but with winter falling, all of the public meeting places had been deserted, the town common and the landing pier and the guest house terrace. For once in his life, Aram did not have the confidence to knock on strangers' doors. The sense that he once had, of being able to go anywhere, do anything, of being universally welcomed and even desired – an impression so many women had together given him, starting with his mother – had diminished in the years since he had been pulled over for a broken tail-light and detained at Dungavel. He had always thought that confidence was a permanent part of him, ingrained as his grey eyes. But now he saw himself as another cragged, middle-aged fisherman, one who would move for the rest of his life from port to port, cold cot to cold cot, and leave each landscape scanter than it had been before he came.

And so he found himself heading, on foot, to the only building in all of Pullhair he had told himself to avoid. If having a simple conversation were enough to lift his spirits, then surely worshipping among other true believers would restore him to a higher state. He hoped that, to Minister Macbay, his would simply be a familiar face from years before. He trusted that Aileen's shame had been strong enough to keep his identity a secret.

The church was just a few kilometres west, in the direction opposite to Gainntir. It was a solemn grey building with tall, peaked windows absent of stained glass. The grass in front was badly burned, turned amber. In the car park were several cars, none of which Aram recognized. Even standing on the outside, he could hear the boys' choir, though he remembered their harmonies being fuller and more florid than they now sounded. He had never been a devoted attender of this church, but he had come on a regular basis when he lived in Pullhair before, in part because he had noticed the minister's redheaded daughter, and in part because the stories he had heard there, of Jonah living in the belly of a whale and Balaam moralizing with his talking donkey, had been in marvellous contrast to the tedious farm days.

He had not known today was Sunday. But when he realized it was, he took that sign as auspicious. At least it would mean there were more bodies in the church, and the minister was less likely to single Aram out among them. He entered the room feeling secure and sat in the final pew. There were about twenty people congregated, plus five boys in the choir and Minister Macbay, huge now, in his pulpit gown. Aram could only see the backs of the congregants' heads as they stood to sing with the choir, so he could not be sure if he had met any of them before. His heart went hard when he saw, among them, a head of tangled red.

Though for a moment he let himself imagine the hair belonged to Euna, he knew she was taller, her body had more waves. This was someone else – the bidse who had stolen his child and his flame.

The hymn was not a standard one, *behold the wretch whose lust and wine/Had wasted his estate*, and so forth. The boys seemed to stumble here and there, having been sheltered from particular lyrics, lust, wine. When the hymn was done, everyone who had been standing sat, and by chance, Aileen peeked over her shoulder to see who had come in to worship halfway through the service. She looked truly, spiritually shaken when she saw Aram. She whipped her neck back around before he could gesture to her, mouth the words *Meet me outside* – or better, *You egg, young fry of treachery.*

He made the choice, then, not to leave the church. He would join Aileen for fellowship after the service, and then over smoky tea he would ask if she knew where Euna had gone. He would in the meantime contain his other tingles, angers. He refused to make a scene in this holy house. If Aileen genuinely knew nothing, he could then admit defeat, finally, and let himself start to grieve the loss of Euna. As miserable as it would be, he could stop reaching for her; his left hand could at last know what his right hand was doing.

After the service, Aram went downstairs, where card tables had been trimmed with treats made by the town matriarchs, as well as bowls of tropical fruits, presumably grown by the minister's wife in her forcing house. He had visited that place on one occasion. The occasion. They had conceived his son there, while a rare Hebridean sun beat down, beaded the wide bridge of Aileen's nose. He had been aching for Euna. He had missed her so much he found a warm form with her hair and entered it bare.

He dyked those thoughts. Not here. Not in the Kirk.

On the far side of the basement, Aileen was pecking at a scone. A man in Highland dress was holding her other hand. He was entirely traditional: kilt of his clan tartan, fly plaid, sporran, brogues. Aram recognized him from years before, when he had come to repair the automatic fish feeders. A fine-looking man, if a bit lanky, with a well-oiled beard. He seemed rather old, until Aram realized he was old now, too, and the man was likely of a similar vintage.

Aram took a bun from the table, as an attempt to fit in, and walked to where they were standing. Hey there, he said to the man holding Aileen's hand. I think we met at the farm a long time ago.

The man let go of Aileen and clapped Aram's shoulder. Aram noticed they were wearing matching wedding bands. Aileen was looking into the distance, where her father was in yawning conversation with the owner of the guest house. That's right, Aileen's husband said. Whether he remembered Aram or not, he was firm about his fellowship. I'm Carson, and this is my blushing bride, Aileen.

Aram. He smiled as he had seen others in the room do, meeting one another, beaming.

A good and glad name, Carson said. Like in the Bible, hey?

Aram would not consent to seeming ignorant, especially not here, so he nodded. He would find the reference later. He

185

had an Old Testament from the castle and a New Testament from Fenella, and between them he would learn the import of his name.

Do you think, Carson, I could borrow your blushing bride for a moment? I have some salmon to give to the church and I just need her to show me where they plan to store it.

Sure thing, Carson said, and kissed Aileen on the cheek. Make sure you set some aside for me, my wee cauliflower.

Aileen peered at Aram finally, for a brief and uncomfortable moment. Then she moved past him up the stairs as he dogged along behind. She led him to a small green behind the church, to a patch of charlock they had tramped on their way to the forcing house that day. Now it seemed so delicate, hurtable, that he stood a few paces from it, where the grass was already charred.

Thank you, he said to Aileen.

For what?

For carrying him.

Aileen looked at Aram now, held and held the look. For the first time he knew how his fish must have felt as he gutted them, his knife moving coldly from vent to head. How do you know that?

Euna, he said.

Aileen reached down into the charlock and tore a handful from the ground. It had started to rain, though gently, and the water ran from the roots in long, crimson strands, staining the hem of Aileen's church dress.

Did you hear me? he asked.

Of course I heard you, you hollow heidbanger. When did you talk to her?

She sent me one postcard, when Lachlan Iain was born. It had a little sketch of him. Where is she?

Aileen started tearing leaves from the mass that was in her hands, tarnishing her nylons, her nails, both cleaned for Sunday worship. The dress was getting soiled. I haven't seen her since I came back to Pullhair a couple years ago, she said. She's forgotten me, I'm sure. She's big time now.

Big time, Aram repeated, confused.

Have you been living in a dungeon? Aileen asked. She's off touring Scandinavia and Lebanon and everywhere you can imagine. Hammer of Witches, biggest band in the country.

Aram remembered the magazine at the corner shop, the name those boys had been spewing, a singer, Euna. But it could not have been his girl. Her charm was in her smallness. His humble, diminutive, modest Euna. And my son? he asked.

I don't have any good news for you, she said. I came back here to marry Carson. That was always the plan. I couldn't bring a boy conceived out of sin.

Coldly, from vent to head. Aram was suddenly worried that Aileen had sacrificed his seed, bedded him under the headland. Is he gone?

Aileen was visibly hurt. I'm not a monster, she said. The boy is fine. He's on tour with Euna. I'm sure her roadie, Muireall, is taking good care of him.

So you do have good news for me, he said. He could not bear to see her church clothes get any grungier, could not stand one more minim of dirt on lace. He took the weeds from her and placed them on the ground where they had, before, been growing. How are you doing with all of this?

My heart was so full of you, she said, at once, as if the words had been hot in her mouth a long time, a smoky tea. And you didn't want me, you didn't ever want me, you just toyed with me like I was a trinket. And when you had enough, Aram, you left me broken in my father's house.

Aram tucked her long hair behind one ear so he could see her face. She was not crying. I never deserved the attention you gave me, he said.

It was not a choice.

Believe me, he said, I know.

I wondered all the time what was wrong with me. I cried so much my nose bled.

He needed to haul them back to the present. He sensed otherwise he could be in for a long spell of this tillage, waiting patiently while she dug up old graves. You're the mother of my child, he said, and I'll do everything in my means to protect you now. From myself, as from others.

Aileen did not seem keen to move on without his accepting some blame. And he knew that was fair. The harm he had caused her was different from the harm he had caused Effie, much deeper, more grievous. The wound would be, even for the strongest woman, immense.

There's one thing you should know, she said to him. Euna was a vestige of you, a kind of limb, and I came to love her, too.

He did not feel protective or shut out; he did not linger on the naked and neon of their late nights. He was covered by a warm wash, thinking of these two women who mattered to him comforting, coming to love, one another. Maybe it trimmed back his shame, knowing Aileen had not been alone with Lachlan Iain. Or maybe any story in which Euna was a living, breathing being brought him pleasure.

And Carson, he asked, do you like him?

You know, Aileen said, he's handy. And he goes all the way to the grocer in Kershader to buy me exotic flowers. I'd say I drew the long straw.

Aileen had glowed up. The indecent, deep-fried teenager he'd met those years before, her mouth a latrine, her laugh a snort, had been cast forth. In her place was a true adult, poised, pert, a self quite hot with mettle. He had learned from his mother that a shrub rose must be pruned, its oldest canes clipped with a sharp blade, so the plant does not overgrow. The baby, the broken heart, the trek home from wherever she had been. All hard. All bladed. And yet together they'd had this effect on her.

Now, Aileen said, you better not have been lying about the fish.

Aram laughed. I'm afraid I was, he said. But I actually do have half a cooler back at my place, and I'd be glad to bring it to you. Are you here every day?

Every day, she said.

Then I'll be seeing you soon, Aram said. He stroked her cheek and then turned to walk away.

Aileen stopped him with a hand on his forearm. No, she said. You wait here. I get to be the one to leave this time.

He submitted. He watched her disappear into a chalet in the shadow of the church. This building was separate from the place the minister shared with his wife, a conventional house with a thatched roof. Aileen would have had to explain her dirty clothes had she entered the church again without changing. Aram guessed she had gone back to the chalet to dress in something tidy.

Aram was iced, his skin a kind of buckram. It was time he went back to the hut. He walked past the chalet and house and through the car park. The fellowship must have just been finishing, because the congregation was coming out of the doors. With them they brought grins and, from above, sunshafts. An elderly woman fastened a bonnet over her hair. But by then the rain was so spare she hardly needed the guard.

*

That evening, Aram searched the Old Testament for his name. He spent hours on his cot doing this, holding a candle to the pages, close enough to light them on fire. The book was cosmic in scope, and searching for Aram in it suddenly seemed as vain as looking for Euna in real life, wherever on earth she was. But ultimately his name did come swimming up through the dim light.

Isaiah 7:8. For the head of Aram is Damascus, and the head of Damascus is Rezin; and within threescore and five years shall Ephraim be broken, that it be not a people.

He knew Damascus was a real city, a mark on a modern map. In the castle he had met a couple of Syrian men, one from the base of Jabal ash-Shaykh, one from Damascus. They had asked where he was from, as if they wielded the answer, then seemed bewildered that he could not locate Sketimini in relation to any other place. He looked like them, they said, the bones just so, the brows just so. After a while, he'd learned to avoid those particular men, because they would not listen to what he was saying, and because he did not know if, maybe, there was some minor truth hiding in their notions.

His mother had never been candid about anything, had chosen instead to hold secrets to her breast, banded. Her lips tended to be closed, he remembered this about her – how often he had wanted to prise that tight line apart, how he'd craved a white glint when she smiled. Please, Mam, just one tooth, had been his refrain. And now he could not stop himself from wondering whether his name had been a silent sign from her, an Easter egg hidden until he was ready to find it. Son, you belong to this land and lineage, your bones, your brow.

She had withheld the truth about his father's death, too, until his absence could no longer go unaddressed. Even when she had offered Aram morsels of the story, she had been looking away, at her sandals, her book laid open on the boat deck. Always holding her voice to a single note.

Where was Sketimini?

On a paper map, on a spread of dirty scenery, where was Sketimini?

His mother was now out walking somewhere, or else lying under a headstone and planted flowers, and because of her silence, that tight line he could never prise apart, he would never find her. That same streak in him – his silence when Euna was set to leave the castle, his dismissal of her curiosity before that, *Euna, you wouldn't understand* – had dashed his chances of seeing her again. How was it that he had assumed this trait of his mother's he so deeply disliked, her dry reserve, and let it strike down all he had learned on his own about womenfolk? How had he, with so many options in hand, ended up alone?

Aram was crying for the first time in as long as he could remember. The feeling was afflictive, the way his nose tingled, the way his eyes itched from the inside. His body had come close to this only when he discovered his sensitivity to mussels, after, of course, having consumed pounds and pounds. He blew the candle out and sat in the dark so he could cry without being humiliated, though even his pet marten was out at that moment.

At the castle, he had braved his pain in private. For other prisoners that would have been an added punishment; others were eager to air their wounds. But Aram would only explore his sadness in his stone room. As a matter of protection, of pride. His mother had been the same way. Now, crying, knowing how it felt to hold sorrow in his own face, and pulse, and belly, he read his mother's silence as he never had. She had not wanted to burden him. She wanted her story, as far as her son was concerned, to begin in the catamaran. Claiming, then concealing, the harm done to her before that. So her son's life could start from a plain, emptied-out place – nothing inherited, not even a homeland.

But she had taught him a language, English, and though she had raised him in the ocean between countries she had, before that, rooted his earliest years in Scotland. It was impossible, anyway, to live among people and be free of origin. He had tried. He had been cosmopolitan, chosen by women of every creed; had worn stylish clothing and a trimmed beard; had learned to use his body to full effect; had advanced beyond the mundane need for friends, and so avoided being defined as they would be. He had done his very best, in other words, to be a man from Sketimini, though part of him had known for years that this was a fantasy. He would sooner succeed in catching a blue man of the Minch and inviting him to dinner.

Aram put the Bible on the ground and huddled under his thin blanket. He longed for a pillow. A hutmate. A speaker in the night. He had convinced himself he was superior to others who were so tribal, clannish, as to be defined by a mutual language, or place, or skin tone. Only on rare occasions had something pierced this thick logic, as had happened at mealtime in the castle, when everyone had clumped in their groups and he had ambled around looking for a place to sit, though he found, each time, that there were no tables for one.

He would bring the salmon to Aileen and Carson in the morning, and he would shake their hands, kindly, so they might know him as a true friend.

*

When Aram arrived at the church the next morning, he found it was much stiller than it had been on Sunday. The sky above the building hung grey and eternal, so lifeless that Aram missed yesterday's rain. That grey stretched all the way into his centre, and just as he missed the rain outside, he missed the way he had felt the night before in the hut, when at least he had been miserable. Anything was better than this dull detachment.

He knocked on the door of the chalet. Carson answered. Aram could see Aileen in the background, well pressed in a linen dress, her hair in four plaits. Aram handed the cooler to Carson. I hear you like fish, he said.

You heard right, Carson said. As Carson turned to put the fish in the refrigerator, Aram looked around. In the next room was a charming, four-poster wood bed, a spoon collection mounted on the walls, a violin in an open case. From the doorway to that room came an intimate light, as if from a bedside lamp, and Aram was envious of the two of them. Your timing is perfect, Carson said, coming back to where Aram was standing. We've just heard some exciting news.

Carson took Aram's rucksack and invited him to sit at the dining table. He did, at the head. Aileen opened a package of oatcakes and set them out on a platter, then she and Carson sat down across from one another. She just phoned, Aileen said. For the first time.

Who did? Aram asked.

Oh, come on, you bampot, Aileen said.

Carson looked over at his wife in surprise, as if he wasn't accustomed to her using curse words. To Aram they were a natural part of her, as vital as her red hair. Maybe she had been showing her husband a separate character.

Aram did not want to seem expectant. Nor did he want to seem, at least to Aileen, controlled by his desire. He asked, attempting reticence, Euna?

Carson winked at Aram. Heard you had a bit of a thing with her, he said.

Aileen swatted at her husband across the table. She was calling from a hospital, she said. It was sad, really. She collapsed while she was out on tour.

This made Aram's nose prickle. He choked down an oatcake so he would have something else to focus on. He wondered if, in taking the oatcake into his shaking hand, in hacking as it went down his throat, he had shown them his discomfort. He would have been better off checking that instinct, linking his hands in his lap.

Aileen faltered. She looked over at Carson, who nodded in his warm way. She's not up to taking care of her boy, Lachlan Iain, she said. So he's coming here.

Her boy. So Carson must not have known. This did not surprise Aram. But it did make the light from their bedside lamp, sublime a minute before, look strained, metallic. When we spoke yesterday you mentioned a roadie, he said to Aileen. Surely she could take care of Euna's boy.

Yes, she could, Aileen said. But she doesn't want the boy to feel adrift, moving from place to place in a tour bus. So she's bringing him here for a while. You'll like her – she's a dear friend of mine.

Well, shite. It sounded as if Euna would not be coming, only the roadie, Muireall. How many times could he weed out this dumb, hardy hope of his? It was a sprawl of knotgrass and he could not quite find the roots to pull. I'm sure I would like her, he said. But I was just heading south to find work.

Aram, Aileen said, you should stay with us until they come. My father would be glad to feed you in the meantime, and he's always looking for fresh voices to help him deliver his sermons.

Carson put his hand on his wife's. My wee turnip, he said, there's not a lick of work here, and it sounds like he has plans.

Aileen flushed pink. Of course, she said. Forgive me. That was a strange thing to offer. Aram, I hope you have good luck down south.

Would your father really feed me? Aram asked. I could

sleep in the church basement. More comfortable than the hut I've been living in.

Now Carson took an oatcake and ate it meticulously, starting with the edges, while Aileen got up to make a pot of pekoe and pour a round of water glasses. Aram wished he could take back what he had said. This was why he kept quiet about all but the starkest things: it is dark today, it is cold outside, I am looking for work. When he moved outside of this scheme it was only to give compliments to people he knew wanted them, people who would not question what he said or, in response, mete out silence. He kept records. He did not tell stories. He watched the days move past. He did not score them with a tender soundtrack.

Carson wiped the crumbs from either corner of his mouth with a napkin. He said, Okay, I think it's time we all came clean.

What do you mean, my dearest?

Carson's mouth was neat, but he kept dabbing with the napkin. What I mean, he said, is that I'm a very lucky man to be married to you, m' usgair. And I'm not one to run away from good fortune. So, if there is anything you would like to tell me, knowing that I am your husband, knowing that I will be your husband until we are side by side in the boneyard, now would be an ideal time.

Aileen sat up and squared her shoulders to his. Do you mean that? she asked.

Of course, he said. You may think you are saving me from some kind of corruption. I would rather just know. It's me, Carson, two boiled eggs every morning, two pieces of rye, two violin scales, Carson. I'm not too keen on the unknown.

She pressed her eyes closed, as Aram always had on the farm when preparing to step into the cold water. Aram and I slept together when I was eighteen, she said.

Carson shifted in his seat. Okay, he said. Thank you for telling me. I'll take some time with that later.

Aram looked over at Aileen, hoping to inspire her to tell the truth about Lachlan Iain's origin. He trusted that Carson would respond evenly, and that, when the boy came, he would treat him with more care, knowing Aileen had given life to him. But her eyes were still closed, and she could not see Aram looking. She said, No, nothing else right now.

Her husband was a smart man. Or, more precisely, a perceptive one. Hey there, pet, he said, I can tell you're holding something.

She started to breathe very quickly. Carson stood and walked over to her side of the table, then pulled her chair out so he could kneel beside it. He took both of her hands into his and whispered something mild and inaudible. Aram felt the urge to turn away, to give them some privacy, but then, that had always been his problem. A man could certainly overdose on discretion. So he stayed watching. Her breath at last slowed down and she stopped worming around, working her heels up and down. I'm sorry, she said to her husband. You're such a good man.

No more talk of goodness, Carson said. We're just here, okay. We're just two people and we're here.

Aileen's freckles were fantastically bright. She opened her eyes. Lachlan Iain is ours, she said, pointing first to herself and then to Aram.

Carson nodded calmly. He shook Aram's hand and kissed

Aileen on the crown of her head. It was very brave of you to tell me, he said to her, his lips still on her scalp. He lingered there for one more beat, inhaling, maybe searching her hair for a familiar perfume. He poured a mug of tea from the pot and went into the next room. He closed and locked the door behind him. A few minutes later, Aram heard him playing a minor scale on the violin.

Aileen was looking, shell-shocked, into the middle distance. Her stare was set tightly to the fridge. Aram had to leave. He could not just stay there while Aileen's body looked over at the magnets and mementoes of her life with Carson. Scraps of notecard, photographs, dried asters from Kershader, it was tragic. Music rarely made Aram feel one way or another, but the slow notes coming from the bedroom, up and down the scale, over and over, needled into the back of his neck. Each hair on his arms went erect.

Do you want me to go? he asked Aileen.

Yes, she said. And then, No.

That's about what I expected, he said. He laughed. She stayed as she was.

Aram went to pour Aileen a cup, then set it before her on the most ordinary coaster he could find. He avoided the ones embroidered with horses, or with field thistle and flax-comb. Those seemed so domestic. Surely they were tied to particular days and feelings. Surely this couple had used them after a particular sermon or ceremony, or on the occasion of their engagement, Aileen's ardent return to Pullhair, and so embroidered them with more than ponies and plants.

He lifted the cup to her mouth and tipped it so a thin stream of tea dribbled down her chin. This woke her from her wool-gathering. She took the cup from him and put it on the table beside the coaster.

It'll leave a ring, Aram said.

If it does, she said, I'll iron it out.

Awright.

The violin scales had stopped. From the bedroom came a new sound, of carving, perhaps, or sanding. In any event, of wood being worn down. This seemed to comfort Aileen. Clearly it meant something more to her than it did to Aram, who did not know Carson's habits, who had never shared rooms with him.

Good, she said. That is good.

Aram asked, gently, How's that?

He's working on a bookshelf for me, she said. When something's on his mind, even something small, he works on that shelf. It's his way of processing.

This language was new to Aram. It came across as second-hand, as if it had been implanted in her by a professional. And that's good? he asked.

Oh yes, Aileen said. Carson has all these ways of working things out, you know, materially.

Interesting, Aram said. He wasn't interested, though, not really. The conversation had taken a turn toward the undefined, the rù-rà he avoided by only speaking concretely, on a surface level. *Working things out* was different from *I am looking for work*. He was comfortable with the latter and not at all with the former.

She said, Yes, it's interesting. He's so evolved.

I'm sure he is, Aram said. Now listen, Aileen. If you still want me to stay until Lachlan Iain comes, could you introduce me to your father? You can tell him I'm a believer and I came to you looking for refuge. He's a man of good faith. He'll have to house me.

Aileen paused. Carson's sanding had taken on a steady cadence. I'd be glad to do that, she said. But we'll ruin our names if we go on telling everyone about our bad choices. So let's keep those between the three of us.

Aram didn't want the minister to know their trespasses any more than Aileen wanted her father to. He said, Lead on, pet.

Don't call me those names any more, she said. She stood and put on a red velvet coat, knotting it at the neck, and a pair of riding boots. Aram had not removed his shoes when he came inside – he was used to floors muddier than the moors – so all he needed was to pick up his rucksack.

They left Carson in the bedroom to work on the bookshelf and went outside, where a horde of crossbills was pecking at fallen pinecones. Odd for so many crossbills to congregate in one place, and then to eat as slowly as they were, with what seemed to be etiquette. He was so rapt by this oddness it took a moment to notice, in the forcing house, a young woman he'd never expected to see in the real world. If Pullhair could indeed be called that.

*

The young woman he had seen, Lili, was not alone in the forcing house. By her side was the minister's wife, a slight, comely woman in her mid-fifties. As far as Aram knew, she did not have a name other than Mrs Macbay. She and Lili were holding opposite handles of a bow creel, the kind fishwives used to carry around Glenfinnan when Aram was a very young boy. In those baskets they used to make the men's weekly catch look handsome, then flank it with a knife and a slate, should anyone want the fish cleaned for an extra coin when the wives came to their home. Aram was so young then his memory could not be trusted, but he had often seen lampreys hiding inside the creels, sometimes even miniature whales, so small they would have fit in the palm of his infant hand. He had seen an ocarina, a tyre, a walrus tusk, the essence of blue, and once an iridescent speech bubble – *'s fhearr teicheadh math na droch-fhuireach*, it had said in its typescript, or, *better a good escape than a bad stay.*

Aileen turned to lead him into the blackhouse, where, presumably, her father was resting. Aram stopped her as gently as he could, with a hand on her shoulder. Do you mind if we say hello to your mam first?

I'd rather we stick to the plan, she said. Anyway, she has company.

I know the young woman she's with. I'd like to say hello.

Aileen sighed. Do what you must, she said. I'll go see my boban. Come knock on the door of the house when you're all done.

Thank you, he said. She sulked for a tick, then slunk across the dry land toward her father's door. The sky above her, plague dark, seemed to swarm. She stepped over some earthwork that went round the house, then knocked in a practised pattern and was welcomed inside.

Aram turned back toward the glass. He could see from where he stood that Mrs Macbay was offering Lili an assortment of tropical fruits, pineapples, papayas, finger limes, green mangoes. Lili looked at each with her dream-eyes, beaming, turning the fruit to take in each smiling colour, so rare in this half of the year. When she had inspected one thoroughly, she would put it in the creel, then move to the next piece on offer. Mrs Macbay chatted with her all the while, their dynamic seeming light and amiable.

Aram came into the heat of the forcing house. Please excuse me, he said. It looks like you folks are having a great time. I'm sorry to interrupt.

Aram! Lili said. She tried to run toward him but realized, still holding the creel handle, she could not go far. Instead she waved with the passion fruit in her hand. This is the best day of my life!

Mrs Macbay looked at Aram with a kindness that came from far within. In contrast to her daughter's wild red, her hair was gelled and well defined, a little helmet of ringlets. This made her look put-together, and so reliable. If she could take such good care of her appearance, she could take equal care of a conversation. You're not interrupting at all, she said. You're most welcome here. Did I see you at fellowship yesterday?

He levelled the cable knit of his sweater. He was sweating already, and he smelled of salmon scales; he hoped the plum blooms would overpower that odour. Yes, I popped by briefly. I had some fish to bring to Aileen and Carson.

That was very kind of you. Are you a fisherman?

Lili said, He's a big shot at the Salmon Company! My friend Euna picked up fish from him once. You should have seen her coming back from getting it, her face all full of moon.

Was it really? Aram asked. That hardy hope of his. Its roots were reaching wider and wider, and he was powerless to stop the spread. I can't really imagine that, he said, trying to come across as cool, unmoved. But anyway, that reminds me, how are you here?

The thrill that had been running visibly through Lili now dulled, disappeared. She put down the passion fruit, not in the basket, but in the shade of its parent tree. Grace really wanted fruit today, she said. She was so low on sugar and sad in her bed. I knew they had it here because a lady came to our door a few months ago to invite us to church. She had a sack of oranges.

Good girl. Does Muireall know you've come?

She finds a way to know everything. But I sneaked out this morning without her seeing me, if that's what you're wondering.

I've never met Muireall, Mrs Macbay said to Aram. Nor Grace, for that matter, though we have tried several times to include them in our congregation.

Aram said, They keep to themselves, mostly.

Lili rattled her handle toward Mrs Macbay, so the woman would hold the creel alone. Lili, relieved of that fruit weight, sat in the dirt. She bunched her hands into fists and rested her chin on them. I was having such a good day before you asked me that, she told Aram.

He sat in the same position as she did, cross-legged, hands bunched into fists. Though he angled himself in front of her, she would not look at him. I shouldn't have asked that, he said. I was too curious. Can you forgive me?

Okay, Lili said. She pegged upright, suddenly vibrant. It was astonishing how quickly the girl moved from one emotion to the next, not like Carson, sanding a whole bookshelf, or

Aileen, still processing anger entrenched over years. Lili was now grinning, drawing a cross-section of an eight-storey house in the dirt around her feet. Aram and Mrs Macbay watched as she decked the interior with chandeliers, televisions, turned-on taps, brimming fridges. Inside were all kinds of beasts – winged horses, giant hares, hairless cats – but not a single person.

Mrs Macbay did not seem impressed by Lili's flitting from feeling to feeling. Actually, she seemed quite concerned. Her forehead, smooth before, was now deeply creased. Is someone at home intimidating you? she asked Lili.

Lili played with the hem of her linen shirt. A strand of its herringbone had started to come loose. No one has ever asked me that, she said. She pulled the thread until it was as long as her ring finger.

You're my daughter's age. If anyone did anything to hurt her, I would stuff their mouth with nettles.

Aram looked up to see if Mrs Macbay was laughing, but she appeared to be quite serious. He needed to dead-end that particular road. Nettles seemed like a nasty lunch. He said, Lili, we want what's best for you. If you tell us the truth, we will go to great lengths to protect you. You have our word on that.

Lili, very quickly, started talking. Muireall had started to bring round men from the Salmon Company, grimy ones who carried lice and bugs and fleas into the house, making the women's beds itchy. Muireall didn't like men, but she kissed them with tongue in the library, sometimes when Lili was in there trying to read or play sgàilich. Almost nightly, Muireall would call Grace fat, too stout to float in saltwater. Just a few weeks before, Grace had made a noose with a belt that no longer fitted her and tried to hang herself from the rafters of the goat barn.

Right after Euna left, Lili explained, Grace had turned horrible, too. She said very mean things to Lili. Now she was on bed rest, Lili cooked breakfast and supper for her and brought it up on a tray, and Grace rarely showed gratitude. In fact, she would often take the chilli marmalade or walnut biscuits and throw them at Lili. Sometimes she even made Lili swallow the tincture Muireall had prescribed to make Grace less morbid, with its essences of gorse, larch, and mustard. The tincture inevitably got Lili sick; her stomach was sensitive to acid. But she forgave Grace because the woman was so wretched inside, and it was making her act like a twat.

Let's try not to use that language, child, Mrs Macbay said. Then she softened her tone. I can't believe this is happening in our town.

Lili looked trodden. Muireall was right, she said. She told me no one would believe my stories. She crammed her mouth with an overly ripe banana that had fallen on the ground by her feet. She put its blackish peel on her head as a little bonnet. With her huge, gloomy eyes and her mouth full of pulp, she looked odd, adorable. Aram wanted to hug her.

Of course I believe you, Mrs Macbay said. You've suffered so much. I just can't imagine that it was happening nearby, and I didn't do anything to stop it.

Lili asked, Do you really believe me? Mush was pushing through the gap between her lips. Sorry, I'm being rude. Do you want some banana?

I'm quite all right, Mrs Macbay said. But thank you, that is very sweet.

The word *sweet* made Aram squirm. He'd already forced himself to sit with Aileen after her friction with Carson. He couldn't gag down all this touchy talk without some roughage. A few shallow words, a bit of bran. He watched Lili eat. Maybe she was thinking precisely the same thought he was, in her own literal way.

Well, Aram said, it sounds like you've got this under control, Mrs Macbay. Lili, would you consider staying at the church for a while, until things are safer at home? I'm hoping to do the same.

Lili did not look up. Now, on the back of one of her winged horses, she traced the figure of a young girl. The girl was ducking so that, as they flew, she did not hit her head on a low-hanging chandelier. No, she said. I'm not like Euna. I won't run away. Grace needs me.

But don't you want to be happy?

No, she said. I mean, I don't think about it too much. But I do know that Euna is a coward and I am a very, very brave girl.

Lili stood up and took the creel from Mrs Macbay. As she did, the banana peel fell from her head onto the ground beside her sneaker, and she came close to comically slipping on it. Thank you so much for these, she said to Mrs Macbay. See ya, Aram.

Come by if you need anything at all, Mrs Macbay called out, as Lili skipped off toward the door.

The girl turned back for a brief moment. Thank you, she said. She pointed to the ground where she had been drawing. Save my house for next time! I don't have any paper left where I live.

Mrs Macbay smiled with hermetic lips, as one does when her heart is a bit broken. Yes, she said, I will be glad to do that. Lili gleamed. She angled herself against the forcing-house door and pushed and pushed. The damp warmth had sealed it tightly, but when her body was well canted, its slant enough to work against the pushback, she managed to get out.

Aram could sense that Mrs Macbay was going to press him to tell her everything he knew about Lili, to fit what she had just seen into a larger context. He hated nothing more than to talk about a person when they had just left the room – it made him feel uncomfortable, and a bit cruel. This may be rude of me, he said hastily, to avoid that particular line of questioning, but I'm looking for a place to stay for a few weeks. Do you think I could sleep in the church basement?

You're welcome to stay, she said. But I insist you sleep in the house with us. We have a guest room, and my husband will even groom you to preach, if you like.

What Aram wanted was a hideaway. Peace and quiet, penetralia, a place where he could read and pray when the mood consumed him. But he reached down into himself and found the other Aram, the one who was only alive on docks laden with people, in flings with new womenfolk. That Aram, since mislaid, would have taken Mrs Macbay's offer without thought. Thank you, he said.

Welcome to the family, Mrs Macbay said. She took Aram by the hand and led him down the aisle of the forcing house, past mandevillas, majesty palms, flame trees, trimmed and partitioned moss. We're sure glad to have you.

Together they leaned themselves against the door until it gave way. No rain was falling, but Aram felt as if he were being submerged in ice-water. Air was not often so cold, so much like the whale-road. He could hardly wait to be in the house. They walked quickly over the heather and the earthwork, then into the cool interior, full of folk art and Shetland lace. Aram's first thought was of his paternal grandmother, though he had never met her or heard mention of her in his father's stories. Then he thought of an old figure his father used to spin into lore about the weather and water – a woman who had been killed, skyclad. Aram could not remember her name. He did not know why these women had occurred to him right then. It was as if the house had a consciousness and he had simply slipped into it.

Aileen came to the entryway to welcome them, holding slippers for her mother and a smoking jacket for Aram. He accepted the jacket, and once its cool silk was on him he perked into his body. So silked, so skinned, he saw how much space he was taking up. He had dragged in some bindweed on his boots and now he knelt to collect it. Weeds did not belong in the house. Then, of course, he was left holding that dirt, those roots, with no place to set them down.

III

WITHIN A FEW days of welcoming Aram into their home, the Macbays had assigned him a central role in the function of the church. He was to lay the groundwork for worship: to mop the sanctuary, distribute the hymnals, stock the tea cabinet in the basement, adjust the height of the pulpit based on who was set to deliver that week's sermon. Today, Sunday, he raised it to his own six feet. The Macbays had heard word of the suffering inflicted on those confined at Dungavel, and though that may have dismayed them before, with Aram temporarily in their family, their care had a stronger tenor. The problem of detention, to them, had a new immediacy, and so they had invited him to share his experiences with the congregation. He had said yes, hoping the words might feel better on the outside.

It was seven in the morning now, and worship began weekly at nine thirty. He had always found the best remedy for tension to be exhaustion, especially as an outcome of labour, so he set to work early. He retrieved an old, hand-crafted broom from Minister Macbay's office. He had learned from Mrs Macbay that, in Celtic custom, brooms held firm import – once, to sweep was not simply to clean, but to demarcate the borders of a home, to set a boundary between domestic and wild. When families lived together on dirt floors, they needed to sweep them several times a day, to keep the space looking liveable. The importance of that act was not lost on Aram, who had survived in a stone castle, who had squatted just recently in an abandoned hut.

So Aram set about his duties. He was amazed by the range of debris that had ended up on the ground, shards of flame shells, even loch lettuce. The old broom was nearly thread-bare, its horsehairs gone hard and unruly. He had to reach around corners, under pews, with both care and force. He found the best way to offset the broom's resistance, and he managed, ultimately, to present the room as a sanctuary again. Looking down the aisle between the pews, he admired its absence of herbs, dust, dead insects.

He sat in the front pew and looked up at the pulpit, settled imposingly in the middle of the raised stage. Behind the podium, the pipes of an organ radiated upwards in a sacred kind of starburst. On either side, the walls were adorned with scenes hand-stitched on felt banners, one of the nativity and the other of Jesus crucified, long, bloodied nails hammered through both of his hands. Aram looked from one to the other, the baby brought into the world without sin, then turned into man, persecuted, treated as a heretic. That arc, Aram knew. That arc, many knew, to some degree. So Aram had found the small mirror in which other congregants might see themselves, even given they had never been incarcerated. He was clear then on what he would say later that morning, after Minister Macbay had warmed the pulpit and called him forth, to cast his own sacred starburst.

An hour or so later, as Aram was placing a hymnal in the back of each pew, he heard a child's voice calling into the sanctuary. At first, he thought he was imagining the sound, having studied the felted nativity scene for too long. But when the voice came again, it was distinctly real. Hello? the boy said.

Aram turned. All the tension he had banished from his body with the broom returned then, tenfold. A young child was there, green-eyed, pigeon-toed, but he was not alone. He was holding the hands of two women. One was unfamiliar to Aram, but the other was unmistakable, as known as breath.

Euna? he asked, though it was not a question. He had simply lost all language beyond her name.

She was there, not phantom but true flesh. She wore a long-sleeved gauze dress, despite December. No gloves, no jacket, just a guitar on her back. One earring was pearl, the other misplaced. She was, of course, lovelier than she had been at eighteen. The bones beneath her face had sharpened slightly, just enough to make her seem settled in her skin. She stood tall, cocksure.

You're here, she said. She let go of the child's hand and hurried toward Aram.

In the castle, time had often come unfastened. It had moved in loops, moments appearing again and again; or sometimes drifting so they seemed interminable, untethered to any clock. But that morning Euna managed to unfasten it in an entirely new way. Suddenly, events made no sense to him. He was a lonely young boy at sea, grabbing brown crabs for his mother, and he was an elderly man, burying a casket in the Pullhair boneyard, and he was a forebear a thousand years before, a hero saving his beloved from a town dank with plague. Time was not floating, nor repeating. It was everywhere.

Euna had at some point, in the swimming of time, arrived by Aram's side. He slid down the pew to make room, and she sat down beside him. She turned her body toward his and put her hands, her soft, hard musician's hands, on his face. To be touched like that...

You look wonderful, she said.

Good, he told her. And what he meant was, Good, because I feel as if the whole world's history just landed on my head.

I didn't expect to see you, she said. She moved her hands to her lap.

Aram gestured to a stained-glass window above them, the Lord rendered in red and gold. He must have brought us together, he said.

Euna scoffed at this, not hostilely, but noticeably, at least to Aram. She said, This is my first time coming home.

The way that word lingered on Euna's tongue. Aram wished time would come unspooled again so he could stay there, living in the echo of Euna's *home*. But it had gone linear, and he was aware of her, there, waiting for him to speak. He tried to say so many things at once they dammed his mouth; from that logjam came only silence.

Behind them he could hear the other two talking. The child was asking, Who is that? and the woman was replying, not unkindly, Someone your mother used to know.

He leaned in close to Euna. He did not want her to hear the others' conversation, in case she placed any words like *used to*. As he neared her, he noticed the gooseflesh on the back of her neck, her high arms. You must be cold, he said.

She told him she was fine. She sloughed off her guitar strap, a length of velvet with bronze stitching, and rested the instrument on the pew beside her. It made a mild sound as she set it down, the strings softly ringing. Relieved of her guitar, she moved into Aram's body. He cloaked her shoulders with his arm. At first he could feel her faintly shivering, and then she settled into his warmth, his fisherman's sweater.

After a few minutes sitting like this – it was so easy, not talking, it was so much simpler just to touch – the other woman came to interrupt them, the little boy in tow. They sat on the pew in front of Aram and Euna's, sideways, so they were looking directly at them.

Hello, the woman said, extending her hand toward Aram. I'm Muireall.

He shook her offered hand. I'm Aram, he said. You may have heard about me.

Muireall squinted for a moment, making a show of thinking. Not ringing a bell, she said. He hoped desperately that she was teasing him.

Euna laughed. That'll take you down a peg, she said to Aram.

The boy started to squirm. He clambered onto his knees, facing Euna. And this is Lachlan Iain, Muireall said. The boy was maybe four years old, redheaded, with cool gold skin. As soon as he heard his name, he dropped his head below the pew. He peeked out above the wood backrest as if a loch creature, lurking.

He's shy, Euna said.

Glad to have you here, Lachlan Iain, Aram said. I've been looking forward to meeting you for a long time.

The boy showed his face up to the tip of his nose.

By the way, Euna said, she was messing with you. Of course she knows who you are, bloody amadan. Having learned that word in the castle, Aram knew Euna was calling him an idiot.

Actually, Muireall added, I have a few things to say to you. And they're not all child-friendly.

This, he had expected. Actually, he was thrilled to know Euna's dearest friends were angry with him. Anger was alive. And so, sensitive, submissive. Excellent, he said, not at the anger, but at the image of them on the tour bus, saying *Aram*. Whenever the time is right, I'm all ears.

Muireall squinted again. She made her suspicion plain. Now the boy, his mouth still behind the pew, repeated, Bloody amadan.

Looks like someone inherited your dirty mouth, Aram said.

This gave them all pause. They knew the boy had not inherited anything from Euna, at least not directly. Unspoken, this shared knowledge settled as silt over their conversation. Are you here for the service? Aram asked.

Euna looked panicked. Is it Sunday?

Aram nodded. I'm actually preaching shortly. Would you stay and listen, Euna? It might explain a few things.

Muireall spat into her hands and started to pat down Lachlan Iain's hair, shaping a clean centre parting. When his hair was perfectly arranged, fit for any church service, Muireall reached into a leather duffel bag she had been carrying over her shoulder. In it was a tasselled, hooded tunic, a silk work of art. She offered the garment to Euna, who luxuriated in its folds, looking royal.

Thank you for the invite, Euna said. But I don't think it's a good idea.

Please, Aram said. Don't go away.

Euna straightened out of Aram's hold. She tucked in the corners of her lips, which she did when she was considering something deeply. Knowing Euna, she thought she was unreadable, but he saw her more attentively than he did any other part of this world. He remembered her tells.

Lachlan Iain said, Màthair, you promised.

Muireall said, Hush, honey. Give her a moment.

You said I don't have to go to church. You said I was a Hammer.

Aram was intrigued. This was the light spilling from under his old lover's door, a hint at the intimate. What's that? he asked the child.

Lachlan Iain began to sing an unusual refrain. *A chrostag! Today I was so mad at my màthair! A chrostag!* Muireall turned the boy around so he was seated tidily on his behind. It's okay, little one, she said. She rubbed his back to calm him.

Aram wanted to hear more from Lachlan Iain, but he did not want to agitate either woman by egging the boy on, so he kept quiet. He placed one hand finely on Euna's knee and stroked the peak of the bone, waiting patiently while she considered his invitation. He had waited so many years, there was no need to rush her now.

At length, Euna said, We'll sit at the back.

Aram's joy was sudden and forceful. He said, without knowing he was going to say it, I missed you.

She looked as if she wanted to respond. Instead, in silence, she strapped the guitar to her back. Bumping his knees, she rushed into the aisle, Muireall and Lachlan Iain following closely behind. Sure enough, they all settled in the final pew, the boy between the two women. Euna pulled the tunic hood well over her intricately braided hair, far enough to cover her identity. Aram wished she would come out of hiding. But then, it was because of him that she had to confine herself, to curtain her beautiful eyes, even on the occasion of her homecoming.

*

Half an hour later, Aram stood at the church entrance with Minister Macbay, welcoming a gentle trickle of congregants. He tried not to think of Euna, of the little family unit in the final pew. Moths were flitting in his stomach. He was nervous because he did not feel inspired, and he believed a preacher could only speak from a place of divine vision. Some days stirred the holiness in him. But now his sense of sàimh, of ascendance, was gone – by being there, red-blooded and human, Euna had grounded him. He could not raise himself to the floating place, parcel of sense and essence, where words moved through him by a greater spirit's hand. Around Euna, the world was made of matter, and that was a world Aram could not leave, not even for the length of a sermon.

Good morning, Aram, said a woman with blue-tinged hair, one of the oldest villagers.

Well, good morning, he said. He was flattered that someone knew his name. Welcome to worship.

Thank you, the woman said. And will you be speaking to us today?

Yes, ma'am, he said.

The elderly woman took both of Aram's hands into hers, which were frosted, unbending. She looked up at him through cataracts, a creamy film over her pale eyes. It occurred to him then that he was not the only one to ever live. This woman had walked the earth for a mythically long time, had almost certainly lost someone she treasured, maybe not a Euna, but someone. I don't hear too well, she said. But if you feel it, I will, too.

Aram cupped his hands around hers, trying to offer some relief, to release her fingers from their tight fate. Though the fingers remained rigid, he did feel an energy move between him and the elderly woman, a gentle alleluia. He was no longer so afraid. He believed in unassuming saints. The congregation having mostly arrived by then, Minister Macbay invited Aram to follow him onto the raised stage. Minister Macbay was meant to deliver his sermon before Aram's, but he changed the order. He must have noticed the moment between the elderly woman and Aram, the confidence it had revealed in him. After the prelude, the processional, and the opening hymn – 'Nations that long in darkness walked' – Minister Macbay offered a short reading from Job, 19:26–27.

> [26]And after my skin has been destroyed,
> yet in my flesh I will see God;
> [27]I myself will see him
> with my own eyes – I, and not another.
> How my heart yearns with me.

He could not have known that Aram had pored over those verses in the castle. Watching the minister from a folding chair near the crucifixion mural, Aram felt wounds open that he thought had closed for good. His loneliness was vast and swift, and it brought him to a place of great vulnerability, which on a day like today would have to double for that inspired, floating state. Minister Macbay introduced Aram to the congregation. I bet you've noticed this handsome fellow around town, he said. He is our friend Aram, our son, really, and he will share a few words about his life that we may do well to hear.

Aram walked to the pulpit. Minister Macbay enfolded him in his enormous form before sitting in the seat Aram had vacated. Aram stood, straight-backed, before the congregation. He was relieved to see Euna, Lachlan Iain, and Muireall, still in the final pew. He noticed Aileen on the other side, wedged between Carson and Mrs Macbay, who was also the organist and director of the church choir. Mrs Macbay beamed her reassurance at Aram. Even in this town, where it seemed any moment a shrub could reveal itself to be a sleeping sheep, or a lovely old farmhouse a site of confinement and cruelty, he could always trust her sincerity.

I want to talk to you today, he said, about the maidenhair tree. He tried to project, hoping the elderly woman whose hands he had held would somehow be able to hear him, or at least feel the vibrations of his voice.

Mrs Macbay did not lose her smile, though his statement may have seemed random. He continued, It's sometimes known as Ginkgo, from a misspelling of the Japanese words for *silver apricot*. A beautiful species called Ginkgo gardneri grew here in the Paleocene of Scotland, sixty million years ago.

Someone had brought a cough into the sanctuary. Was it the owner of the guest house, or maybe the herbalist rumoured to live in a home of uncaged rabbits? Someone, anyway, was coughing, and for a moment Aram was thrown. He could see the villagers in front of him losing their concentration. He began again, more assertively, raising his words as high as the roof beams.

I learned about this unusual tree, he said, while I was in prison. At that, everyone returned their focus to him. A man in the front row waved his hand as if to encourage Aram to continue on this route, rather than with the maidenhair.

Aram said, And you might be interested to learn that there is only one living Ginkgo species, biloba. The others have gone extinct because of their unusually slow rate of evolution. The maidenhair tree evolved in an era before flowering plants, but when those came along, they adapted better to disturbed environments and gradually replaced the many types of Ginkgo.

There is a reason I mention this particular tree, here in Pullhair, in your beautiful church, he said. The room was quiet. The cougher had stopped coughing. The waver had stopped waving.

It was very kind of Minister Macbay to invite me to speak, he said. But now I'm here, I don't know what more to say. He looked from face to face. He wanted to share more of his thoughts on evolution, about the dangers of stagnation, really, but in that moment he realized he was still speaking to them from a distance. And no one wanted to have their ways dressed down by a guest, a non-member – he had seen how poorly that worked on his visit to Gainntir.

Aram was ready to get off the stage, or at least stop talking. He feared the judgement not of God but of the congregation. But he might never have Euna's attention again, so he could not be silent until he had addressed her. He said, While on the inside, I had one special visitor. He hesitated, wanting to name Euna, but not wanting to out her to the villagers. If I could do one thing differently, it would be to tell her how much it meant to me that she came. I know she walked away from her haven.

He was quiet for a full moment. He wanted to gesture the choir in, to hide him as Euna's hood hid her, but he did not. He stood exposed in the silence. At last, Mrs Macbay stood and faced the five-boy choir. She lifted her hands in the air, and the boys breathed in together, then began to sing 'Angels we have heard on high'. He was grateful for their voices, blanketing his talk, as wildflowers used to blanket the ground in this part of the Outer Hebrides. There were holes in their song, too, patches unreached by the flowers, but those were barely perceptible among such cream and bloom.

He glanced at the family in the final row while the boys forged ahead with their song. Euna was still invisible beneath the tunic, while beside her, Muireall had a slight and calming smile on her face. Lachlan Iain was standing on the pew, drumming his torso in a style Aram related to his own father, playing the bodhrán.

When the song was finished, Mrs Macbay sat down and motioned for the choir to do the same. Again, Minister Macbay and Aram switched positions, the minister behind the pulpit and Aram in his seat on the side of the stage. As they passed one another, Minister Macbay looked at Aram with eyes so blue they seemed stolen from a man of the Minch. He whispered, You did well, son.

The rest of the service passed in a blur, the benediction, the lighting of the Christ candle, the Communion. Before Aram knew it, they were all joining together in their final hymn, 'There is a happy land'. He remembered this same song from when the congregation was more full-bodied, its sounds wider. But today its strength was in its starkness. How gorgeous it was to pick out individual voices warbling, Come to that happy land, come, come away;/Why will you doubting stand, why still delay?

After, Minister Macbay invited everyone to the basement for fellowship. Aram considered bolting right then, but he was too great with gratitude toward Minister Macbay and indeed toward the whole congregation, who had listened to his attempt to communicate, to offer a sermon. So he went to the basement with everyone else. Everyone, that is, except Euna, who had evidently ducked out of the building after the service.

He first saw Lachlan Iain, stack of oatcakes in hand, and Muireall. They were meeting Carson and the three Macbays, and the exchange seemed simple and harmonious. Of course it was not Lachlan Iain's first time meeting Aileen, but either he had been young enough then to avoid forming memories of her, or he had already learned the fine art of affectation. Aram hoped it was the former.

Minister Macbay knelt and kissed the boy on both of his freckled cheeks. And who is this handsome child? he asked.

His mother used to live here years ago, Aileen said. Euna and I were quite close for a while.

And where is Euna today? Mrs Macbay asked.

She'll join us later, Muireall said. She just wanted to take a spin around her old hometown.

Funny, Minister Macbay said. I don't remember her at all. I thought I knew everyone in Pullhair.

Mrs Macbay knelt by the child. It's wonderful to meet you, she said. And then, looking up at Muireall, We're praying Aileen gives us a grandchild of our own one of these days.

Muireall smiled her same consoling smile, while Carson left to collect a plateful of black cookies. Aram took that as his opportunity to enter the conversation. He came into the circle, hand extended, and even Lachlan Iain shook it.

Beautiful words, Muireall said.

Thank you, he said. Sincerely.

We're happy to have you here, Minister Macbay told Aram. Breathing new life into the congregation.

Muireall leaned in and spoke to him, semi-privately, of course knowing their exchange was audible to the others. He was relieved when she told him Euna had gone onto the heath – despite the strange weather, he preferred the air out there to that of this basement, gummy, dense.

Minister Macbay asked, Do you know this Euna, son?

I do, Aram said. I did.

The minister said, winking, We'll save you some shortbread.

Aram nodded and said his goodbyes as politely as he could. In his flight from the basement, he took the stairs two at a time. He hurried through the side door onto the heath. A fine mist had started to settle on the heather and low sedges, forming a sheer film, as if gossamer. Aram climbed over small hills, looking for her, into a stone enclave, looking for her. Euna had in that short time gone a long distance. Then he saw it, a small teardrop in the grass, her pearl earring. Whether it was the missing one or the one he had seen, hours earlier, clinging to her ear, he could not know. He stopped to pick it up, tiny and wet, delicate. He brushed the damp dirt away, polishing the treasure with his thumb.

No more than a hundred metres from him, on turf somehow both dead and overgrown, he saw Euna lying on her stomach. The tunic was tented over her head, skin only showing on her fingers, adorned with runic rings, and her ankles, poking out from under her gauzy dress. She gave the impression she was lifeless. Aram cantered to her. The ground was cold, a punishment even through his soles. From up close, he could see the velvet tunic lifting, ever so gently, when she breathed.

He lay down flat beside her, near enough that he was touching her least finger with his. He felt a rounded shape pushing into his spine and reached under his back to recoup an apple, bruised though whole in his back arch. He was, after fellowship, too full to eat the fruit, but he remembered an old method of divination his mother had taught him – he twisted the stem in his hand, reciting the alphabet, until it gave way. *E.* He did not put stock in that kind of prophecy, and yet.

Euna rolled over at the sound of the stem separating from the fruit. Her cheekbones caught what light leaked through the grey sky. What are you doing? she asked.

Just an old game my mother taught me.

I know it, Euna said. She was flushed now. Cool, reticent Euna, icon of control, betrayed by her own face.

Have you played? he asked, moving his least finger on top of hers.

A few times, she said. After you and I met. I was locked in the goatshed most days. Grace would bring me apples.

Aram did not want to open any wounds that Euna had taken care to heal. So, sensing it had been a place of pain, he tiptoed away from the goatshed. What did you do with the apples? he asked.

You'll think it's silly, she said. But there are a hundred ways to read the future with an apple. This was before I got your postcard, of course.

This was teenage Euna talking. For a precious moment, her feelings were plain as primary colours, and for once she allowed him to see them. I think that's lovely, he said. I'm flattered.

At that, Euna hardened. Her flush had gone deep, the blood now so near to the surface. I wasn't trying to flatter you, she said.

He reached over and carefully clipped the pearl earring he had found onto her lobe. It was the absent piece. Now she had a set.

Her interest in him was indistinct.

Her lips were blue from cold.

Their son was in the holy house, an acre away.

There were many sound reasons for him not to kiss her, and only one reason for it – his one generative reason, over-riding all else, as if a sea change. When he told others that God gave him reason to wake up in the morning, was this not what he meant? Was he not talking about love, or more precisely, agape?

He pressed his red to her blue. All his thoughts stopped and for a spell he lived through her lips. They were a portal to a world in which grass still grew greenly, and gannets still flew overhead, in the right season. One hand on his chest and the other in his hair, Euna bonded him to her body, the land.

The mist around them had turned to snow, burned grass to fresh meadow. All the days of deprivation, not only his, but his mother's, his father's, his beloved Euna's, seemed to have converged in this vital end. All this time he had carried a flame for her, she had kept hers fuelled, too.

Aram, he heard. He thought at first the voice was coming from Euna. But no, it sounded furious, and Euna was anything but furious right now, her gaze gentle as the mist. How could you do this? the voice asked. Then he saw Aileen, full of a separate kind of flame, hustling up the tall hill.

We cooked for you, she was yelling. We gave you your own bedroom. You disgusting dìol-déirce.

Euna scampered away from Aram and curled into a stone, the tunic over her head again. Aram sat up, attempting to face the harm he had done head on, though he was at the same time dreaming of the warm portal. Aileen had tears in her eyes. Snow on her lashes enhanced their shine. She went over to stone-small Euna and removed her hood. Why are you acting as if you don't know me? she asked. Even in Aram's state of enchantment, in which all edges seemed so smooth and conforming, in which the hills could well have dissolved into level meadow, her tone was hard with sadness.

Euna looked at Aileen and then away from her, at her own runic rings, the bare and tapered ends of her legs.

The camper van, the library, Aileen said. She crouched in the bell heather beside Euna, thumbing the filigreed hem of her tunic. The way we slept every night.

I shouldn't have come home, Euna said, vacantly, from the same lips Aram had just been kissing.

Aram wondered about the legitimacy of Aileen's interest in Euna. He wondered if, in part, this performance was for his benefit. He was troubled by the thought – surely Aileen was not so mercenary. Maybe this thought was his way of safe-guarding his love for Euna, by making sure it was unusual, a sentiment unshared by any others.

Aileen said, Aram, you aren't supposed to touch her any more.

Aram was still planted on the ground he had been sharing with Euna. He peered down into the frosted clover and saw her body's imprints, the troughs of her thighs, the stabs of her elbows. He said to Aileen, I didn't realize you had made rules.

At that word, Euna looked up with a start, returning her full attention to the conversation. She seemed unsettled. Having glimpsed Gainntir, its ugly, strangling rigidity, he was not surprised by her response. He wished he had thought of its impact before he used the term. Aileen said to him, Kindly keep quiet. You've hurt her enough.

Aram chafed the scruff under his chin. He was exasper-ated. He wanted to place all his focus on Euna, on darning the holes between them, and instead he had to contend with Aileen, turned bitterly backward, lording the past over him. Are you going to be like this forever? he asked Aileen.

You expect to be forgiven so soon, Aileen said.

So soon? he asked. I've done a lot of time.

Aileen peered from side to side, the way a trapped animal sometimes does, in search of an escape route. Euna offered one instead. She started to whimper from the cold. She was so self-contained it was possible, sometimes, to neglect even her essential needs. But the fact was, she had been out on the heath, nearly bare against the rudiments of winter, for the better part of an hour. Her skin had been drinking all that cold, and now her cheeks were going greyish, her lips scaling as if belonging to a fish.

We need to get her home, Aram said. I'll carry her.

You'd like that, I'm sure, Aileen said.

Aram felt his anger mounting at this tiny, petty child posing as an adult woman. He saw himself slapping her, her falling to her knees, subservient in the wild grass. He pictured the blush on her face, the chastised look in her wide, suddenly powerless eyes. But he held back, and without much work. He had learned along the way to control himself. He had not known this until Aileen had tested his bounds.

We both want the same thing, Aram said to her, as gently as he could. We both want Euna to be safe. Please, let me carry her.

Euna swallowed with some effort, forcing her trachea down its iced column. Yes, she said. Yes.

Fine, Aileen said. Take her.

Thank you, Aileen. I know that wasn't easy to say.

Hurry up, she said.

Aram stripped his fisherman's sweater and drew it down over the high neckline of Euna's tunic. To see her nuzzle into its folds, pull the sleeves to cover her slight, trembling wrists, filled him with affection and, in some muted way, hope. He knelt beside her and asked permission to lift her. She granted it, and he scooped her into his arms, now covered only with a long-sleeved jersey.

You know, Aileen said to him, this doesn't make you some hero.

I know, he said. Believe me, I know.

This tempered Aileen a small bit. She nodded to him, then trotted off toward the church. Clearly, the stress was affecting her deeply. When Aram climbed from his knees to his feet, it was with great, prayerful attention, as if ready for the final, most vital hymn.

IV

A FEW WEEKS had passed since Euna's homecoming, since the scene on the heath and its attendant emotional hangover. After that morning, Aileen had grown gradually withdrawn, while Euna, who had made a full recovery from her bone-chill, tried in brave and unobtrusive ways to integrate herself into the community. She, Muireall, and Lachlan Iain had come for meals at the Macbays' on several occasions, and they had helped to bake oatcakes for fellowship. Muireall had even taken little Lachlan Iain to the home full of uncaged rabbits, where he had brushed their long ears and washed their dusted tails back to their original white.

Then, just like that, it was Christmas. For Aram, the holiday had always seemed narrow. When he was a boy on the boat, his mother would pick a day at random and say, Wake up, son, it's Christmas! They would pray together for a life of lovelier things, plush red seats at the cinema, abundant pot roasts, recordings of the most sublime operas. Then they would embrace, eat some scallops, and return to the repetitive, if peculiar, reality of their era at sea. And that would be that, until the next year.

Only at the castle had Aram realized that Christmas, like many other spiritual holidays, was not narrow at all. It was wide, alive; it was a day, for some people, that made further days possible. But he had never been around enough people, let alone enough people of one shared faith, to understand what it meant for a room – or a detention centre, or a village – full of them to observe a holy day together. The sense it fostered was close to sàimh, though of course mightier, more formidable, held as it was not by one person but by many.

Today, everyone in Pullhair had been invited to a Christmas potluck. Aram had been asked to bring salmon in whatever form he pleased. He chose to bring jerky, as then he could do all the preparation beforehand, reducing the margin of error. He had vowed to never make a mistake again, no matter how minor. This was one of many ways he was pressing himself to repent.

Mrs Macbay had invited the women from Gainntir to the potluck, and according to her, they were planning to come. She had extended the invite through Lili, who had come to visit her at the glasshouse the week before. Aram's strategy for the potluck was fairly simple. He would stay invisible as much as he could, unless a situation arose in which he needed to intervene to protect someone he loved.

Aram tidied himself in his bedroom mirror, shaved with a straight edge, and tied his bow tight as a noose. His mother, rest her soul, would have told him he looked handsome.

He was still living in the blackhouse, and quite comfortably. A tart smell was now rising from its kitchen. Even nearly destitute residents gave generously to the church collection every week, and a significant portion of that pool, Aram had been told, went to importing food for this annual Christmas feast – saffron from Iran, lavender from France, cocoa from the Ivory Coast. At first, Aram had been sceptical of the collection, until he moved in with the Macbays and saw that they were, as promised, holding the money for this sole purpose. They lived within their humble means and would never have dreamed of skimming from the top.

Dressed, Aram went into the kitchen. Mrs Macbay was curved over the stove, stirring. She turned briefly to him. Don't you look handsome, she said.

He smiled. Mrs Macbay was wearing a garland of hazel and dried bluebells over a festive wave in her hair. She looked superb, in a sort of modest, homespun way, and he basked for a moment in that floral visual, in the kitchen's rising, ripened scent. Thank you, he said. Merry Christmas.

To you, too, she said. Try this.

She fed him from her long wooden spoon. He was not sure he liked the texture, buttons of fruit in such a dense seep, but the slightly burned sugar touched a tender place inside. His mother's seaberry preserves, cooked in a skillet on the heat of the boat deck, had that same fluorescent taste. He felt so close to Mrs Macbay then, a spoon's length away. It's delicious, he said.

Glad you like it, she said. Have you had cranberry sauce before?

Never, he said. Though it tastes very familiar.

She looked faintly confused, but she kept her *Merry Christmas* smile constant. The sureness of her reactions always made Aram feel safe, the way he had once felt safe, as a fish farmer, with the succession of seasons. Aram kissed her gently on the cheek, an act he had learned over time to separate from any sexual subtext, and she patted him on his lapel.

He went into the adjoined living room and found Minister Macbay there, crammed into his wing chair, drawing on a sketchpad.

Merry Christmas, Aram said.

Minister Macbay did not glance up from his sketch. His expression was distant. Aram walked near to him and peered over his shoulder. Usually, drawing was the minister's private enterprise, and he got short and even petulant when someone asked him to let them look. Today, maybe cheered by the smell of cream buns rising, or by the sun-sliver over Pullhair after weeks of fair hoar, he showed Aram the page without hesitation. For some reason, Aram had expected crude, rudimentary work, but here was an intricate metropolis, crammed with chrome and fibreglass. In this imagined city, everyone wore tartans, sporrans, garters, clan badges, but with unusual adornments: crescent moon-shaped masks, velvet chokers, elbow-length gabardine gloves. The linework was so fine, so lovingly done, it made Aram somehow homesick. I wish we lived there, he said to Minister Macbay.

The minister smiled. I call this one Eden.

Where is it supposed to be? Aram asked.

If I knew, Minister Macbay said, I would move there tomorrow.

It may have been a naïve assumption, but he had always believed the minister loved Pullhair, worshipped its knolls and dells and even its quirky, somewhat diminished community. That thought had been a comfort, a root system in otherwise unsettled soil, and to have it negated now made him feel troubled, almost abandoned. Can I ask, then, he said to Minister Macbay, what keeps you here?

The minister tapped the pen against his chest for a moment, considering the question. I've always dreamed of living in a larger city, he said. London, Glasgow. I have a very solid life here. But I guess I never burned through that desire.

He went back to drawing, as if he had not just revealed a profound chasm to Aram. He shaded the windows on the far side of a high-rise, where the sun could not reach. It's funny, Aram said to him. I always envied people who had the choice to stay in one place.

The minister set his pen down, holding the sketchpad even so it would not roll onto the carpet. You know, he said, that's not lost on me. I think about the Highland Clearances, how badly some of those tenants must have wanted to stay.

Aram perched on the wing of Minister Macbay's chair, knowing it was a precarious position to be in, and looked more closely at the drawing. He saw, in the lower left-hand corner, perfectly calligraphed Gaelic: *O mo dhùthaich 's tu th'air m'aire*, or, *Oh, my country is on my mind*. Below such a modern, itinerant image, the words were heavy with history, as if stones in a boneyard. They bore down on Aram's heart.

Aram did what he always did when unsure of his own language, and he quoted the Gospel, this time according to Luke. He said to them, 'Wherever the body is, there will be eagles gathered together.'

Yes, Minister Macbay said. Though in this corner of the world, it's more like seagulls.

Aram laughed, not because it was that funny, but because it felt good to release such a carefree sound. Mrs Macbay came into the living room holding two unnaturally coloured jellied salads, one orange, one deep pink. She asked for their

233

help carrying them to the church basement. Minister Macbay seemed deflated, desperate as he was to keep drawing. He would clearly have chosen his illustrated world over his inherited one, today, given the opportunity. But he did not protest, nor did he make his wife feel sheepish about asking this reasonable favour. He took both salads from her, and they waited for Aram to collect his container of salmon jerky from the kitchen.

Thank you, Mrs Macbay said, and rested her head on her husband's shoulder for a spell. He kissed the wave in her hair. Then she went into the living room and returned the sketchbook to its distinct place in their heirloom cabinet.

For you, mo mhilseag, anything, he said. And the glimmer in his blue eyes told Aram he was being sincere.

Jerky in hand, Aram followed Minister Macbay to the church. Both men walked with faintly heavy heels. In the basement, they pushed together a dozen card tables and placed on each a bramble-and-blackcurrant centrepiece, tatted lace napkins, tall rush candles. At Minister Macbay's request, Aram set each place with cutlery and a Christmas cracker. Hidden in each cracker, he explained, was a paper crown, a toy, a shiny trinket, and a riddle on a strip of paper. Coming to this ritual from the outside, Aram found it endearing, if altogether strange.

Aram did not see any nametags, and he wondered about the Macbays' decision to not assign seats, considering how many wires could be crossed at this feast, and explosively. He wondered if a whit of control might be effective here, to sidestep any blow-ups. Still, he said nothing to undercut the Macbays' authority – they had been hosting this feast for decades, so surely by now they had streamlined their method.

They had done so much for Aram, and he refused to show his gratitude by questioning their common sense.

Soon the other congregants began to trickle down the stairs, armed with sides, devilled eggs, cock-a-leekie soup, bannock, cullen skink. Peppered among those familiar dishes were imported foods Aram had never seen, and though they intrigued him, he had no desire to try such alien things.

The air in the room thickened as the Gainntir women skulked down the stairs. They carried with them a chill from the fells, a hard nip of winter. As far as Aram knew, he was the only person in the congregation to have met Bad Muireall, and still the others grew palpably tense the moment she entered the space. Lili and Grace were several steps behind her, holding hands in a way that seemed less about showing affection and more about forming a physical boundary. Lili looked sweet in a pale yellow snowsuit, while Grace was covered head to toe in cotton-lined Highland lace. Whoever made the garment had cut out a small face-hole, presumably to allow Grace to breathe. Aram wondered how she manoeuvred in and out of the costume – for instance, if and when she had to use the bathroom – but then, the Gainntir women worked in shadowy ways.

Aram, Bad Muireall said, greeting him with an uncomfortably warm embrace. He wilted into her hold.

Muireall, he said. Merry Christmas.

She pulled away and stared at him. He felt confined by her glare, as if he were suddenly wearing Grace's lace getup. Thank you, she spat out.

Aram saw his error. He knew these women disdained holidays such as this one. Instead of addressing the misstep, he hurried ahead. How have you been? he asked.

Lili was invited, Bad Muireall said, by the minister's wife. She should have known we do everything together.

Aram was surprised by her response, as it answered a question he had not asked. He nodded, afraid if he spoke again he might elicit another strange, instinctive reply. At the sound of her name, Lili let go of Grace's hand and came to Aram, throwing her arms around his neck. Hi hi, she said. Everything looks so nice in here. I love the tinsel.

Thank you, he said to Lili. We have lots of good food for you, too.

Good, she said, I'm starving.

Believing her, he doubted the congregation's decision to have a huge annual feast, instead of feeding Pullhair modestly and regularly, throughout the calendar year. Would Christ himself not have done the latter? But there Aram was again, an ingrate, questioning the Macbays' expertise. Grace moved beside them then, though she still stood hushed and rigid. Through her face-hole, Aram could see lips pressed into a line, a gentle sheen in the corner of each eye. He wanted to tear the material from her face; he was suffocating just to look at her.

Is there any wine? Bad Muireall asked.

We're in a church, Aram said, then winked. Of course there is.

The Macbays kept a store of communion wine in the cellar next door. Aram knew it would be rash, even sacrilegious, to retrieve one of these bottles for Bad Muireall's consumption, especially since he knew her to be unstable, capable of any number of outbursts. He could not have explained why, but a significant part of him wanted to please her – he supposed she had that effect on many people.

Lili clicked her tongue. I don't think that's a good idea, she said.

Bad Muireall took her by the wrist and twisted it slightly to the left. Darling, she said. This is not your concern.

I apologize, Lili said. She waited limply for Bad Muireall to release her. When she finally did, Lili rolled a cramp out of her wrist and then stretched her hand toward the ceiling, toward some of the tinsel she so loved. She clawed at its furrow, the only section she was tall enough to reach, so its silver glitter came loose and rained down on her hair, her arched eyebrows. She was mesmerized, as if, having shaken free of the wrist-hold, she had willed her thoughts to a far corner of the world.

Only when Mrs Macbay went over to greet Lili did she stop playing with the tinsel. Cupping Lili's face in her hands, Mrs Macbay said, Sùileag buntàta, which Aram knew to mean *little potato*. Her adoration for the young woman was clear, and witnessing it again, he wondered why she had never run from Gainntir into Mrs Macbay's doting arms. This detail gave him a new appreciation for Euna, the dogged spirit that had driven her from the gaol she was raised in to Glasgow, then to Scandinavia, to Lebanon. Not that Aram knew where to put this new appreciation – he was brimming with it already.

Will you introduce me to your friends? Mrs Macbay asked Lili.

Lili inhaled. They're hardly my friends.

Mrs Macbay looked concerned. Lili must have noticed the change in her expression, as straight away she introduced her to Bad Muireall and Grace. When shaking Grace's hand, her eyes lingered on the lace covering her fingertips. Grace, mionag, she said. Is everything all right?

Aram expected Grace to hold her silence, but instead she said, Just don't like strangers to see me. Her voice was clipped and low-pitched. Maybe her cords had been damaged when she tried to hang herself. Aram was intrigued that all it had taken to make her speak was an invitation.

I understand, Mrs Macbay said. To be perfectly honest, I sometimes wish I had an invisibility cloak.

Bad Muireall let out a whinnying laugh Aram had never heard. To him, it sounded affected. Don't we all, she said.

Muireall, Mrs Macbay said, I think we should have a word.

Bad Muireall's affected smile morphed into a look of astonishment. She was clearly not used to others speaking to her in this manner. Aram excused himself from the conversation. Anything Mrs Macbay said, Bad Muireall would attach to Aram, and he was afraid both of receiving her wrath and of forfeiting the cool fondness she seemed to have for him. He excused himself under the guise of preparing a blessing with the minister, though in truth he was headed to the cellar to retrieve a bottle of wine for Bad Muireall.

He could not have been gone for more than five minutes. But when he returned, red in hand, it was to an almost entirely new climate. A storm, it seemed, was hovering inside the church basement. The walls were damp, as if perspiring, and the overhead lights had dimmed. Half the candles Aram and the minister had lit had since been smothered, and the soundscape of the room – before, the whirr of trivial conversation, the gentle clinking of dishes being added to the spread – had taken on a faintly higher pitch, a pale kind of noise Aram associated with the radio. But then, he could have been imagining this interior shift, as the transformation was so hard to see empirically, and he was for some reason, today, especially unable to trust his instincts.

Aram noticed that Euna, Good Muireall, Aileen, and Lachlan Iain had arrived and were loitering at the foot of the stairs, perhaps unsure where in the room they would feel most welcome. He flashed to himself in the mess hall at the castle, hovering, waiting for a wave from some gracious stranger. Then Aileen made Euna giggle, girlishly, and Aram's throat tightened. He could not stand to see them redressing their old bond, afraid Aileen would manage to turn his love against him. He needed to wrench the two of them apart, and he swore at this feast he would do just that.

Aram returned to where Bad Muireall and the others were standing beneath the now drooping tinsel. He did not offer the bottle of wine to Bad Muireall yet, since Mrs Macbay still had her confronted, and he was confident Mrs Macbay would not approve of their drinking the blood of Christ for fun. Bad Muireall's back was to Euna, and Aram wondered if Bad Muireall had seen her enter. Then Aileen made Euna belly-laugh, and at the sound, Bad Muireall whipped around. Seeing Euna, she started instantly to cry.

Eudail, she called, doubled over, my love.

Now it was clear to Aram why Bad Muireall had come to this basement, despite hating the institution above, despite fearing the congregation. And he could not say that he blamed her.

For a moment, Euna looked doelike, panicky. Though she was wearing jeans and combat boots, her guitar strapped to her chest, she hardly looked the rock star, her inner child so obvious. Lili ran to her, clinging to her waist, weeping, squealing, while Euna kissed the girl over and over on the crown of her head, still festooned with little silver shavings. Grace waved with spider fingers though, maybe overwhelmed, she kept a slight distance.

Minister Macbay moved to the middle of the basement, where a single stone column seemed to save the roof from caving. Welcome to you all, he said. And especially to those who are joining us for the first time today. We're honoured to have you here. Let's take our places now, and we can say grace.

Everyone hurried to snag seats nearest to the foods they wanted to eat. Within two minutes, each guest was tucked in to the table, even the most elderly congregants, whose appetites had apparently given them sprightly energy. To Aram's disappointment, Aileen claimed one side of Euna, Bad Muireall the other. So he assumed a place at the head of the table opposite to Minister Macbay, settling into his role as second-in-command.

He noticed that Bad Muireall was stroking the back of Euna's hand. I missed you, Bad Muireall said. As she had when Aram said precisely the same words – why he had spoken to his cridhe teòma so insipidly, he did not know, forcing on their love a language that was not limited to them – Euna remained silent. She moved her hand away from Bad Muireall's, not as an impulse, but as a slow and deliberate movement.

Would anyone like to say grace? Minister Macbay asked.

Euna stood partway, leaning by her hand-heels on the tablecloth. I would, Ministear, she said.

Brave soul, Minister Macbay said, eyes twinkling. Be our guest.

Euna thanked him. She twisted her neck toward Bad Muireall, addressing the woman with her sunken cheeks and her combed but abnormal bowl-cut with great serenity. Here's to cleanliness and godliness, she said. To electricity and to freedom. Here's to living life without fear of the strop.

Well, all right, Minister Macbay said, laughing. I was imagining something a bit more traditional.

Euna glanced briefly at the minister and said, I'm sorry. For a moment she seemed ready to sit down, avoid causing any more commotion. Then from between her teeth she said, To normal human haircuts and to not being an arsehole all the time.

Minister Macbay turned suddenly stern. His eyes, until now twinkling, were a blank and thankless blue. Enough, he said.

Head low, she cowered in her chair. Aileen kneaded her nearest shoulder. I'm very sorry, Ministear, Euna said. This is not an easy day for me.

Minister Macbay said, I understand, feudail. But in this church we all have to take responsibility for ourselves. Then he turned to Aram and said, Son, do you think you could say grace?

Aram did not want to seem as if he were undermining Euna, trying to save the room from some destruction she had caused. But the minister had asked a simple favour, and he had to comply. And so Aram – parroting a scene he had seen in films? Fenella's novels? his subconscious? – asked that everyone around the table hold hands. Grace, on his left, offered her lace-covered one, but on the other side he could not convince his son Lachlan Iain to touch him. The boy stuck his tongue out and perched on both hands. Aram did not want to draw any attention to his son's rejection, or to his son in general, so he hurried ahead. Everyone else was connected and quiet, even Bad Muireall, shaking slightly ever since Euna scolded her, so he began.

I am going to share with you, he said, some poetry I wrote when I was alone in my hut this autumn. I ask that you be kind.

> O thou, in whom we live and move;
>   Who made the loch and moor;
> Thy mercy day on day thee prove;
>   Our stains turn thee no less pure.
> If it please you, O Good and Just;
>   To grant us grain and meat;
> A town that we can trust;
>   We will sit now, and we will eat.
> In the name of Dia. Amen.

Amen, the others said. Bad Muireall sucked on her teeth, while Aileen tapped her fork tines on the edge of her plate. Aram was mortified. It had been a mistake to share this poem with a room of strangers, several of whom were clearly indifferent or even hostile toward him. He had done so much in life to avoid holding himself this plain and public, had loved so many women to deaden the chance of being seen.

Well, he said, thinking of the fastest way to force the congregation's focus from him, let's eat.

As far as he could tell, this tactic worked. They started

to pass the food clockwise. Bad Muireall piled her plate so mountainously she left almost no scalloped potatoes for anyone else; in a similar show of self-regard, she poured her tumbler full of club soda, chugged it down, and brimmed it again. As the dishes circulated, Grace and Lili both made sure to take precisely the same amounts of brandy butter and mince pies as did Mrs Macbay, for instance, or Good Muireall. Euna fixed a heaping plate for Lachlan Iain and a small, birdlike smattering for herself – noticing this, Aram sneaked some extra rumbledethumps and mealie pudding onto a side plate, should she still be hungry after that snack.

Conversation was token as they ate. Over the course of the meal, Lachlan Iain hid beneath the card tables. Occasionally he peeped out at Aram and showed his by then gravy-dyed tongue. Good Muireall at one point crawled under the table to retrieve him and instead stayed down there for a while, playing makeshift draughts with peas and soda bread the congregants had dropped from their plates. Aram barely knew her and he liked her already.

Where's your better half? Minister Macbay asked Aileen.

She shot her father an unimpressed look, as if she could not believe he was asking this in front of the entire table. Carson? He has a toothache.

Lili perked up. I'm a dentist, she proclaimed, showing several holes in her own smile. I've pulled so many teeth I could make a necklace!

Aileen smiled. I'll tell Carson to give you a call, she said.

He can't, Lili said. We don't have a telephone.

This opened a new conversation, and Aileen seemed glad to have the limelight turned from her. Each person, now fuelled by their first round of feasting, was eager to enter the discussion, incidentally about how advanced their own lives were relative to their neighbours'. *No telephone? We have a toaster that changes colours! No telephone? We have an automated garage door!* All wanted to prove how inventive their homes were, what widgets they had in their kitchens, what tools for climate control. Grace, in her cropped voice, said, We don't have running water.

Bad Muireall threw a pheasant bone across the table at her, then looked penitent, as if she had unveiled a private matter by reacting that way.

Lachlan Iain showed his eyes above the table. He was hyper now, having eaten so many small portions of energy. He started to sing an updated version of that same strange number he had revealed to Aram weeks before, in the sanctuary upstairs. *A chrostag! Today I drew a lady with a double bum! A chrostag! Today I wanted to pee in everyone's cups!*

Bad Muireall stood at once. Though most others were looking at the child with adoring faces, she would not even glance cold at him. Where is your outhouse? she asked the minister.

The bathroom is just upstairs, by the Sunday School entrance. He laughed. An outhouse, really. You must think we're barbaric!

Bad Muireall gritted her teeth at the barbaric bit. She thundered up the stairs. As soon as she was gone, Aram felt the dampness that had been gripping the walls dry, just slightly, almost imperceptibly. He looked around to see if the others had noticed the shift in humidity, but most of them had started into their seconds, and were so absorbed by neeps and partan bree they seemed not to care.

Lachlan Iain insisted that Euna open her Christmas cracker, and to appease her boy, she did. In it was a red crayon, and with it he began to doodle on the tablecloth. Where are the other kids? he asked. I want to show somebody.

Mrs Macbay's face was always a clear barometer, and Aram could tell this question depressed her. Oh, darling, she said. We don't have too many in Pullhair. The brothers in the boys' choir went to Inverness to celebrate the holidays.

The boy sighed and rested his chin in his hands. I don't want to draw any more, he said.

Lili excused herself from the table and found a private tract of carpet a few feet away. She pulled a torch from her snowsuit. Come here, Lachlan Iain, she said. As far as Aram knew, this was their first time meeting one another, but the sunny, natural way she spoke to him, the tender carpet-pat with which she invited him over, implied a high level of trust. He scurried over and sat on the carpet beside her. Let's play sgàilich, she said. It's my favourite.

Lili and Lachlan Iain started to cast shadow shapes against the wall, giggling each time a deer or hare or monster appeared in the ring of light. They gave each creature a distinct voice, though none used formal language, only an array of noises. While they played, Aram cleared the refuse of the meal, bones, pits, stems, ligaments. Conversation had started again, amiably, moving from news of deaths and marriages, to the congregants' latest health concerns, to their increasingly marginal crop yields. Aram went to the alcove to settle the desserts onto a cart. It felt natural to listen to the conversation from this slight remove.

At last he wheeled the treat-cart to the table and arranged

the dishes in the middle, a tad closer to Euna's end. He passed the dishes one at a time, observing how lovely the border tarts were, the shortbread, the cranachan. He had always thought this the one defect of Scottish life, the paltriness of all desserts, the slight anticlimax they introduced to even the most delicious meals, but he knew how hard the womenfolk had worked on these treats, so he felt a duty to appreciate them out loud. Most of the guests ate generous helpings of the cranachan, by far the most tempting dessert, clots of cream adhering to beards and mouths. Euna refused a helping when the dish came to her.

After the meal, Minister Macbay read out loud from the Gospel according to Luke. They all listened to the story of Christ's birth, for the fifth or hundredth time, though Aram noticed Lili covering Lachlan Iain's ears. Bad Muireall had not yet returned from the bathroom, which Aram thought perhaps a mercy. When the minister was finished, the Christ child wrapped in cloths and snuggled in his manger, his folks having found no room at the guest house, the gathering began to dissolve. The goodbyes were many, the blessings sincere. This meal had heartened the congregation in a vital way, and as they prepared to leave, the room pulsed with eager dialogue, laughter. Mrs Macbay made a show of divvying up the leftovers evenly, wanting everyone to be well fed and fairly treated. Aram was happy to see her sneak extra soda bread into Lili's container.

The townsfolk left as they had come, in a gradual trickle, though noticeably merrier than when they had arrived. Minister Macbay asked Aram to wait with the remaining guests while he sent the others onto the moor with a beannachd. Aram agreed. With the Macbays and the majority of the invitees gone, only two clumps – Aram did not want to call them families – lingered. The Gainntir women, minus Bad Muireall, who was still in the bathroom; and Good Muireall, Euna, Aileen, and Lachlan Iain, who Aram had begun to name-bundle in his head as the Hammers. It struck him as selfish that he had never learned Euna's family name, but then, he had never learned his own, either. His father had insisted it was Sealoch, his mother Sundew. Perhaps they wanted to attach to him their most darling things, his father water, his mother land. When at Dungavel he had been forced to use his surname, he had selected Sealoch.

Aram went to crouch beside Lachlan Iain. In Lili's circle of light, Aram cast the form of a salmon. Want to know something? he asked the boy.

Lachlan Iain nodded. He was mesmerized by the fish, more than he had been by the deer or hare. Aram wondered if the boy had inherited this love from him, from the Sealoch-Sundews, or if that was a kind of covetous thinking.

You and I know each other, he said.

Lili, clearly intrigued by Aram's proclamation, turned off the torch. She hooked a hand around Lachlan Iain's waist, as if to brace him against the impact of the coming conversation.

Do you know what a father is? Aram asked.

The Gainntir and the Hammer women had, by now, all crowded around the child. Euna dropped to her knees beside Aram and he fretted, given how worn out the carpet was, this descent would cause her pain. But if it did, she showed no sign. Aileen sat down cross-legged, while Good Muireall, evidently not one to bear discomfort for no reason, pulled up a chair for herself and one for Grace.

Are you really going to do this? Aileen asked him.

Why not? Aram asked.

Go ahead, Euna said. Just don't use him to work out your own cac.

As ever, he was moved by Euna's unassuming wisdom. He took a moment to undress his reasons for announcing his paternity. He tunnelled down into his interior world, away from the faces, expectations, sentiments glutting the basement. And finally he saw nothing but virtue in his drive to reveal his identity. There was no guarantee he would be received well by Lachlan Iain, or by any of the watching women, but he of all people was sure a boy had a right to know his father.

So he looked into Lachlan Iain's eyes, while Lili continued to hold the child, and explained he had fathered him. He wished Aileen would step in then and explain her role – Lachlan Iain did, after all, still believe Euna to be his biological mother – but then, Aram had learned long ago he could only speak for himself.

Lachlan Iain shrugged and said, All right. He did not seem especially shell-shocked, to Aram's relief and disappointment. Having spent minimal time with children, he had lost track of how mutable they could be. Lachlan Iain nudged Lili to turn the torch on again.

Before she could do that, Bad Muireall, clearly having heard what Aram said to his son, came clomping down the stairs and jumped onto Aram's back. She clawed at his eyes, monkeying over his left shoulder, and then they were rolling together in the tobacco-and-burned-coffee stench rising from the prehistoric carpet. He had never grappled like this, had only fought with honour or else been sucker-punched, only rolled when he had intended it to be sensual. This was anything but sensual. From outside came a babel of thunder and dense rain. The church basement was surprisingly well insulated, and free of windows, so only the most violent sounds ever permeated its walls. Lachlan Iain had started to cry, in his infantile way, where every ten seconds he would stop to make sure everyone was noticing how sad and scared he was, and then he would start to cry again. Meanwhile, Bad Muireall cupped her hands over Aram's eyes, blinding now rather than clawing. Apparently she did not want him to see his son's emotions, perhaps afraid this would bond the two of them.

You stupid toll na tòine, she said to Aram. Look what you've done.

The rain intensified. When the thundercloud boomed, the room trembled, as if the storm were directly overhead. Grace prised Bad Muireall's hands from Aram's face and in the process was steamrolled, her hand and shoulder forced brutally into the weight-bearing column. Rounds of blood appeared in the lace. Ach, she said. I was just trying to help.

Aram pinned Bad Muireall's two wrists to the carpet. He climbed onto her low belly and straddled her, by then breathing heavily. Her haircut, severe before, had been ravaged by the rolling, her whole person slick with sweat. She looked weak like this. Assailable. And yet any desire Aram had to hurt her, primal or mindful, faded as quickly as it had come.

What hurts? he asked.

Her face changed. Where before her features had been distorted by fear, anger, now they were phenomenally still. The thunder blanched and gradually began to diminish. Bad

Muireall looked silently at Aram. She looked at him until her looking made him sheepish and he had to speak. He said, leaning in so only she could hear, I don't know what happened to you. But I believe it's not your fault.

Now his temple was soaked with her sweat, or maybe tears – he was too close to have any perspective. He was still afraid of what she might do were she totally free, so he kept her pinned lightly in place, as a boy might a butterfly whose wings he did not want to tear. A strange endeavour, finding the midway between reasonable measures of safety and all-out domination.

Euna said to Bad Muireall, If I'd had you in this position a few years ago, I might have done something terrible.

Bad Muireall closed her eyes, as if, body trapped, her only retreat was toward sleep or some likeness of it. Aram had secretly wondered if Bad Muireall were somehow controlling the rain, but now the downpour had diminished, he felt ridiculous for even considering that a possibility. If she had that power in her arsenal, surely she would be mustering it right now, in this defenceless moment.

Aram looked at Euna. What should we do with her now? he asked. He liked this arrangement: Euna felt she was in control of Bad Muireall's fortune, while in truth Aram was the one with his knees tight around her ribcage.

Euna thought for a moment, using her clipped, guitar-shredding nails to force back her cuticles, one so far she drew blood. Aram's mind went first to formal punishment. There was no gaol in Pullhair, no standard means of justice or restraint of dangerous persons – they could have ferried and charged her farther south, in a more populous area of

Scotland. In theory, Aram no longer believed in holding folks in captivity – he knew how degrading that fate was – though he was not sure how he would behave in practice.

Lili covered Lachlan Iain's ears again. She seemed eager to safeguard his innocence. Euna turned toward Good Muireall and asked, Would you help us figure this out, Muireall? Your word is basically gospel.

Bad Muireall flared her nostrils and opened her eyes at the sound of her own name. She seemed enraged to learn she shared *Muireall* with someone else, especially someone Euna genuinely loved. Aram felt the ribs between his knees inflate and then tighten, a fast and repeated pattern.

Absolutely, Good Muireall said. I mean, what the feck do I know, but it might be helpful that I have the least stake in this.

You're a wise woman, Euna said.

The breath-pattern between Aram's legs hastened. I think what's important, Good Muireall said, is that everyone who's been hurt gets some time to talk about it.

Aram groaned inwardly. This sounded like a nightmare. Luckily, he had never been hurt, so he did not have to say a word. He could sit there straddling Bad Muireall and pretend to listen while Good Muireall conducted her little bohemian, fringy, free-and-easy circle. He could wait for everyone to share their grievances, air the wounds well beneath their daily armour, and when that chatter, like the thunder, had subsided, they could return to the practical matter of what to do with the villain who had upended all their lives.

Good Muireall said, We might need to do a few circles like this one. There might be unresolved matter after today.

Shite, Aram thought. That's okay, Euna said. We don't expect miracles.

Grace nodded so the lace on her neck furrowed and flattened. She said, If you only knew how low our expectations are...

Nothing better than low expectations, Good Muireall said, laughing. So here's how it works: participation in the circle is voluntary. I'll be the keeper, and I'll direct the movement of the conversation. She looked around and retrieved Euna's guitar pick, a thin, hot-pink piece of plastic, from her fretboard. When you're holding this pick, you're allowed to speak.

At that point, Minister and Mrs Macbay came back down the stairs, presumably having blessed all the guests and waved them out onto the heath. The Macbays took one short look at the scene and a long one at each other. Well then, Minister Macbay boomed. We'll let you get on with... this.

Aileen beamed, a sight Aram had rarely seen since she was eighteen, by the forcing house. She said, I'll explain later, Boban.

I trust you, dearc-dhearg, he said. *Redcurrant*, Aram thought, was appropriate. Mrs Macbay motioned with her hands to say she would be waiting above, in the sanctuary. She seemed to direct this message toward Lili in particular. The Macbays left the basement with a few concerted glimpses over their shoulders, as if nervous parents leaving their children alone for the first time.

When they were gone, Good Muireall combed the room and found the communion wine Aram had fetched for Bad Muireall hours before, then squirrelled away in the Sunday School supply closet. She uncorked the bottle with a camping knife from her pocket and poured its contents into a casual assortment of teacups, steins, and Mason jars, one for each person, save Lachlan Iain. This isn't exactly recommended before a circle, she said, but it's more fun this way.

Aileen raised hers, a chipped, commemorative Stornoway United FC mug, to toast. Everyone followed suit, other than Bad Muireall, who was still trapped beneath Aram. Aileen said a benediction first in lilting, golden Gaelic, and then in blunted English: May the Lord keep you in His hand, and never close His fist too tightly on you. Aram found the words vaguely ominous, more of a warning than a blessing, but hey, any excuse to drink.

Within a few minutes, thanks both to the wine itself and to the act of imbibing together, the energy in the room was looser. Good Muireall must have sensed this, because then and only then did she explain the parameters of the circle. First, they would build a list of the crimes committed. Second, each person would explain how these offences impacted them physically, emotionally, and spiritually. Third, the offenders – she looked at Aram, *what the hell?*, as well as at Bad Muireall – would explain why they had committed those crimes.

Euna said, Damain, Muireall. I wish you had lived here all along.

Good Muireall beamed at Euna. No, she said, you don't. Then you wouldn't be a fucking rock star.

Euna made devil horns and deep-drank the wine, staining her gorgeous, carnivorous teeth a richer shade of red. Let's do this, she said to Good Muireall.

She offered the guitar pick to Euna. Why don't you get us started? Good Muireall asked gently.

Euna, who had fled Pullhair on foot to find Aram at the castle, Euna, who had seen rare niches of the world, of course dived in with complete abandon. The pick held naturally between her pointer finger and thumb, she laid out the crimes she believed she had been victim to, though she used the word ainneartachadh, more *oppression* than *crime*. She spoke of strops and horsewhips and hairbrushes and switches, then of the silent treatment, of emotional manipulation. Then, turning her attention to Aram, she accused him of pilfering her virtue; of humiliating her, leaving her young and forlorn on the moors; of tearing her pearrsag, causing it to burn through urination; of thoughtlessly, narcissistically, ruining Aileen's life.

As she waded through this tender, decades-long catalogue of wrongdoings, Aram knew he would not be able to sit there in silence, inwardly rolling his eyes. He either had to run, to avoid being dragged into the circle, or he had to commit himself to his family and homeland, despite the discomfort, to anchor himself in place as any good seasonal fisherman knew how to do.

Grace spoke. Lili spoke. Grace's list was short, and pivoted on the shame Bad Muireall had implanted in her about her attractiveness, especially her weight, culminating in Grace's attempt to stop living. Lili's list was long and rambling, but full of lighter items, like the sheep trampling a little patch of clover she kept in the garden, or Muireall never wanting to play with her, or Euna making her feel lonely by leaving. Aileen spoke. She, of anyone, was the most furious, though she had never lived a day at Gainntir.

He tried to stay peaceful and focused while Aileen vented for half an hour. He had to admit, though, it was a struggle, and ultimately he had to separate from her unbridled anger and arrive in his own private landscape, where he was alone with Euna on a trawler, watching fireflies flicker in the sky.

Thank you, he heard Good Muireall say. I believe we've started to do this already, but if anyone wants to add to the ways in which these crimes have impacted them, now is the time.

After Aileen's long diatribe, Aram's knees, still straddling Bad Muireall, were beginning to get sore. He could feel the acid building up in his thighs. He raised his hand and waited for Good Muireall to pass him the guitar pick. I don't want to seem impatient, he said, but my legs are starting to ache.

All right, Good Muireall said. Maybe we have had enough for one day. She looked around the circle, and everyone who could nod, did. Lachlan Iain was asleep on the carpet, curled into a tight shape.

I just want to say, he added, in case this helps anyone sleep tonight: I will answer to all my offences.

Euna smiled at him, minimally, from across the circle. Good Muireall said a secular benediction to close the day's events, and then she stood up. Lili turned Lachlan Iain awake with great care, as if flipping an over-easy egg. All quietly collected their belongings and prepared to leave the basement. Aram assured them he and Bad Muireall would catch up soon. They agreed, and once they were upstairs, even through the closed basement door, Aram could hear Mrs Macbay exclaiming how lovely it was to see them.

Aram went to the buffet and retrieved two large urns. Even when he was no longer straddling Bad Muireall, she remained in her prone position. Though she made no noise, he could see when he faced her that she was crying. He placed both urns in the corner of the basement and said, These are for waste, number one and two, if you need them. There's running water in the kitchenette, and plenty of tinned food in the cupboards. I will come to visit you tomorrow.

She stared at Aram. He wondered if she were going to buck, to turn feral, but she stayed where she was, tamed, tearing up in silence. He waited for ten or twenty minutes like that, to make sure she had genuinely submitted. Then at last he walked backwards up the stairs, training his eyes on Bad Muireall the whole time, and stepped into the sanctuary. By then the sun had set, the others gone home. He locked the basement door behind him.

*

Walking back toward the house, ashamed by the others' accusations, Aram accidentally stomped on a twinflower. He had not seen one in years, not since leaving Pullhair for the first time. The two tiny heads, bent by his boot toward the ground, saddened then stunned him. Their gradient. From such a deep pink at the sepal to pale, almost white, at the end of the bud. How had they survived the loss of land, the desiccation? Seeing this delicate, nostalgic show of beauty, he was nearly inspired to return to the basement and free Bad Muireall. He resisted the urge.

A world of weather overcame him, panes of snow, a sub-arctic bite, winds so severe they could have blown him all the way to the salmon hut. He was not wearing a coat, and in the two minutes it took him to move from the church to the blackhouse, he picked up a pale burn on his wrists. He had not intended, of course, to be out so late, so he had not brought with him any extra layers.

He could hardly digest everything that had been said in the circle. What stunned him was how persistently the Gainntir women, between full-frontal sweeps of anger and grief, had defended Bad Muireall. *She's been through a lot.* Or, *We were disobedient. She had no choice but to punish us.* Or, *If I'd stayed in the house I was born in, I might have been killed. She saved me and I should be grateful.*

Neither Euna nor Aileen had defended Aram, given similar opportunities to do so. They reprimanded him without the slightest trace of compassion. They both seemed to feel comfortable, completely guilt-free, chastising him. He was missing the manipulation skills Bad Muireall had so clearly mastered.

Though his self-esteem had taken a hit, Aram was at least consoled to know his failings were now laid bare. No more secrets. No more sour feelings lurking beneath the surface, escalating into violent fictions, bitterness, estrangement. After rotting teeth were extracted, even sweet Lili knew, a person could expect to be in pain – but they could tolerate that pain, knowing they were heading down the line of healing, knowing the poisoned roots were gone.

V

THE WEEK AFTER Christmas, a brutally cold chain of days, Lili and Grace stayed free of charge at the guest house, returning only intermittently to Gainntir to tend to its remaining livestock. Aram knew the proprietor from his time selling Scottish Salmon Company wares there, and once he explained their predicament to the freehanded elderly woman, she agreed without hesitation to shelter them. She had not had a paying guest in months anyway, she explained to Aram. Few ventured to the Outer Hebrides in the winter unless they had serious business there.

Turns out, he said, there is lots of room at the inn.

Like most folks in Pullhair, the proprietor had a sense of humour, and after she bonked Aram on the back for his cheekiness, she laughed at his joke.

The Hammers were still living with Aileen, who had extra space in her chalet since Carson had driven to Glenrothes to visit his ailing parents, or so Aileen said. She assured everyone he would return in finer spirits than ever, a dyed-in-the-wool devotee of his wife, though no one but Minister Macbay had asked. On first meeting them, Aram had wondered if Aileen wanted her husband at all. Now, that distance between them,

Aram felt the weight of her longing, what some – not he, but some – might name love. Aram visited the Hammers daily, and even when Aileen barred him from seeing the other women, she gave him unfettered access to Lachlan Iain. He taught the boy to ferret out peat, then set a house-heating fire with it; to tie a bowline; to identify toxic plants, like foxglove. He tried to impart as much practical knowledge on the child as he could, considering he did not know how long this living arrangement would last – considering, too, no figure had taught Aram any of these skills.

Bad Muireall remained locked in the church basement, which, Aram imagined, surely confirmed to her all she thought she knew about religion and tolerance. The Macbays protested against holding her there in confinement, and Aram engaged them in several multilayered debates on the matter. His whip hand: this was the only way to keep Pullhair safe, especially – he took a long look at Mrs Macbay – Lili, who was the most susceptible to Bad Muireall's cruelty. This trick worked. Maybe he had learned a few techniques from Bad Muireall, after all. His desire to detain her was, truthfully, only partly related to the community's safety. What he would not admit was, he revelled in the fact that he had another person in captivity, especially after being detained for so long himself. It was oddly gratifying to control her supply of food, monitor her visitors, limit, or curb entirely, her range of movement.

On New Year's Eve, Aram went to the chalet to collect the Hammers for a date at the guest house. Good Muireall greeted him at the door, where she was helping Lachlan Iain to slip into layers of fleece and sheepskin, to double-tie his little boots. He gave her a kiss on the cheek and Lachlan Iain a kiss on the tam, then joined Euna in Aileen's bedroom. Euna was pulling the quilts as high as Aileen's cheekbones, stroking the sweat-dappled part of her brow. Sleep well, she was saying. Aram felt he had stumbled upon a private vignette of the women's past in Glasgow.

Stay, Aileen said. Please. She clung to the hem of Euna's velvet coat, where a fine thread curled like liquorice smoke. She was a child afraid of being abandoned. Her desperation about Carson had reached a fevered high, and Aram, several feet away, could see its effects in her reddened cheeks, her tight grip.

He said, Aileen, pet, what's wrong?

You wouldn't understand the pain, she said. It's fuil mhìosail.

I once got my foot caught in an aerator at the farm, he said. Does that compare?

Hardly, she said. She looked at him with anger, not resentment, as she had before their circle in the church basement. The distinction was marked.

He gently separated her fingers from Euna's hem, then kissed her knuckles one at a time, with what he hoped was not seduction but slow kindness. Aileen tucked her whole body back beneath the quilt. She clutched the fabric from below, fluting its pattern of pink sea rockets. We have to go now, Aram said. Lili and Grace are expecting us.

So you're going to leave me alone in agony? she asked him.

Your parents will come check on you in a few hours, he said. You'll live.

Awright, Aileen said. You stupid prick.

He grinned. Her dirty mouth made him feel strangely loved, comfortable. Stroking Aileen's forehead one last time, Euna said, We'll miss you, m' usgair. Happy New Year.

Happy New Year, she said, soft as baby's breath, to Euna. To Aram she said, Go eat a juicy bag of baws.

He blew Aileen a kiss, to which she rolled her eyes. He led Euna by the hand to the front door, where Lachlan Iain was clearly boiling through his winter getup. Good Muireall asked them, Everything good?

You know Aileen, was all Euna said.

Good Muireall beamed. Oh, you two, she said. Ever the odd couple. I remember in the camper van...

Aram prickled at this talk. He hurried the others out of the chalet before Good Muireall could share any more of her recollection. He led them past the town common, which had, before he left Pullhair, been a handsome place for townsfolk to gather. Picnic benches once rimmed the green, pits for charcoal fires, baths for migrant birds. These trappings were now gone, and even if the season had been more hospitable, Aram doubted anyone would be there sitting, reading verse, drinking tea, as they had even five years prior.

A kilometre farther, they came to the guest house. From the outside it looked deserted, its eaves come loose, leaves iced and piled high on the threshold, though on the inside it was much more hospitable. Aram knocked brightly on the front door, knowing warmth waited for them on the other side. Feasgar math! the proprietor said, swinging the door wide open. She was a doughty, eighty-something woman with horn-rimmed glasses and a blue rinse over her lovely white hair. Come, come, she said, brushing flakes of snow from Aram's fisherman's sweater, Euna's velvet coat.

They gratefully hurried inside. Good afternoon, Aram said to the owner. Thank you for having us.

Lili came scrambling to the doorway. She switched places with the owner, who tidied Lili's hair before shuffling off into the kitchen, promising gingerbread. Lili dragged him and Lachlan Iain by the hand into the drawing room. They sprawled on the floor, softened as it was by a monumental, hand-loomed rug. Though he had not thought about it for years, he remembered now that his mam had a matching one in their boat hold – it was the only thing, she said, she had managed to import from Sketimini. The drawing room was so crammed with kitschy figurines, antique chairs, curios that made the place homey and Albannach, he might not have noticed the rug were it not for its deep-rooted familiarity.

Grace joined them in the drawing room then, wearing a plain tan sweater and tweed pants, her face bare and a bit pallid, but at least exposed to the air. Euna and Good Muireall lay intertwined on the sofa, an old country plaid number in which holes revealed tufts of stuffing.

Lachlan Iain called out, Boban, watch this! He nudged Lili until she flicked on a nearby torch. It was still daytime, so the beam was only faintly visible against the wall. But Aram would not miss an opportunity to see his child perform. For years, he had caught larger and more impressive fish, becoming the most efficient farmer on the coast, with no father to witness his prowess. Aram squinted now as he tried to see the slippery, one-eyed shadow his son was making. It was unrecognizable as a fish, but that did not matter.

Aram cried, Would you look at that salmon!

No, dummy, Lachlan Iain said. It's a sardine. Only he did not yet know the proper pronunciation, so he said *saw-been*.

Aram would have to stay in his child's life, he decided then, if mainly to discipline him. The boy was already becoming a brat, and no seed of Aram's would be so disrespectful. Aram moved his son's hands to form a perfect salmon, and together they held the shape in front of Lili's pale beam. Aram noticed that his hands complicated the outline, so he dropped them, leaving the boy to compose the image on his own. The shape he came up with was remarkably precise. A shaoghail, Lili said. Now that's a great salmon.

Lachlan Iain grinned magnificently. He took full credit for the fish, instantly forgetting the help his father had given him.

Euna must have seen Aram's reaction to this slight, as she laughed, open-mouthed, at him. He's just a boy, she said.

Aram shrugged as if to say, Of course, but the truth was he could not slough off the feeling. He did not see himself reflected in the child. He supposed this was what happened when a person was raised by womenfolk. Wolves might have been preferable. At least then he would have sharp teeth.

This time of year, evening fell firmly and fast. The sky shifted from pale grey to gun-smoke to pitch black in the matter of minutes. The proprietor of the guest house bustled into the drawing room and brightened all of the standing lamps, lit a candelabra and then a fire in the woodstove. Gingerbread is in the oven, she said. And I have good news.

Lili clapped her hands loudly together. I love good news, she said. What is it?

I've invited everyone in town for a cèilidh. She turned to Euna, Would you play for us, love?

Euna leaned back, her ear poking, elven, through her hair. Aram saw the pearl earring, a small chip in it from when the drop had fallen on the ice, on the upland. He loved the small-est parts of her. I didn't bring my guitar, she said.

I'll phone the minister, the owner said. He can bring it for you when he comes.

Euna seemed surprised, pleasantly, at the mention of the telephone. Of course, she said. I would be glad to play.

Wonderful, the owner said. It's been so long since we had one. The last one would have been at Carson and Aileen's wedding.

Beautiful, Aram said. It would be an honour.

The owner clapped her hands together, clearly exhilarated. She had the comportment of a much younger woman. I'll bring the cookies when they're done, she said.

Thank you, Lachlan Iain said, and Aram felt momentarily reassured.

Grace sat cross-legged behind Lili and began to braid her hair. At the sight of this, Euna bounded toward the women and joined their line, combing Grace's hair with rigid fingers. Good Muireall took the rear of the train, working Dutch milkmaid braids into Euna's hair. Aram did not know how to integrate himself – watching felt perverse, participating impossible. So he invited his son to sit on his lap, which the boy did gladly. Aram was seeing, in small glimpses, the appeal of children. How could you feel isolated with a child around, how could you question your worth with a little self trawling your lonely feelings for a smile?

With Lachlan Iain perched there, Aram felt grounded. Not weighed down. The distinction was subtle – like that between Aileen's anger and her resentment – but Aram grasped it deeply. He had, after all, searched low and high for the feeling that had just now landed, squarely, in his lap.

When the townsfolk arrived for the cèilidh several hours later, they really and truly arrived. Their energy was markedly different than it had been at the Christmas feast just one week before, though that occasion had been similarly light and festive. But tonight, the guests were glimmering, moon-bright, as if brought into the world by incantation. Aram had never witnessed anything so enchanting, maybe in his life, and certainly not in his life in Pullhair. But he was not going to let habit blot out the present. He was going to meet this delight, both divine and entirely ordinary, with his own. Fuck it, he was going to have fun.

As scores of guests came pouring in – they must have driven in from other towns, as Aram only recognized about half of them – he went to the well-stocked whisky cabinet, a source of pride in a town of frequent dearth. He downed a few drams of Balblair whisky, of Ben Nevis, of Tobermory, then brought as many bottles as he could carry into the drawing room, in which guests were by now packed like *saw-beens*. They had started to spill into the hallway, the kitchen, to spread their rowdily chatting selves all over the main floor. Euna pressed her way to Aram's side and said, You started without me? before pinching the bottle of Balblair and catching up to him shot for shot. Soon she was kissing him on the scruff of his cheek, then nuzzling into his neck, in full view of the Macbays, who had just arrived with her beloved guitar. They did not seem upset, but why would they? They did not know about Aram and Aileen, nor did they ever have to. Sometimes secrecy was a poison, of course, but sometimes – today – it was a simple boundary.

Euna, tipsy, a Caledonian queen in blue jeans, grabbed her guitar from Minister Macbay. She thanked him with an eagerness that betrayed her slight intoxication and he laughed. Even he, even devout he, accepted a swig of whisky when Aram offered him the bottle. His wife seemed to approve and off the minister was, a bit ruddy, greeting all the good souls who had travelled to Pullhair. Euna thrust her way into the corner of the room and made a makeshift stage by pushing tables and benches together. She tuned her instrument, which had, in the Macbays' icy outdoor journey, gone a little flat. A couple of the other townsfolk had brought fiddles, one a bodhrán, one a hammered dulcimer, and they rallied around her as a slapdash quintet. Euna said something inaudible to them and then, all of a sudden, they were elevated by the tables and benches, playing 'Highland Welcome' in an impeccably tight arrangement.

Within a few bars many of the guests had launched into a formal country dance, a round-the-room number in which sets of couples stepped, turned, made arches with their arms, under which other couples eagerly swanned. Aram did not know the dance, and he did not especially want to fall over his own feet in front of this many people, so he inclined against the wall where a few hours prior his son had been casting salmon. And though Aram was not dancing, he did not feel excluded, simply standing there, watching. He was still a heartened part of the sweat and energy.

Mid-song, Aileen hurried into the drawing room. She seemed to have made a full recovery, or perhaps to have taken some strong painkillers. Her cheekbones were streaked with pale gold sparkles, slicked then with oil. Her whole being gleamed. Aram felt a pang. He figured it was just the liquor talking.

Aileen greeted Good Muireall, who by then had Lachlan Iain in a piggyback and was somehow, at the same time, stomping to the melody. Though the wind was shaking the guest house's thin panes of glass, the room was warm, the storm-sounds drowned by the joyful swell of fiddle, guitar, bodhrán, feet on floor, and then, gorgeously, miraculously, Euna singing.

Aram downed more Balblair, now near to the clear glass bottom, if only to elevate himself closer to that sublime sound. How had he gone so long without hearing Euna's voice? Nothing mattered before or beyond it. Aram imagined this was what God's had sounded like when he said, on the first day, Let there be light. And there was light. And Aram saw the light, and it was good.

He had the wildest ideas in his head, hearing her sing. Now she was leading the band in 'St Bernard's Waltz' – one he knew from his tender, early years, before his father died – and she was crooning, Come let's dance tonight… Just as they did in the old days… and Lord above, was he overcome. Drunk and unchecked after years of holding himself so tightly, obediently together, tanked up and wanting, at long last, to breathe. And there was Euna's falsetto. And his heart red and rug-soft beneath all these couples' stomping feet.

Grace came in on the harmonies and the meld was deeply, immortally beautiful, especially with her clipped cords. Who knew an imperfection could make her tone so resonant? The timbre turned her to a natural baritone. Euna seemed inspired by the sound and smiled with all her teeth, somehow not neglecting a beat in the waltz. Aram moved through the dancing couples toward the band. He asked for permission then lifted the bodhrán into his arms, hoping to see if his heritage, his inborn cadence, was enough to keep him in stride with the next song. Euna winked to show that she saw him. She started in on the next tune, a version of 'I'll Lay Ye Doon Love'. It quickly became clear to Aram that there was nothing innate about drumming skills. He hammered away at the bodhrán for a full verse before realizing the others were playing in spite of, not in response to, him. So he eased off the percussion. And when he did, Euna raised a hand to ask the others to do the same, to give her space to sing this ballad a cappella.

Euna looked at Aram when she sang, and the sensation was so strong he had to clutch the drum to his chest as a kind of breastplate. I hae travelled far frae Stornoway/Aye, and doon as far as Glasgow toon/And I maun gae, love, and travel further/ But when I come back, I will lay ye doon. The room had gone from riotous, rollicking, to nearly silent. He could not break his eye-line to Euna, but he thought he saw in his periphery someone wiping away tears. A lady had to be pretty confident to interrupt a drunken, dancing crowd, and yet, here she was, bringing the room in tune with their rawest emotions.

When she was finished, she set her guitar on the ground. She grabbed the bottle of whisky from Aram and drained its last dregs, to a chorus of cheers from the audience. Then she took the bodhrán from Aram and said, impishly, Never try that again, okay? before reuniting the drum with its proper owner.

I promise, Aram said.

She held on to him while the band started up again, this time led by the fiddlers. Outside or upstairs? she asked.

He pocketed her hand, taking her through the guest house and up the creaking staircase, in time with the rowdy down-beat. The heat from the visitors in the drawing room was rising, blanketing Aram and Euna, warming them beyond what the whisky and tenderness had already managed to do. The month had been so terribly cold, it was life-affirming to have that temperature saturating them, as if they were tropical plants in a glasshouse. Aram led Euna into a guest room, where he had overnighted on occasion when delivering salmon in the midst of a particularly harsh storm. The bed had been made too tightly, and he tore away the quilt and top sheets. Euna latched the door behind them, then flipped on the beaded lamp by the bedside. He hauled Euna on top of him, slipping her chipped earring between his lips. The jewel sweat.

As she ran her hands across his beard, her guitar-player calluses caught on its greying spines. For once their bodies were both hard-worn, carved through acts of living. Neither was to be exalted. Neither to be blamed. The pearl only granted him a taste, of melancholy, sea salt. Then she tilted her chin toward him, an offering. He leaned in. And held there. And looked at the loudest story of his last ten years. And looked at God's creation, delicate and hardy as the twinflower that had, against all natural reason, appeared behind the church in mid-winter.

And when they did what he had thought so long of doing, when she pulled him by the skull and the collar of his cable-knit sweater, it was not with callow wanting. When they loved one another on that stranger's bed, the mattress trembling with the insistent, rising sound of folk fiddle, it was sàimh. Richer than their afternoon in the hut, less carnal, more celestial. A hash of pleasure and peace.

Last time, as soon as they were finished, he had noticed a shift in Euna. She had turned her back to him and tugged her pants up to cover dribs of blood. The Aram on this bed would have asked, Awright? well before that red cue. Euna curled into the crook of his arm, not to make herself smaller but to bond more of her skin to his. This was the best part, he thought now. Not the soaring itself, but the soft landing after. The way she burrowed her face into his underarm, an animal in search of a familiar odour, a home. He stayed at anchor for a long time, letting her use his body as a haven. Then eventually, the first strains of 'Auld Lang Syne' rose through the floorboards.

Euna shook off her trance and looked suddenly at Aram. We can't miss the New Year, she said, jumping up and pegging into her jeans. He wanted nothing more than to stay in this blessed bed, if not forever, then for the night, but he had vowed to never disappoint her again. So he dressed, too, and hurried down the stairs behind her, bustling into a sea of sunny Scots and uncorked champagne bottles. Minister Macbay wowed the crowd by hauling a set of bagpipes from a closet and filling the lodge with their pining notes. At midnight, everyone in the crowd kissed one another, toasted with thunderous pleasure. The wild merriment, what in Gaelic he might have called meadhail, was so boisterous it was surely carrying across the heath – to the church basement, perhaps all the way to empty, echoic Gainntir.

*

The next morning, Aram woke in ear-splitting, eye-pinking pain on the floor of the church, near the Sunday School entrance. Euna was not with him. His post-midnight memories only came in flickers, here and there, none too cogent or complete. He needed to stand in spite of the pain. Bad

Muireall was waiting in the basement for him to feed her, empty her chamber pots. He knew what it was like to be left too long without attention – the monologue, the stench. He grimaced as he dressed and then, face rinsed of residual whisky and potential hints of vomit, he headed toward the basement door. Coming from behind it was an unexpected sound, a lowing, as if from a cow. He unlocked the door and climbed down to see Bad Muireall in an arch-backed bridge, her inverted face unnervingly calm. She slowly moved into a normal seated position and patted the ground in front of her, inviting him to sit.

Hello, Aram, she said.

Muireall, he said. What's going on?

Just keeping limber, she said. How long do you plan to keep me here?

Aram moved toward her and, against his best instincts, sat on the stretch of carpet she had been patting. Now that he was so near, he could feel a warm force of hers circling him. She seemed to be radiating something brighter than body heat. Her posture was that of a holy woman, one who had spent significant time in quiet contemplation. From her palms came a tremolo. Aram felt pulled to truth-tell.

I don't know, he said. I have no plan.

No surprise there, mè bheag, she said. How can I convince you to let me go?

He was thrown by the question, as by the tacit command she was somehow exerting over him, now their bodies were so close. It's my choice, he said, and he felt pathetic the moment he heard his words out loud.

She nodded thoughtfully. Was the light in the basement

muted, or did she somehow look kinder today, her haircut less severe? She put a hand on his knee and gently stroked the bone, a soothing motion. You're in pain this morning, aren't you, she said. She slid so she was sitting directly behind him, then began to massage his temples, his pounding forehead. In his current state, he welcomed her warm hands.

While she continued to knead his head and shoulders, softening his tightest knots and twinges, she spoke to him. Let me tell you, she said, about my ancestor, Cairstìne. Perhaps your father told you about her before he died at sea?

How did Bad Muireall know about Aram's father? He barely recalled anything about the man, save for his faint, fading infant memories.

I was an uncommon child, Bad Muireall said, and sometimes incompatible with others. Or at least, they thought so, though I tried desperately to be like them. You might understand what I'm talking about, Aram. He tensed at this implication, but then, massaging just the right muscle, she tempered his response. Cairstìne hosted me every summer at her farm, the place you refer to as Gainntir, and those were the only days I truly felt I belonged on this earth.

When she said *Gainntir*, revealing she knew the way others privately referred to her cherished home, he felt briefly ashamed. He wanted nothing more than to deny he had ever used the term.

When she was murdered, I took my inheritance seriously, she told him. I promised myself I would make Cairstìne's home into a sanctuary, by following all her customs, rituals, eating what she ate and using only the resources she had. There was just one difference. I knew from her private diaries how lonely Cairstìne was at the farm, so I decided to start a coven, to make sure I always had others around me.

Nothing wrong with that, Aram said, as long as they wanted to be there. But when they wanted to leave—

What this building means to you, Bad Muireall said, indicating the church sanctuary above, Cala means to me. And I had to protect its boundaries.

A new rivulet moved through Aram. She moved her hands away from his head and turned him by the shoulders to face her. His hangover was gone entirely. He felt truly, preternaturally light. Not just because the pain was gone, but also because someone had noticed it. He said to Bad Muireall, I hear what you're saying. But do you see at what cost it's come?

She turned her attention to the carpet, pulling at its loops until one end came free. I was setting down our roots, she said. History does not come at a shallow cost.

A sadness clutched Aram, from nowhere, by the throat. He missed his mother. He missed something arcane and afflictive – a faraway country, a folk song, a broken horse, a woman skipping through grass of Parnassus – the thoughts were as indistinct and fickle as his memories of the drunken night before. What am I feeling? he asked Bad Muireall.

I'm sorry, she said, but I'm not sure how you expect me to know that.

I don't believe you, he said. You're the one doing this.

She glanced up from the rug, confused or performing confusion. It's lovely you think I have such power, she said. But I'm a normal woman. And a hungry one at that. Will you take me to have a proper breakfast with your family?

Aram knew the Macbays would be glad to feed Bad Muireall,

and more so, they would be thrilled to know she had been released from his crude custody. But Mrs Macbay had promised they would celebrate Hogmanay with *saining*, a blessing of the household. They would sprinkle water from a nearby river ford in each room, then fill the sealed home with the smoulder of flaming juniper branches. When they could hardly breathe any longer, they would fling the doors and windows open, to let in the cold, vitalizing island air. And Aram did not want to share that ceremony with Bad Muireall. He supposed he understood what she meant about protecting the boundaries of the home.

Maybe we can do that another day, he said. He went to the kitchenette and sliced the lid from a can of tuna using his favourite penknife. Though he had initially agreed to give Bad Muireall free rein on the tinned goods in the cupboards, he had decided at the last minute on Christmas to take all the openers and sharp utensils with him to the blackhouse. She looked disconsolate as he handed her the opened tin, which he agreed, as a fisherman, did seem wretched. For a moment Aram felt remorseful. But then he busied himself by carrying the chamber pots to the toilet upstairs and back, while Bad Muireall sucked down the wet flakes. Once he had attended to her needs, his guilt was at least in part gone. He returned the emptied chamber pots to their corner and then, by her side again, placed a hand delicately on the back of her neck. Muireall, he said, I don't know if I can let you out today. I'm just not sure I trust you yet.

She placed the tin, slurped to the last drop, on the carpet. When she turned toward him, his hand moved naturally to the front of her throat – had his grip been tighter, he would have been choking her. I would have the same concerns if I were you, she said. Seems like we are two of a kind.

How he hated to hear that *two of a kind* bit. Her words were breakers and he was sick at sea. He sucked his teeth. We're nothing alike, he said, if mostly for his own benefit.

Be that as it may, she said. Thank you for coming to take care of me.

This irked him even more, watching Bad Muireall as she tried to take the high road. Aram was the good one, she the deeply bad, and if she could not see that, she was not fit to step outside this basement. Where before he had been considering freeing her, if not today then some time soon, now he wanted to add irons and chains. Rach thusa, he said, standing.

Mè bheag, she said again, only this time the endearment did not have the intended effect. He instinctively spat on the ground by her feet. If you ever want to talk, she told him, you know where to find me.

He headed to the stairs, choosing not even to glance back at her. He did not want to be like Lot's wife after peering at Sodom, turned to a pillar of salt – Do not look behind you, nor stop anywhere in the Plain. Instead he took the stairs two at a time, then double-bolted the basement door behind him. He dragged a spare pulpit from a few feet away to rest against the wood. He inhaled. He felt a brief amnesty from the damp, musty discomfort of the basement, until he heard a familiar voice gliding to him down the church aisle.

*

Aram wished, when he saw Euna rushing down the aisle, that it was under other conditions. He wished she had juniper braided through her long red hair, and not carried in her

275

hands, burning, a bough for a more mundane ritual. He wished she were in white lace, or black velvet, or whatever she wanted, really, as long as she felt comfortable enough in the dress to say she would have and hold him.

Good morning, she said, when she was close enough for Aram to choke on the juniper smoke. I'm surprised you're not hungover.

Tough constitution, he said.

She beamed at him. I guess so, she said. Come on. She nudged his shoulder with her nose, summoning him to follow her through the church as she scattered the smoke. He did not need to be convinced; he would shadow her to the bottom of the loch. As he watched, she filled every crook and corner of the sealed space. She climbed onto and under the pews; stood on the bench of the organ; crawled around the cloakroom. Though Aram was entranced by her, an oasis in that Hebridean burn, some part of him wished she would stop. He loved the ceremony in theory, but he and Euna had different mindsets at the moment – she had just come in, elatedly, from the cold, while he had been trapped inside this building for an hour that had felt interminable.

I think you've filled the space entirely, he said. Isn't it time we open the windows?

Not yet, Euna said. We have to make sure the evil spirits stay away.

Aram wondered if Bad Muireall were smelling this smog in the basement, if it were filling her wicked lungs. Even as he wondered this, he started to cough uncontrollably. He could no longer breathe through the grey thickness, its exhaust obstructing his throat.

Awright? Euna asked.

He was becoming fevered, frantic. Instead of giving him the one thing he needed, a dose of open country, she flirted, kissing fresh air from her mouth into his. He continued to choke. Please, he tried to say, please.

Just a minute more, she said. It's an important tradition.

He wished he could beg her to open the windows, drop to his knees and entreat her, but he was coughing so violently, his throat so straitened, that he could not reach his voice. He could die like this, his love surveilling but seeing nothing. He forced his way toward the doors. He needed a hit of the heath. The life he wanted with Euna – the having, the holding, the stroking of hair, the smoking of salmon, every day, every night, every window open, every town another, every refrain flowing straight from her mouth to his ear – would never appear if he suffocated in this beautiful, safe room.

His flight toward the door must have been a dramatic one, because Euna suddenly noticed him drowning in all that air. Or maybe she simply felt the ritual had run its course. Either way she wrapped her arm around his shoulders and helped him toward the exit. When she swung the doors open, elatedly, to a world of blowing snow, Aram could have broken into song. He thought he heard a banging on the basement door, that sound so like a cow lowing, but it was easy to ignore with so much free space ahead of them. Euna gripped Aram by the wrist. The new year stretched, as yet untouched, across the moor.

ACKNOWLEDGEMENTS

Thank you to:

Madeleine O'Shea, Clare Gordon, and everyone at Head of Zeus. Will Francis, PJ Mark, and everyone at Janklow & Nesbit.

The Toronto Arts Council.

Dania Bhandal, Randy Boyagoda, Ruth Donsky, Katie Kitamura, Chris Adrian, and Annie Koyama.

Louise Sider, Ilana Speigel, Lisa Bevilacqua, Smrita Grewal, Kyle Gatchalian, Inaam Haq, Maria Golikova, Rochelle Basen, Mimi Ashi, Kristy Wieber, Annika Kirk, James Herbert, Blake Robert Campbell, Tala El-Achkar, and Michael Deforge.

Amrit, Kiran, Mike, Sanjay, Kalwant, Kamal, Nani-ji, and the whole Phull family.

Danny King Chau and the whole Chau family.

Aunt Heather, Uncle Aurel, Aunt Janet, Biafia, Nate, Uncle Robert, Aunt Kathy, Uncle Ken, Nina, Elias, and Niall.

Violaine, Jean-Pascal, Aunt Valerie, Aunt Marilyn, and Uncle Michael.

Matt, Meg, Mom, and Dad.

This book is dedicated in sacred memory of Grandma Joyce, Grandpa Garth, Grandma Helen, Grandpa Howard, Aunt Betty, Uncle Wool, and Uncle Gary.